# Out, Proud, and Prejudiced
By Megan Reddaway

Out, Proud, and Prejudiced
Copyright © 2018 by Megan Reddaway

Published by the author
meganreddaway.com

Cover art: Natasha Snow natashasnowdesigns.com

This book is written in British English. If you're not used to reading British English, please be tolerant of variations in spelling and usage.

This is a work of fiction. Names, characters, places, and incidents are either the product of the author's imagination or are used fictitiously. Any resemblance to actual persons living or dead, businesses, events, or locales is entirely coincidental. Any persons depicted on the cover are models used for illustrative purposes only.

All rights reserved. No part of this book may be copied, reproduced, translated, or transmitted in any manner whatsoever without the written permission of the author, except for brief quotations included in reviews. To request permission and all other enquiries, contact the author at meganreddaway.com/contact

Please do not copy or share this ebook. Support your favourite books and authors by posting reviews instead, and keep the supply of good books coming!

First edition 1.0
June, 2018

ISBN: 978-1-912735-01-3

## Also by Megan Reddaway

Shelter Me
Big Guy
Two In One

Subscribe for free stories:
meganreddaway.com/free-reads

## About *Out, Proud, and Prejudiced*

*One's proud, one's prejudiced, and they can't stand each other.*

Quick-tempered Bennet Rourke dislikes Darius Lanniker on sight. Darius may be a hotshot city lawyer, but that doesn't give him the right to sneer at Bennet, his friends, and their college. It doesn't help that Bennet's restaurant job has him waiting at Darius's table. So when his tutor recommends him for an internship at Darius's Pemberley estate, Bennet isn't sure he wants it. He's also not sure he can afford to turn it down.

Darius is a fish out of water in the small college town of Meriton, but something keeps pulling him back there. He's helping out a friend with business advice, nothing more. If he's interested in Bennet, it's not serious. Sure, Bennet challenges him in a way no other man has. But they have nothing in common. Right?

Wrong. Their best friends are falling in love, and Bennet and Darius can't seem to escape each other. Soon they're sharing climbing ropes and birthday cake, and there's a spark between them that won't be denied.

But betrayal is around the corner. Darius must swallow his pride and Bennet must drop his prejudices to see the rainbow shining through the storm clouds.

A modern retelling of Jane Austen's *Pride and Prejudice*.

In homage to Jane Austen and all the other storytellers from whom I draw inspiration every day, consciously or not.

# Chapter One

BENNET ROURKE'S YOUNGEST housemate put his head around the bedroom door. "Guess what? Nigel says a hot young gay guy's bought the art gallery in the marketplace."

Bennet didn't take his eyes from his phone. How could the payment on another credit card be due? He'd paid the last one . . . he counted on his fingers. Five days ago.

"Earth to Bennet?"

"Don't you ever knock, Leon?"

"It was open, kind of. Did you hear me?"

"Sure. Some guy's bought an art gallery. Why should I care?"

"Because he's hot. Because he's young. Because he's gay. Because as far as we know he's single, so he must want someone to love, and tonight is Rush."

Rush, Meriton's gay club night, took over the town's one nightclub on the first Friday of every month. Right now, Bennet couldn't care. But wait, if it was the first Friday . . . "So we're in March?"

Leon gave an exaggerated sigh. "Yes, March has come along in its usual position this year, straight after February."

That was it. Mystery solved. *But February, all alone, has*

*twenty-eight days clear.* He'd learned that rhyme when he was tiny. And now here he was with two payments in one week, all because of those stupid missing days that should have been on the end of February.

He dropped the phone on his rumpled bed. He shared the house with four other students and their middle-aged landlord. Two of the students stood in his doorway now: Leon, short and pale, and Kofi, short and dark. Bennet was in the second and final year of his Higher National Diploma course. Leon and Kofi weren't much younger—first year HND students—but somehow the difference was huge.

"What will you wear?" Kofi asked.

Bennet looked down at the grey hoodie he'd put on when he came back from college. "This? Although I'm not sure I'll go."

"Oh, Bennet, you have to, with this new guy in town. Can I . . .?" Kofi inched towards the wardrobe.

"All this on the word of our landlord?" Bennet raised an eyebrow. "Nigel thinks anyone under eighty is young and hot."

"He might not have said *hot*," Leon admitted. He came in and flopped on the end of Bennet's bed. "I might have added that to make our new citizen sound more enticing. But young, gay, and rich enough to buy an art gallery—that makes him hot by definition, doesn't it?"

"Money has nothing to do with it. Anyway, I may have to work tonight."

"You can't, Bennet," Kofi said. "We need you. If you and Jamie go, Charlotte will go, and Charlotte knows him."

"From home?"

"No," Leon said, "from snooping round houses at weekends for that estate agent. She showed him the gallery, and she knows his name—Tim Wilson. So she can introduce us."

"Otherwise, no chance," Kofi added, riffling through Bennet's shirts. "He'll be mobbed, I swear. Turning up halfway through the college year, when everybody's already had everyone they're interested in—except nobody's had Jamie, of course."

Leon snapped closed a quilt fastening that had come undone. "I think we should cross Jamie off the list. Any man who's keeping himself pure for marriage doesn't count."

Bennet frowned. "Don't mock Jamie's principles."

"I didn't. I just said he was keeping himself pure for marriage. You're so defensive, Bennet. A person can't make the briefest remark about the beautiful Jamie without you jumping down their throats. Anyone would think you were in love with our golden-haired Jamie yourself."

"He's not, though," Kofi said. "We'd know if he was. He'd be in misery, because nobody gets to first base with Jamie. How about this, Bennet?" He waved an ice-blue top on its hanger. "Brings out your eyes."

"It'll be dark. Everybody's eyes look black," Bennet pointed out. "So who told you this Tim Wilson will be at the club? Charlotte or Nigel?"

"Neither, but he has to be there," Leon said. "It's only once a month, and Meriton has nothing else resembling a gay scene. Why wouldn't he go?"

Bennet could think of plenty of reasons. "If he's just

arrived, he might not know about Rush."

"Oh my God," Leon said. "I never thought of that. Potential catastrophe, Ko."

Kofi said, "We could put one of the flyers through the gallery door?"

"Yes! Oh, brilliant. We might even meet him. Steal a march on the rest of the crew." Leon bounced off the bed, planted a smacking kiss on Kofi's cheek, and dashed out of the room.

Kofi thrust the blue top at Bennet and followed.

Bennet got up and closed his door. He called the duty manager at the Black Lion, where he worked Saturdays and Sundays. Did they need anybody tonight? They did not. Next week? Yes, but on the one evening he was on duty in the college's training restaurant, so he had to turn it down.

No extra shifts, and he couldn't miss a credit card payment. He'd already renegotiated the payment plan twice. He'd just have to wring more pennies out of his budget until next term's student loan came in. And he'd be leaving college in four months. Other students had careers lined up, but he had nothing. He shouldn't go to Rush tonight. He ought to stay here and start applying for jobs.

But all of his housemates would be there, and they always had a laugh. He lay on his bed and stared up at the ceiling. He wouldn't have to spend a lot of money if he didn't go to the pub first. It didn't cost much to get in, and he could drink water all night. As Leon had said, Rush only happened once a month, and it needed their custom. Use it or lose it.

Besides, he had to admit to a sneaking curiosity about this new guy. What if Bennet missed out on the night of his life by staying at home?

He was still holding the shirt Kofi had picked out. He grabbed clean underwear and headed for the shower.

---

CHARLOTTE'S CAR PULLED up in the marketplace with a jolt and a squeak of brakes. She'd driven Bennet and Jamie into town, saving them a cold cycle ride. She flashed Bennet a quick smile from bright-red lips as she pulled on the handbrake.

"Why do you bother with makeup when there's no chance of meeting an unattached straight guy?" he asked her.

"God, you're grouchy tonight," Charlotte said. "You might as well ask why Jamie bothers dressing up."

Bennet glanced over at his best friend in the back seat. "Well, yeah." Jamie looked stunning in a russet silk turtleneck, but he'd have looked almost as good if he hadn't taken such care.

Charlotte stretched up to see herself in the mirror and poked at one of her false eyelashes. "Because it's not about picking up guys. It's about feeling good and having fun. Right, Jamie?"

"Right." Jamie shot him a grin behind her back. He'd know damn well that picking up guys was a big part of the fun for Bennet—the hope of picking up a guy, anyway. It had been a while since he'd actually done it.

Charlotte opened her door. "Pass me my bag."

Bennet handed over the turquoise leather pouch he'd had on his lap through the ten-minute journey, and they clambered out of the car. Charlotte locked the doors and dropped her keys in the bag before hoisting the strap onto her shoulder.

They crossed the road to the club. A bright rainbow banner flapped above the entrance: *RUSH! YOUR LGBTQ CLUB NIGHT*.

Bennet nodded at the sign. "And here we are at the hub of West Hertfordshire's gay scene."

Jamie raised an eyebrow. "You can be sarcastic now, but I remember the first time we came here. You were thrilled to bits to see that sign."

Bennet laughed. "That was eighteen months ago." It was true, though. He'd been touched and excited to see *LGBTQ* written in huge letters over the entrance. It seemed so open, so *out*. The town where he'd grown up, on the other side of the county, had nothing at all. And even now, if he was honest, he felt a shiver of anticipation as they walked in.

The club had once been the town's cinema. The rows of seats were gone, but the floor still sloped. Energetic or drunk dancers gravitated down until they were clustered in a sweaty huddle near the far wall, below the lights and videos flickering across the old screen. The floor surface was a black rubbery substance that stuck to the feet—like dancing on tar. Tacky as hell, in every sense, but it was theirs.

Kofi and Leon were already there, wriggling to the music but staying near the bar, keeping a close watch on the door. Bennet left them to it. He danced with Charlotte and Jamie, greeted a few people, and watched this month's new pairings without getting involved. Just before midnight he went back to the bar for more water and found Charlotte and Jamie trying to coax Kofi and Leon—now sulky with disappointment because no new guy had come—onto the dance floor.

Then, at last, a smiling stranger stepped in and hesitated at the entrance.

The people in Rush were not subtle. Everyone who saw him nudged someone else, and soon all heads were turned. Faces were wiped of expression, postures straightened. But when the stranger came into the club and they could see behind him, everybody slumped.

"He's brought someone," Kofi wailed.

Both men were toned, well-dressed, the same height, and around the same age—mid to late twenties. But the similarities ended there. The first one came in with open hands and genial smiles—the kind of guy Bennet would be glad to work with, because he'd be into teamwork and cooperation.

The second man was the opposite. He looked good, with dark hair and fine, chiselled features, but his mouth was set in a sardonic grimace. With him around, a person would have to watch every step.

"Which is Wilson?" Leon shouted above the music. "Please tell me it's the smiley guy."

Charlotte nodded.

"Who's the other one?" Bennet asked.

"Don't know," Charlotte said. "Ha, it'll put a spoke in everybody's wheels if he's the boyfriend, won't it?"

Leon gave her a nudge. "Go and say hello." But Tim Wilson caught sight of her before she took a step. His smile widened, and he started towards them, with his friend following.

Charlotte greeted Tim, then offered her hand to the second guy. He shook it with a cold nod.

Tim's eyes fastened on Jamie, who took his cue from Charlotte and put out his hand. Tim Wilson grasped it, shook it, and went on holding it. He maintained a polite smile as Charlotte pointed to each of them in turn. Bennet saw his own name in the movement of her lips, though it was drowned by a heavy bass line from the speakers. It didn't seem to matter to Tim. He barely glanced at anyone but Jamie.

Leon put on a big grin and said something to Tim's friend, but the other man ignored him. His gaze passed over them all without a flicker of interest and he turned to the bar, raising his hand to attract the attention of the two staff who stood chatting by the till.

Leon dismissed his rudeness with a shrug and gazed longingly after Tim Wilson, who was heading for the dance floor with Jamie. "Somebody should tell him."

Bennet made a quarter turn so his eyes couldn't linger on the man at the bar. "Tell who what?"

"Somebody should tell Tim he's wasting his time with Jamie," Leon shouted.

"No need. Jamie will tell him." It was happening already. Jamie was keeping his distance, discouraging touch, making it clear that one-night stands were not on his agenda.

"Dance?" Charlotte said.

"Why not?" Bennet answered, and they went down to join the other dancers.

He didn't look back until five or six songs later when the DJ put on "It's Raining Men," always an iconic moment at Rush. People flooded the dance floor, arms in the air, singing along. Charlotte's whole body rippled as she belted out the words.

Up at the bar, Tim Wilson's friend stood motionless. Behind him, even the staff were jiggling their hips, but he was as stiff as a pillar, staring down the sloping floor at the dancers as if he were watching the mating rituals of some insignificant and rather disgusting animal in a zoo.

*Well, fuck you too.* Bennet turned his back on him.

The song ended. Bennet wiped sweat from his forehead. Charlotte shouted, "I'm going for a ciggie. Do you want one?"

It would cool him off, so he nodded, and they made their way up the stairs to the gallery. If they'd used a ground-floor exit, they'd have had to ask the door staff to let them in again. Up here, they could go out on the fire escape, where someone always wedged a beer mat in the crack of the door to stop it closing all the way.

He followed Charlotte out onto the L-shaped area of flat roof, welcoming the chill of the air against his overheated skin. At the edge, an old metal staircase led down to the club's smelly backyard.

Charlotte laid a couple of Kleenexes on the top step and sat on them, but she jumped straight up again. "Shit, that's glacial. I'm not parking my rear there. Will you look round the corner? We could sit on that little sheltered wall, but I don't want to interrupt anything."

Bennet put his head around the angle of the L. The space beyond was empty. He beckoned her on, and they settled on the low wall by the door to the old projection room.

Charlotte shook two cigarettes from her pack, gave him one, and lit them. "I'll make you buy your own, one of these days."

"It isn't worth it. I smoke, like, one a month. I'll buy a packet for you sometime."

"That'll be the day." Charlotte inhaled, holding her breath for the maximum hit, and puffed out a thick cloud of smoke. "So what's the story with you and money? Why are you always so skint?"

"Trying to keep the debts down." With luck, she'd think he meant he wanted to minimise his student loans. In fact, he took the maximum there. He switched to a safer subject. "Tell me about this Tim Wilson. What did you think of him when you showed him around the gallery?"

"Seemed all right. Not the toughest of businessmen, but plenty of money, I'd say. The back room was in a right state, with mould and crumbling plaster, but his only concern was time—how long it would take to fix up. The cost didn't seem to matter." Charlotte blew a wobbly smoke ring. "He and Jamie look hot together, don't they? It would do Jamie good to have a little romance. He needs to loosen up a bit."

"He's loose enough. He just does things differently." Bennet took a puff of his cigarette and let it out without inhaling much. He didn't smoke, really, but he liked the smell of tobacco—it reminded him of his grandparents. "What about Tim's friend? Did you meet him before, too?"

"No. Doesn't look impressed, does he?"

"Looks like he thinks we've all crawled out of a sewer." Bennet kicked his heel against the wall.

"His name's Darius, if I heard right. They can't be together, the way Tim's carrying on with Jamie."

"I expect he's straight, and he's uptight about being surrounded by queers."

"Nah. Straight guys either stare at my tits or look around in panic for something else to stare at, and he did neither." Charlotte shivered. "It's freezing out here. I'm going in."

She took two more deep drags, blew out her last lungful of smoke, and ground the half-smoked cigarette against the wall.

Bennet didn't move. "I'll stay a bit longer. I feel stifled in there."

"Okay. I'll leave it wedged open for you."

She headed back around the corner. Bennet heard her steps crossing the roof, then the creak of the door.

He hugged himself against the cold and gazed up at the clear, starry sky. It wasn't just the club—he was beginning to feel stifled in this town. When he'd first come to college, leaving home had been a liberation in itself. Now he was impatient for the end of his course, so he could move on . . . except he didn't have anything to move on to.

The cigarette between his fingers had burned out. He flicked the stub into a pot of sand by the projection room door, then picked up Charlotte's and sent that the same way.

It was time to focus, to narrow down the possibilities, to take one path and let all the others go unexplored. Next week he'd see Monsieur Philippe, the head of the college's hospitality department, and . . .

A voice cut through the night. "I wouldn't call this *fresh* air. It stinks."

Someone else was on the roof, out of sight by the other door. The voice was confident and derisive, with the clipped accent of the upper class. Not a voice he'd ever heard before. It had to be Darius, Tim Wilson's friend.

"They come out here to smoke, I expect." Conciliatory. That must be Tim.

"And suck each other's cocks. For God's sake, how can they call this a nightclub? The description is virtually actionable."

Bennet's blood ran hot, and he sat up straight. Okay, Rush wasn't perfect, but it was all they had. Who did this Darius think he was?

Tim said, "It could be worse. I'm sure there's never any violence, for example. Try to be nice, please. I have to live here."

"You don't *have* to. You've chosen to, for reasons that remain obscure. I hope you'll change your mind, now we've seen what I assume is the whole gay population of the town and the surrounding countryside. There isn't a man here that doesn't make me want to run screaming back to London."

"Nonsense."

"Tim, there's *one* good-looking guy. You haven't taken

your eyes off him, so you have no idea what the rest are like."

Unfair. Bennet clenched his jaw. Sure, Jamie stood out, but he wasn't the only attractive guy in the club. There were plenty. A person just had to see them as individuals instead of writing them all off at a stroke.

A sigh, and Tim said, "Isn't he the most gorgeous thing you ever saw? And he's got an amazing kind of graceful strength."

"Whatever you say. But is he old enough to be in here?"

"Of course. I did ask. He's well over eighteen—almost twenty-one."

Footsteps sounded on the asphalt roof, approaching the corner. If the man in those shoes came any further, he'd see Bennet and know he'd heard. Bennet pushed at the projection room door, but it was another fire door, not designed to be opened from outside, and it held firm. Why hadn't he shown himself when they first started talking? He stood up, steeling himself for the mortification of meeting them.

But the steps stopped short of the corner and went back. Tim said, "I thought you might go for his friend."

"That pushy little blond?" The voice was full of scorn. Poor Leon.

"No, the dark-haired guy in the blue shirt. Don't tell me you didn't notice him—I won't believe you."

That was Bennet. He couldn't let this go any further. He didn't want to listen to them discussing him. He coughed and strode around the corner.

Tim jumped back, startled. At least he had the grace to look embarrassed. His friend just stared, his eyes like black ice.

Bennet had to pass within inches of them to reach the door. He moved like a wooden puppet, stiff with self-consciousness.

Darius looked him up and down and said, "Just about fuckable, I suppose, but hardly up to *my* standards."

Fury lit a fire in Bennet's veins. He forced himself to keep walking as if nothing had been said, but he didn't breathe until he stepped over the threshold into the club. Then he tugged the beer mat out of the hinge and pulled the door towards him, slamming the bar up and locking them out. The bastards could climb down the stairs or freeze until the next people went out and rescued them.

Why had he wasted a whole evening to meet these idiots? And why hadn't he brought his bicycle? He always did this—came out thinking he'd be spending the night with some hot guy, only to end up walking home alone.

He didn't look around for Charlotte. He'd jog back to Longbourn. He didn't want to be in the club when Darius came downstairs.

No way would he put himself under that cold gaze again. Ever.

# Chapter Two

"HE WAS GORGEOUS, Jamie," Leon said. "You were crazy not to jump on him. This whole no-sex-before-marriage thing makes no sense."

Bennet yawned. It was Saturday morning, and he'd been up early to work the breakfast shift at the Black Lion. He was due back there later to serve dinner. Meanwhile he'd brought his ancient laptop downstairs where the wireless signal was stronger, to scour the internet for jobs.

Jamie was baking. He wasn't studying management, but training to be a chef. Leon leaned against the counter flicking through Jamie's recipe book, and Kofi sat hunched over a cup of coffee. The shower was running overhead—Charlotte must be in the bathroom.

"It makes sense to me." Jamie opened the oven door to push a skewer into his chocolate cake. Bennet's mouth watered at the aroma that filled the room, and he took another bite of the sandwich at his elbow.

"But why would you want to marry someone you haven't even had sex with?" Kofi said. "All those ancient rules give me the creeping fantods. I swear, I wouldn't survive in Ghana. My gran saved my life, keeping me here when my mum and stepdad went back." He picked up Bennet's plate and peered into the sandwich. "Oh my God, Bennet, not peanut butter and cucumber *again?*"

Bennet took the plate from him and put it on the other side of his computer. "Why not? They're healthy. All the food groups." He'd grown up on peanut butter and cucumber sandwiches—it had been the only way his mother could make him eat anything green—and they were still the mainstay of his diet.

He added, "There's no point arguing with Jamie. I've known him a year longer than you have, and nobody can change anybody else's mind on this one. Can't we just respect each other's way of life?"

"And what's your way of life?" Leon asked. "Why don't we see you bringing home guys?"

Bennet shrugged. "I do. Or I did. It just hasn't happened lately."

"They're both romantics," Kofi said. "They want luuurve."

"Don't we all, but that's a different thing." Leon turned back to the counter to pick up the wooden spoon, scraped cake mix onto his finger, and licked it off. "Anyway, Jamie, it was selfish to hog Tim all night when you never had any intention of going home with him. Next time, give someone else a chance."

Leon stalked out with his nose in the air. Kofi followed, wriggling his arse at the door and turning to see if Bennet was looking. Bennet laughed. He couldn't take them seriously.

"Maybe you've had an influence on me," he said to Jamie

when the others were gone. "I'd rather have a relationship too, if I had the choice. But casual sex is better than nothing—only I don't seem to get that either." He turned to his computer and clicked in the search box. "Do you know any good sites for jobs, apart from the obvious? I don't want to take an internship with some faceless hotel chain if I can avoid it."

"You should talk to Monsieur Philippe."

"Yeah, I keep meaning to. I'll try to catch him next week."

He gave up on the major employment sites and typed *events management jobs* into the search bar. That was better. A lot of the results were about starting a business, and that was his aim. Not now, of course—he needed experience—but in a few years.

He glanced across the kitchen. Jamie was standing at the window staring out at the rain with a soft, dreamy smile.

Bennet grinned to himself. "So how about Tim, then? Is he The One?"

"I don't know. How could I know that, after one evening?" Jamie turned round, biting his lip. "*You* understand how I feel about sex, don't you?"

"I think so."

"I don't like being pawed. I've had people staring and trying to touch me ever since I was a child. They only wanted to cuddle me or pat my head—there was never anything sinister—but I hated it."

That, Bennet could understand. He'd seen pictures. Jamie had been a gorgeous little kid with a mass of cherubic white-blond curls that had now turned to gold. He'd stood out in a family with two rowdy-looking big brothers and a huge clan of aunts and cousins.

"I don't want that from someone I just met," Jamie went on. "I prefer to wait. It doesn't have to mean no sex before marriage, but I'd want some kind of commitment. I need to be sure I have the right guy. It's not something I would know after a couple of dances at Rush."

"Will you see him again?" Bennet asked, expecting a *no*.

"Maybe. He said he'd call me."

Bennet sat up. "You gave him your number?" This was new.

"Yes. He was respectful, you know? And there was something about him, like I already knew him. Have you ever felt that?"

Bennet arranged his knife on his empty plate. "Love at first sight? Not sure I believe in it."

"I didn't say *love*. More as if something settled into place when I saw him."

Could that happen as soon as two people met? Bennet couldn't imagine it. Or was it just that it had never happened to him, and he didn't like Jamie having an experience first?

He shrugged. "I've had the opposite—instant antagonism. With Tim's friend, for example."

"Darius? You didn't like him?"

"No, and it was mutual. He called me 'just about fuckable.' As if he'd ever have a chance."

Jamie laughed. "Poor Bennet. That's not what you're used to, is it?" He came to sit at the table, looking over

Bennet's shoulder at the computer screen. "Don't worry about jobs. You're top of your class. The right one will come along."

"I can't afford to wait. I'll need to start work as soon as our exams are over."

"Are you in trouble? Is it money? I wish you'd let me help."

Bennet shook his head. "Bad idea. That kind of thing ruins friendships."

"I don't understand how you already owed so much before you started college."

"It doesn't take much time to run up a debt, believe me." He typed *quirky jobs in hospitality*. "Hey, this could be it. 'Wanted: outstanding team player. Distinctivent—stunning events in unique locations.' Southwest London. And they're hiring . . . but they want a degree. Shit."

"I thought the Meriton HND was equivalent."

"It's supposed to be, but employers don't think so."

"You could convert it. You'd only have to do one year at a university."

Bennet gritted his teeth. "Another year is not an option. All those fees, just for more theory? I want to be out there working and earning. I'll learn more that way than I would in some university library."

---

BENNET CYCLED TO the Black Lion for the dinner shift. He went in at the front door—oak painted black to match the beams—and glanced into the manager's office. He'd been drawn back to Distinctivent's website and had fired off an application during the afternoon, degree or no degree. But he'd need stellar references to give him any chance.

The regular manager had left for the day. No point talking to anyone else on this one. He pulled his head back.

"Bennet?" The duty manager called after him. "Can you go in the bar tonight? We're one down."

"Sure." Bar, dining room, cleaning, or portering, he didn't care, as long as they paid him—and he'd have done the work for no pay if he hadn't needed the money, because he picked up experience he couldn't get from books. If his assignments came back with the highest marks in the class (and they often did), his weekend job was a big part of the reason.

The bar here was the most expensive in town, and it was never crowded. Bennet polished glasses, cleaned tables, and took the occasional order, part of a process that went like clockwork. He moved smoothly though the hushed atmosphere, until Tim and Darius walked in.

Every muscle in his body tensed at the sight of Darius. The classic stress reaction—fight or flight.

He went for flight, excusing himself to the other staff member and slipping out through the hatch before the two friends could reach the bar. He cleared a table in the far corner and picked some tiny scraps of paper off the thick, dark carpet. At the bar, Tim paid and took the glasses, while Darius carried an ice bucket containing a bottle of wine. Time for Bennet to move. He drifted around the edge of the room and reached the safety of the bar as they settled at an isolated table, far from other customers.

They saw him, however. Tim fluttered his fingers in a wave, and Darius glanced up with his cool, distant stare. Then Tim pulled a computer from his bag, and they both focused on that.

*Forget they're here.* But Bennet's muscles stayed tight, and his movements were clumsy. Glasses clanged together when he emptied the washer. Whatever he did, his eyes were drawn back to the pair at the distant table—or to one of them.

Darius was like a man in a painting, one of those old portraits where the subject's pose is too stiff to be real. He looked good. Dark hair waved over his temples. His brows were straight and his nose razor-fine. With a little more animation, he could be gorgeous. But his face was a mask, holding too much back.

Tim came up to the bar, alone, at a moment when Bennet was the only one there.

"You have peanuts?"

"Sure. Dry roasted, honey roasted, bacon, or sweet chilli flavour?"

"Sweet chilli sounds interesting!"

Bennet reached for the stupidly expensive plastic pot of nuts. Tim's head swivelled as one of the waiters came through, his face lighting up with hope. But he turned back, disappointed.

"Does Jamie work here too?" he asked, as Bennet gave him his change.

Bennet smiled to himself. "No, sorry."

"I wanted to send him something—something I need to mail. I have his phone number, but I don't have the address. Could you . . ."

Bennet didn't want to give out Jamie's home address, however nice the guy seemed. "You can send it to the college. James Kershaw, Hospitality and Catering, Meriton College. He'll get it."

Tim nodded and typed it into his phone. He thanked Bennet and turned away.

"Your peanuts?"

"Oh yes!" Tim blushed—he went pink to the tip of his nose—and took the plastic pot. Just an excuse to get in touch with Jamie. How transparent he was, and how friendly. How unlike Darius.

---

BENNET TRIED TO make an appointment to see the head of hospitality and catering a couple of days later.

"I'm sorry," the secretary said, "Monsieur Philippe's in a meeting."

"How about this afternoon?" Bennet persisted. "I need some advice about jobs."

"I can't say when he'll be free." She paused for a second before she said *he*—giving it a capital H, as if she were talking about God. "Why don't you talk to the careers officer?"

That hadn't crossed his mind. Philippe Hennice was a complete fake in some ways—he put on a French accent, but Nigel had once let slip that his real name was Philip, and he'd grown up in Birmingham—but he had a vast web of contacts in the catering industry, and he knew Bennet. He was the person to see, no question.

"If I came by at five . . .?"

She pursed her lips, gazed at the appointment book that Monsieur Philippe preferred to an on-screen diary, and shook her head. Bennet wouldn't be granted an audience today.

On his way out of the office, he checked the students' mail pigeonholes. In Jamie's, along with the usual memos from the college, lay a handwritten envelope of thick, cream-coloured paper. Bennet took it to the kitchens, where his friend was making savoury choux pastry buns.

Jamie pulled a vinyl glove off one hand and gripped the corner of the envelope between his teeth to open it. Inside was a card inviting them to the art gallery's opening party that weekend. *All your housemates*, it said.

Bennet was curious about Jamie's potential boyfriend and his gallery, so he went along. He planned to ignore or avoid Darius, if he was there. It shouldn't be difficult. Darius would have more important people to talk to—people who wouldn't make him *want to run screaming back to London*, as he'd said.

And sure enough, the gallery was packed with well-dressed citizens clutching champagne flutes, huddled in chattering groups, paying little attention to the paintings. The average age was close to sixty, and if there was any music, it was drowned by the jabbering voices.

"How can he call this a party?" Bennet muttered to

Jamie. "The description is virtually actionable."

"Pardon?"

"A joke. Never mind."

Tim broke away from an animated discussion to greet them. "Hello!" He smiled at all of them and touched Jamie's arm. "Let me show you the paintings."

As Tim drew Jamie away, Nigel, their landlord, stepped through the door wearing a brown poncho, complete with cowboy hat and boots. Monsieur Philippe came in one minute later.

"Sweet," Leon whispered. "Arriving separately, as if nobody knows they've been a couple for, like, forever."

"I don't know why they bother to hide it," Bennet said. "They should move in together."

Leon made a face. "Please, not at Longbourn Manor. Imagine bumping into our head of department in his undies in the morning. Awkward, much?"

Charlotte grabbed a glass and spotted a colleague from Credlands, the estate agents. Kofi went looking for the food. Bennet was standing in the middle of the room with Leon, wondering how soon he could leave, when Darius came out from the back room and strode up to them.

He gave a nod that might have been intended as a greeting to one of them, or both, or neither. "Good evening. Are you enjoying the gathering?"

*I was, until you showed up.* Bennet had to choke back the words. What kind of answer did the guy expect? Polite chitchat, as if he hadn't been hurling insults at Bennet on the roof of a club only last weekend? Well, he wouldn't get it.

Not from Bennet.

But Leon gave Darius a bright smile, said hello, and asked what he did for a living.

"I'm a barrister."

"Oh, in a coffee shop? Which chain?"

Darius blinked and stared down his aristocratic nose at Leon.

Bennet felt the heat rising to his face, as if he'd made the mistake himself. "A barrister, Leon, not a barista. It's a kind of lawyer."

Darius's face cleared. "Yes. Traditionally, the kind who argues in the higher courts, although the distinctions between barristers and solicitors are beginning to break down in England."

"Right," said Leon, unfazed. "Silly me—imagine not knowing that. But then, our minds are trained to focus on catering establishments."

Darius's brows drew together in a momentary frown. Bennet said to him, "Why not talk to the local worthies, who might at least understand you?"

"*You* seem to understand me well enough," Darius said.

Bennet's shoulders stiffened. "I couldn't fail to, the last time we met. You made yourself very clear."

Darius's mouth twitched as if the memory amused him.

Leon looked around at the walls. "Do you think he'll sell all these pictures tonight?"

"I doubt it," Darius said.

Bennet challenged him. "Why not?"

"Most of this crowd are too old to fit the target

demographic. Retired people don't buy art. They already have their houses decorated the way they like them, and when they next move, they'll downsize. An art gallery needs a population of child-free high earners in the thirty to fifty age range, who don't tend to live in a Home Counties backwater."

Bennet couldn't wait to get out of Hertfordshire himself, but that didn't mean he wanted to hear some hotshot lawyer dissing the place.

"This town may not seem much to you," he retorted, "but it attracts huge numbers of tourists. There's tons going on in summer—a regatta on the river, a historic fair—and the surrounding forests and hills are so unspoilt, they're often used for film locations. A person doesn't have to live here to buy a painting. I think your friend's made a good decision, and there's no reason why he shouldn't make a success of this gallery."

"I didn't say—"

Leon interrupted him. "People don't just come to see the river and forests and stuff, either. Our actual college used to be a stately home called Netherfield Park. You must have heard of it. It's the country house in *Bridgemaston Days*—or its outside is, anyway."

"The country house in what?" Darius asked.

Leon made a face of mock astonishment. "Hello? *Bridgemaston Days*, the TV series? Winner of God knows how many awards? What cultural desert did they ship *you* in from?"

"A different one from yours, clearly," Darius said stiffly. "I don't have time to waste sitting in front of a television."

Leon flashed a pink tongue at him, just as Monsieur Philippe came up behind them. The head of department ignored his students and held out his hand for Darius to shake.

"You must be Darius Lanniker. Delighted to meet you. I'm Philippe Hennice. Your aunt Catherine and I are old friends. In fact, she and I together put Tim in touch with the agent selling the gallery."

A flash of annoyance crossed Darius's face. "She's not my aunt. A connection by marriage, that's all."

"But you must see a lot of her at Pemberley?"

"I'm not often in Derbyshire. I live in London."

"Ah. Sad for you to lose your childhood home."

Darius's posture tightened, and his words were clipped. "It's not lost."

He looked uncomfortable. That was a first. Bennet wanted to know why, but Monsieur Philippe dropped the subject. "How do you like our little town? Are you planning to visit often?"

Darius avoided the first question by focusing on the second. "I doubt it. I was advising Tim on the purchase, but once the gallery's established, I imagine he'll be glad to get back to London when he can."

"You think?" Philippe turned to watch Tim, who was venting his enthusiasm in front of a wire and plaster sculpture. A circle of smiling ladies surrounded him, but Tim was addressing every word to Jamie. Darius frowned.

Philippe nodded at Jamie with pride. "One of my students."

"You teach at the college?" Darius asked.

"Yes, indeed. We offer vocational training at the highest level. In my department, we provide students with all the managerial and technical skills required for hospitality management and other professional positions."

Darius looked blank for a moment. Then he said, "A further education college? And they're studying catering? That explains a certain ignorance that was puzzling me."

Leon made another face at Darius and stalked away.

Monsieur Philippe drew back his shoulders. "Our students aren't ignorant just because they're not at university. If their ambition is to manage certain businesses in the service industries or to become a top chef, they wouldn't choose a degree course, however intelligent they were. They would come to Meriton, if they were good enough."

Bennet edged away after Leon, but Philippe gripped his shoulder and drew him back.

"For example, this is Bennet Rourke, one of my hospitality management students. He'd have had no trouble getting a university place if he'd wanted one, but finding the best vocational training was what mattered to him. An extremely able young man, specialising in facilities management."

Darius turned to Bennet. "Hotels, conferences, that kind of thing? Sounds like a lot of hassle for not much reward."

"I enjoy a challenge," Bennet said, looking straight at him.

One side of Darius's mouth curved up in a wry smile. An actual smile? Bennet was too surprised to respond.

Monsieur Philippe pointed out the other students. "Leon's in the first year of the same course. The young man of African extraction is in the business studies department, I think. What's his specialism, Bennet?"

"Kofi? Travel and tourism. Charlotte too."

"Not my department," Philippe went on, "although there's a lot of overlap. And of course James. One of my final year professional cookery cohort. He's proved to be an exceptional talent at French patisserie."

Darius stared at Jamie and gave a short bark of a laugh. "You mean he's a *pastry cook*?"

As if nobody who worked with their hands deserved respect. Bennet didn't plan to listen to any more of the man's put-downs. He made his excuses and pushed away through the crowd.

---

"Bennet?"

Bennet turned unwillingly at the door. He'd done his duty. He'd met Charlotte's colleague, eaten his share of weird marzipan-flavoured canapés, and drunk another glass of the wine, which had turned out to be sparkling Vouvray, not champagne. He'd earned the right to leave, and he'd almost escaped.

But not quite. "Darius."

Darius cleared his throat. "I believe you have some kind of restaurant at your college, run by the students?"

"The training restaurant? The college runs it, really, but the students staff it for work experience. We serve lunch at midday, then it's open to the public five evenings a week."

Darius shrugged off the explanation. "Tim's interested in seeing it, anyway. He's heard it's in a good location, with views?"

"Well, yes—the main college building is an old mansion, as Leon told you. The restaurant's in what used to be the ballroom. If you're seated at the back, near the windows, you can see out over the ha-ha to the river in summer."

Darius opened his mouth to speak, but Bennet wanted to end this conversation as fast as he could, so he went on talking.

"But at this time of year, it's already dark when we open. Tell him to wait a few weeks until the clocks have changed."

He turned away, but Darius called him back. "He won't wait. He's arranged to eat there with your friend on Friday night. I wondered if you'd like to go along?"

Bennet couldn't hide his surprise. Words tumbled out. "You mean—me go with Tim and Jamie? Or *you* and me and them?"

"All of us, yes." Darius's face gave nothing away.

"You're asking me for a *date*?" It made no sense. Darius wasn't interested in either Bennet or the college, he'd made that clear. "No, wait, I get it. You're inviting me as a kind of alibi so you can crash *their* date."

Darius didn't deny it. He didn't even look embarrassed. "That's not the correct use of *alibi*."

Unbelievable. Any chance he had to put somebody down, he took it.

"Whatever," Bennet said. "I'm on the rota to work there next Friday, so I can't. Sorry."

Half true. He was on the rota, but he wasn't the least bit sorry. He slipped outside before Darius could answer, grabbed his bike, and headed back to Longbourn.

# Chapter Three

Bennet hit the button on the shower in the college locker room and stripped off while the water warmed. He was the training restaurant's maître d'hôtel tonight, with a full day of classes behind him and a long evening ahead.

It was a tiring role, but meal service gave him a buzz. When it went right, it felt so clean, so smooth and easy. Dishes flowed in and out of the kitchen with a Zen-like effortlessness. The dining room was a world of its own, where everything was a perfect fit.

When it went right.

He showered, shaved, and shrugged his shoulders into the jacket that only the maître d' wore. He'd be in charge in the dining room, but the true power lay with Jamie's classmate, the head chef in the kitchen, and above her, whoever was there to supervise and assess them—Monsieur Philippe, tonight.

Bennet winked at himself in the mirror and grinned. *Looking good.* Stay calm and in control, that was the way.

Out in the dining room, he turned a critical eye on the tables and on his waiting staff, younger students from the Ordinary National Diploma or the first year of the Higher. Leon was one of them. Bennet stopped them chatting, sent them to their places, and took up his position at the island near the entrance, checking the bookings.

He wouldn't have been surprised to see Tim's name against a table for three, but no. He found two reservations in the name of Wilson, a two and a four, both for eight o'clock. Darius wasn't coming, then. The two must be Tim and Jamie. The restaurant would be full, as usual on a Friday, but he made plans to keep one of the best tables for them. The college—and the restaurant—had to make a good impression on Tim, for Jamie's sake.

Richard Jones, a student from his own class, hurried in five minutes late. He saw Bennet looking at his watch, and his chin came up in defiance. He didn't like Bennet, and it was mutual.

Right behind Richard, the first guests arrived. At this hour, most of them were college staff enjoying the chance to have a cheap meal out at the end of the working week, some with colleagues, some with a spouse or partner. Bennet seated the first two couples and a group of five. The serving students peeled themselves from their stations, electronic notebooks at the ready, while Richard Jones, as sommelier, stalked around the occupied tables taking wine orders.

Then Leon went to check on an order in the kitchen. He came straight back to Bennet and said, "It's chaos in there. I think we'd best keep clear for a bit."

"Keep clear? What are you talking about? Most of these tables are booked twice. We can't have delays."

"Yeah, but there's nobody with an ounce of sense in the kitchen. The chef cut herself, and the next in line had to drive her to hospital. Nobody else seems to have a clue how to cook anything."

Bennet shook his head. "It doesn't matter. Keep taking the orders in to them. We need this lot to eat and leave. The sous-chefs will soon start to focus—unless it's serious enough for us to close, and that's up to Monsieur Philippe."

"He's stuck in traffic."

"Traffic? In Meriton?"

Leon shrugged. "He must be on his way back from somewhere."

"But they've talked to him, right?"

"I assume."

"Okay, so he's dealing with it. Back to your station. You've got another threesome by the window there."

"Ooh, a threesome! My fave." Leon giggled and went to greet his new customers.

Bennet turned away. Chefs who bled all over the kitchen shouldn't be put in charge on a busy Friday night. But hey, it wasn't his problem. Two more groups had arrived for another pair of tables. He'd seat them and have his staff take the orders. The rest was out of his control.

Still, when a few more minutes had passed and things should have calmed down a little, he slipped through the swing door.

Bad move. Students in white coats and aprons were tripping over each other like ants whose nest had been dug up. Vegetables lay on counters, half-chopped, and pots were boiling over on the stoves.

Then someone came in from the locker room, shrugging

into a chef's jacket—someone familiar.

Bennet strode up to him. "For fuck's sake, what are you doing, Jamie? You've got a date."

Jamie shook his head. "Monsieur Philippe phoned me from his car. You heard about the accident here? She sliced her hand open to the bone, and there are two new specials on the menu tonight, her own recipes. They couldn't cope."

"We'll cross those dishes off the menus."

"The ingredients won't keep until Monday, and they're too expensive to waste. I called Tim and explained."

"Can't someone else cover?"

"Half the class have gone to London for the weekend, for someone's birthday."

Bennet threw up his hands. "Okay. It's your call." The price of working in a service industry. "Shall I cancel Tim's booking? We could use the table."

"No, I think he's still coming, with Darius."

Darius. The last person Bennet wanted in the restaurant on an already stressful shift.

An overheated pan spat oil. One of the students shrieked. Jamie went off in that direction.

"Keep the customers cool out there, Bennet," he called over his shoulder. "We might be a little slower than usual."

"Right," Bennet said to vacant space.

---

WHEN TIM AND Darius arrived, the restaurant was only running a little late. Bennet had to park one group of six in the waiting area, but the table for two that he'd allocated for

Tim was clear and clean. Only problem—Tim and Darius weren't alone. A dapper young man with slicked-back auburn curls and a pert tilt to his nose hovered at Darius's elbow.

"This is my cousin Quentin," Tim said. "Quentin, this is Jamie's friend, Bennet."

Bennet said hello, and the redhead nodded with pursed lips. He might be Tim's cousin, but Bennet would bet it hadn't been Tim's idea to bring him along. Darius had found someone else to crash Jamie's date. As for Darius, Bennet ignored him, but he was aware of the barrister's gaze.

"Table for three?" Bennet ran a finger down his list, although he knew there was nothing free.

"I booked for four," Tim said, "but Jamie's working?"

"Oh, right. Of course."

So they were the Wilson for four, not the Wilson for two. Okay. Some other pair would enjoy the well-placed table he'd set aside.

The way Bennet felt about Darius, he was tempted to seat them by the kitchen door, or better still, by the toilets. But that wasn't fair on Tim. So he led them towards number sixteen, two rows in from the windows.

Tim brought them to a halt in the middle of the room. It was dark outside, and the bare windows glittered with reflected lights. Bennet waited, letting them gaze around. People often did this the first time they came, and even when he was busy, he liked to be reminded how beautiful the former ballroom was, with its oak-panelled walls and the intricate plasterwork on the ceiling.

Tim's eyes sparkled like the chandeliers. "I think my family might have lived here once. There's a painting of Netherfield Park in our laundry room. Do you remember it, Darius?"

"I have no recollection of your parents' laundry room."

"I never suspected we had such illustrious antecedents," Quentin said. "I thought we were filthy nouveau riche."

"Oh, not the Wilsons—the Bingleys, on my mother's side." Tim turned to Bennet. "Is it true that *Bridgemaston Days* is filmed here?"

"Yes, but only the rear façade. The interiors are shot in a studio, and they use another house for the front."

"Technically, the façade *is* the front," Darius said. "*Rear façade* is a contradiction."

Bennet bit back his irritation. He hadn't been talking to Darius.

"But a lot of the action happens on the lawn at the back," Tim broke in. So he didn't share Darius's disdain for television. "And I heard they'll be shooting the next season soon."

"That's right," Bennet said. "Before, they've filmed in the summer or at Christmas, when we're not here, but this time they're coming at Easter, and the vacation isn't long enough, so they're setting up next week. It'll be weird. Those windows will be screened off on the inside, and we won't be allowed around the back of the college at all."

Darius cleared his throat. "Are we here for a guided tour or for dinner?"

Tim laughed, so maybe that was meant to be a joke.

Bennet shrugged it off and led them a few more steps to their table. It was one of Leon's, which would have been okay if he'd been as competent as usual, but he hadn't finished resetting it from the previous guests.

Bennet took him aside and said in a low voice, "You've missed the napkins."

Leon put his hands on his hips and thrust out his chest. "So seat them somewhere else. I don't want that Dari-arse in my area, thank you."

"They're staying right where they are. You'll be professional. Pretend he's a complete stranger."

"Complete *wanker*." But he flounced off to fetch the napkins.

Darius studied the menu. "Lobster, that's ambitious."

"Shall we have that?" Tim said, smiling. "There's no wheat in it, is there, Bennet? I'm allergic."

"Oh please, not lobster for me," Quentin put in. "Way too messy. Besides, I agree with Darius—I'd only want to order lobster in a *good* restaurant."

If this guy was Darius's date, they were a perfect match, Bennet thought. And judging by the way he kept touching Darius's arm, Quentin was up for it tonight whether they were together or not. Which shouldn't bother Bennet. So why did it?

Two more couples were waiting by Bennet's station. He excused himself and left Tim's party with Leon.

He checked on them later. Tim and Darius had ordered the lobster. It wasn't messy at all. The meat had been removed from the shell in the kitchen, and it came served over fennel risotto with watercress, red pepper, and one orange claw to punctuate the plate.

Quentin looked envious. He had *boeuf bourguignon*, which always tasted fine but was nothing special to look at. He was compensating by knocking back the white wine.

Darius clicked his fingers at Bennet and tapped the side of his full glass. "May we have another bottle of this?"

"Certainly. I'll tell your waiter. Is it the Graves?" Bennet was brusque. Okay, no bottle stood on the table, and whoever had taken the empty one should have asked if they wanted more... but who did Darius think he was, summoning people with a snap of the fingers?

"The Chablis *premier cru*. Excuse me, I thought you *were* a waiter."

"I'm the maître d'hôtel. You may have noticed that I'm wearing a jacket, and the others are not?"

"Ah. I'm afraid I'm not au fait with the niceties of dress for serving staff—although a man in uniform always has an edge."

Quentin made a show of stifling a laugh. "Oh, Darius, you are naughty. As if waiters counted as men in uniform! What do you go for, really?" He swept back his auburn locks and fluttered long eyelashes. Someone should tell him his skin went bright red when he drank.

"I rather like the blue eyes, dark hair combo," Darius said, looking at Bennet.

Quentin grabbed his glass with a pout, tipping the last drops into his open mouth.

Darius went on, "But equality matters more to me than

appearance. I do enjoy a challenge."

Bennet gave him a sharp glance. Enjoying a challenge—hadn't he said something like that himself, at the party at the gallery? And was Darius taking the piss with that swipe about equality? No way were they equals, the high-flying barrister and the penniless student whose parents drove buses and cleaned offices for a living.

Monsieur Philippe sailed into the dining room through the kitchen door, making straight for their table. He nodded to Bennet and took the vacant seat. Bennet didn't nod back. That was Jamie's place. If the crisis was over, couldn't Jamie have come out?

They still had no wine, and Philippe might want some. Leon was nowhere in sight, but Richard Jones was leaning against one of the waiter stations near the kitchen—a station where a pretty girl was based. Bennet walked that way and beckoned him out.

"Someone's left table sixteen without wine."

Richard scowled. "Wasn't me."

"They want another bottle of the Chablis *premier cru*."

"Okay, okay."

Richard felt in his pocket for the keys to what they called the wine cellar—a temperature-controlled walk-in refrigerator in the kitchen—and stalked away. As he went, he turned to wink at the girl. At the same moment, Leon burst through the kitchen exit door carrying four dessert plates. His attention was focused on balancing them on his arm, and he didn't see Richard.

"Watch out!"

But Leon didn't hear Bennet's warning, and Richard only looked at Bennet instead of the girl. A second later, he cannoned into Leon.

Custard went all over the floor, and a portion of ice cream landed on the back of the nearest diner, a middle-aged woman in a thin blue dress. She shrieked.

Leon stood immobile, doing a face palm. Richard was almost as useless, bending to pick up a plate as if the customers weren't there.

The woman's companion, a man, got up and dabbed at her back with a napkin. She was quiet now, but shaking. Bennet recognised the couple. They'd eaten here before, and they'd been at Tim's party.

He moved fast, going straight to their table. "I'm so sorry. Please bring us any receipts for dry cleaning. There'll be no charge for your meal."

The woman managed a smile. "Accidents will happen. Luckily it was nothing hot."

Thank God she was taking it like that. Bennet turned to Leon and Richard.

"It was his fault," Richard said, pointing at Leon.

"I saw it," Bennet said. "Neither of you was looking where you were going."

Richard hissed, "You've been on my case all night. Fuck off."

Bennet froze. Leon's eyes went wide. The man at the table straightened up. "Excuse me! There are ladies present."

Bennet stared at Richard. *I'm not bloody apologising for him again*, he thought, as Monsieur Philippe appeared at his elbow.

Philippe placated the couple with his own effusive apologies, then said, "Bennet? Are you in charge here?"

He'd better show that he was. "Leon, back to the kitchen and ask them to repeat that order, then start cleaning up. Richard, stay here until Leon gets back, to stop anyone slipping on this mess. Then the Chablis for table sixteen. I'll check Leon's other tables."

"And all three of you in my office after the last diners have gone," Philippe added.

So much for giving Tim a good impression of the college restaurant. Bennet glanced over at their table. Tim was acting like he hadn't seen a thing, and Darius had his back to the scene, but Quentin had a hand to his mouth as if covering a laugh.

The kitchen door swung open and Jamie came through it, shrugging out of his white coat. He headed for Tim's table. So they'd have a few minutes of their date, and maybe that would wipe out the disaster in Tim's mind. Bennet didn't give a shit what Darius and Quentin thought.

---

"LET'S HEAR IT," Monsieur Philippe said. "Leon, what happened?"

"Why are you asking him?" Richard objected.

"I'll be asking all of you. Leon?"

Leon shrugged and tipped his head on one side. "An accident? I used the right door. Perhaps he wasn't looking."

"Richard?"

"*He* wasn't looking. He barged out of the kitchen and ran straight into me."

"Bennet?"

"Neither of them was paying attention, but that's not the point. It's what followed. They didn't deal with the customer who had ice cream dripping down her back—"

"Only because you got there so fast," Leon said. "I was still in shock."

"—and Richard swore at me in front of customers. The f-word."

"Bullshit," Richard said.

"He did," Leon put in. "I heard him."

Philippe waved him away. "All right, Leon, you can go."

"I won't fail, will I? It wasn't my fault."

"You need to pay more attention to what's going on around you. When you're in the maître d' position next year, you can't afford to be caught up in your own little world."

"Whew. So I'll still be here next year? What a relief."

He left, and Bennet pushed the door closed behind him.

"He was carrying too much," said Richard. "He couldn't handle it, and he dropped the lot. Nothing to do with me. And if I used any bad language, which I don't believe I did, it was *his* fault." He flicked a hand towards Bennet.

"*My* fault?"

"He was in my face the whole evening, accusing me of not keeping up with the wine orders, when it was that airheaded little drama queen who'd cleared away the bucket without telling me. Oh, and they happen to live in the same house. What a coincidence."

"This is—"

Monsieur Philippe held up a hand to stop Bennet speaking. "So what do you think would happen here in real life, Richard?"

"He'd use it as an excuse to sack me, and I'd complain to an employment tribunal."

"On what grounds?"

"Discrimination by the f—by the gay mafia in this college."

"*Gay mafia*?" Bennet said.

Philippe didn't seem surprised. "It's not an uncommon accusation in the industry, Bennet. You'll have to be careful not to favour other gay men, especially those you've slept with or would like to—"

"Leon is not in either category."

"—or discriminate against women and straight men. Richard, watch your mouth in front of customers. I heard the gentleman reminding you that ladies were present, so you must have said something. Perhaps you use the word so often, it slips out without you noticing?"

Richard didn't answer.

"I want two pages from each of you by Monday morning on the legal ramifications of an incident like this—the employment law, and what could happen if the customer got nasty. Not an essay. Bullet points."

"That's harsh," Richard said. "You didn't give that first year any punishment at all."

"It's not a punishment, it's a learning opportunity. And consider everything from the management side. I'm not interested in the employee's point of view. You'll be managers, if you pass this course."

Richard's head snapped up. "*If* we pass? You know my contract in Dubai depends on it. If I don't pass, I'll—"

"Do the work you're assigned, and you should have no trouble. Now, get off home, both of you."

Bennet followed Richard into the locker room. Richard thumped a fist against his other hand. Bennet ignored him. Let him start a fight if he wanted. If he thought a gay man couldn't defend himself, he'd find he was wrong. Bennet had been fighting all his life.

But Bennet wasn't Richard's target. "The fucking bastard," Richard said as they changed, out of sight of each other on different sides of the bank of lockers. "If he fails me, I'll have him in court."

"Now who's being a drama queen? He won't fail you."

Venom filled the voice that filtered back around the lockers. "Oh, you know him that well, do you? I wonder what you've been doing for your grades. You wait. You might find things don't go all your way in the real world. There you are, all cosy in the manor house with Philippe's bum-boy. But you don't have a job yet, do you?"

Bennet pushed his uniform into his bag and left, careful not to let the door slam. He wouldn't give Richard the pleasure of knowing his last dig had hit home.

## Chapter Four

Bennet called Donna Clare, the operations director at Distinctivent, the day after their deadline. They claimed to be a vibrant, open, and innovative company, so they damn well should consider him, and he didn't want some junior assistant weeding out his application because he wasn't studying for a degree.

"My head of department will tell you I'm heading for a distinction," he told her. "I'm in the top five percent of my class. I could get a degree in another year with no trouble, but I want to be active, I want to be working. And from what I've seen online, I want to work for you."

"Where do you see yourself in ten years?"

"Either running my own business or in a senior position with a young and dynamic company like yours."

She laughed. "Do you mean like our company, or like my position? No, don't answer that. I could well be ready to give you my job in ten years. Okay—I haven't seen the applications yet, but I'll keep you in mind. Meriton College has a good rep. Bennet Rourke, right?"

The email came two days later. The call had won him an interview.

He took the train to London for it. The offices were in

Richmond, not far from the Thames. Not a bland tower suite, but the top half of an old engineering workshop. Outside, the building was dusty brick. Inside, bright colours and laughter, though no one was slacking off. They seemed to have plenty to do. That was fine. Bennet worked best under pressure.

They gave him coffee and a doughnut while he waited. Some of the staff smiled and said "Hi!" as they walked past. The oldest looked about thirty-five. The receptionist wore roller skates.

Bennet could see himself working here, with this office as his base and the city as the loom where he'd pull together all the threads of his work. He'd sit at one of these workstations, when he wasn't on the move. He'd design events that would flow like cream around obstacles, growing and adapting, sparkling through every moment from the opening of the doors to the bagging of the last faded ribbon. Events that people would talk about for the rest of their lives. Events they'd call The. Best. Thing. Ever.

But a chill hit him when he stepped into the interview room. Two people sat behind a low table—a man in a suit, and a woman who looked nothing like the photo of the operations director on the website.

"I thought I'd be seeing Donna Clare?"

They exchanged a glance, and the woman said, "Donna couldn't be here today. Family crisis."

The excitement he'd felt in the outer office drained away in seconds, like water through a sieve.

"So, uh—" The guy glanced down at his papers.

"Bennet. I think the advertisement was clear in that we're looking for a university graduate for this post. Perhaps you could start by explaining how you feel your background makes up for your lack of that qualification?"

Bennet went through his argument again, but their faces were set like masks. How could he convey his enthusiasm when the man spent the whole time tapping a pencil against his copy of Bennet's application, as if he were slapping Bennet down?

They said they'd let him know, but the interview was over in fourteen minutes, and the outcome was obvious. Without Donna Clare, they weren't prepared to take a chance.

---

"YOU'RE COMING TO Rush, Bennet," Leon announced. "You are coming, don't argue."

"Give me one good reason." It was the Friday after his interview. Bennet had heard nothing from Distinctivent.

"Filming's started! The actors will be there."

Kofi and Leon now spent every lunch break hanging around the caravans on the edge of the college grounds. Leon's big fantasy was to appear in *Bridgemaston Days*. It left Bennet cold. The real stars came and went in darkened cars, and he couldn't work up any interest in the C-list celebrities who walked the streets of Meriton.

"Actors?" Bennet said. "Last month you made a big deal out of Tim, and what did that amount to? One new guy."

Kofi pointed an accusing finger at him. "You're just

grouchy because you thought Jamie would always be around when you wanted to go out, and now he's met someone, so he's not."

He had a point. Jamie would be at Rush, but he'd be with Tim. Charlotte was sick. Only sourness made Bennet want to refuse to go.

So he went. And three new guys did come in. One was around Tim's age, with a heavy forelock of light-brown hair and a wide smile. The others were older—balding, heavy-bellied bears. Not Bennet's type. But the younger guy . . . yes, maybe.

Kofi and Leon didn't seem interested. They checked the men out and turned away.

"What's up?" Bennet asked Kofi, who was near enough to hear him over the music. "Aren't they TV people?"

"They're crew. Cameramen. We want the actors or the directors."

"Maybe they go home at weekends."

Kofi gave him a scornful look. "Of course they don't. That's when they do most of their filming, when we're not there."

Actors, crew—whoever they were, Bennet didn't care. The brown-haired guy had an expressive face, flickering and laughing. Bennet liked his broad, easy smile. The dimple in his left cheek was cute too. Yes, Bennet wouldn't mind getting to know him. He straightened his shirt.

But before he could make a move, Darius came through the doors.

Darius stared at the brown-haired guy and stopped in his

tracks. The brown-haired guy stared at Darius. Then Darius spun around and strode out, without a glance at anyone else.

The film crew guy stood still, watching Darius leave. Then his grin came back, but he didn't look so confident now.

Bennet put his glass down on the bar. One of the staff came over, wanting to take his order. Over the music, it took Bennet a while to make her understand that he didn't want anything else. When he turned back, the brown-haired guy was gone.

*Damn.*

And weirdly, days later, when he asked Jamie if he knew why Darius had left like that, Jamie said Darius hadn't been in Meriton that weekend, as far as he knew. Tim had said he was expecting him, but he hadn't arrived.

Darius must have driven up, come into Rush looking for Tim, spotted this guy, and climbed straight back in his car without ever saying a word about it to Tim.

So what was going on there?

---

BENNET DIDN'T GIVE up his hope of a job with Distinctivent without a fight. Donna Clare might still agree to see him, when she came back. He called and called again.

"She'll be out of the office for a few weeks," they told him, finally.

"Is she sick?"

"No, she's on leave. Can I put you through to somebody else?"

He didn't remember the names of the people who'd interviewed him. No point talking to them, anyway. They'd made it clear they wanted a degree.

Monsieur Philippe didn't seem able to spare him a moment. Bennet made an appointment to see him, only for it to be cancelled. Another week and they'd be into the Easter vacation.

To work off his tension, he went to the college gym one afternoon between classes and found Jamie there. Bennet warmed up and joined him in the weights area, picking up a pair of dumbbells.

"I heard there might be a job coming up at the Black Lion," Jamie said.

"Yeah, one of the sous-chefs is leaving. You're interested in that—full-time? I never thought you'd want to work there, or I'd have told you." Bennet finished a set of bicep curls and shook out his arms. "They might want someone who's available now. Hotels have to keep the kitchen running. But it might be worth a shot. Do you want me to pick up the information for you?"

"No, I've got it."

Bennet did another set and then said, "Wait. Would this be about staying in Meriton to be near a certain art gallery—or its owner?"

Jamie laughed and shook his head as if embarrassed. "It's a good hotel. Great kitchen. Respected head chef."

"True, but it's not world-class. And there's not much scope for your patisserie."

"They do afternoon teas. Anyway, it's only an idea. I

might not apply."

"Have you talked to Tim about it?"

"Oh no, it's too early for that."

Bennet grinned. "So it *is* because of him."

Jamie looked away. "Shall we do some pull-ups?"

"Okay, I'll let you change the subject. Three sets of thirty? Got to keep the biceps and lats in shape for climbing."

They went for the bars. "Have you done any climbing lately?" Jamie asked at the end of the first set.

Bennet wiped his brow with the back of his hand. "No, it's not worth paying the entrance fee for that little boulder wall at the Meriton sports centre. I'm over it in five minutes. I'll wait till I'm back in Beldon. There's a real wall there."

"Tim's talking about going to Brighton."

Bennet laughed. "With you?"

Jamie frowned. "What's funny?"

"Just that if you tell people you're heading to Britain's gay capital for the weekend with Tim, they'll jump to certain conclusions."

"It won't be a weekend. That's the busiest time for the gallery. He's thinking of going on a Wednesday in the Easter vacation, coming back on the Friday."

"Whenever, everyone will think you're going to spend the whole time in bed."

Jamie's expression darkened, and Bennet could have kicked himself. He didn't want to stop Jamie going.

"Take no notice," he added quickly. "You'll love Brighton. I bet you've never seen the south coast, have you?"

Jamie came from the northwest, near Liverpool. "No,

but it can't be that different from Southport or Blackpool, can it? It's all English seaside. It's not like going to Greece or somewhere."

"Maybe not, but the Channel's more sheltered than the Atlantic. And I think you'll find Brighton's trendier than Blackpool—not that I would know what Blackpool's like."

Jamie turned away to reach for his water. "Have you been to Brighton?"

"Once."

"You should go again." Jamie took a long swig and wiped his mouth. "Come with us."

Bennet froze with his hand on his own water bottle. "What? You're joking."

"No, man, I want you to. I don't want to go away alone with somebody I just met."

Bennet laughed. "There's so much wrong with that statement, I don't know where to start. But first, you must have known him, what, six weeks? That's not *just met.*"

"Four weeks last Friday."

"Of course, yeah, Rush. Still, it's not yesterday. And second, I can't afford it. I'm skint until the next loan payment comes in, and it's got to last until I start working and get paid, which means at least a month after the end of next term. That's if I find a job."

"You won't need much money," Jamie said. "A little cash for going out, that's all. Tim will drive us there, so no train fares—and nothing for accommodation, because I'll book a twin-bedded room we can share."

Bennet uncapped his bottle and swallowed a couple of

mouthfuls while he thought about that. "You'll pay for me? That doesn't seem right."

"It would cost the same if I took the room alone."

"Maybe, but third question—what does Tim think about this? I bet his plans for a romantic break didn't include having me along."

"He's fine with it. And you could climb. They have cliffs down there, and sports centres with good climbing walls—better than the one in Beldon."

Bennet looked across at his friend. "You've researched the climbing walls?"

Jamie shrugged. "Yes, because I wanted you to come. Please. You'll have a good time."

Bennet set his water back down. "Let me think about this."

He thought about it through the last set. A free ride to Brighton. Gay men everywhere—in the clubs, in the sports centres, on the beach. He couldn't fail to score, probably more than once. Adrenaline fizzed through his veins.

"Tim's really okay with it?" he asked when they'd both collapsed face down on their mats.

"It was his idea. I said I wouldn't feel comfortable going away with him alone, and he said why didn't I bring you? He understands I won't sleep with him, and there's less pressure if we're a group."

"Three is a group?"

Jamie didn't meet Bennet's eyes. "Four is a group."

Four? And guess who the fourth would be. That vaporised Bennet's fantasies of hot days and hotter nights. "Oh no.

No way. I am not making up a foursome with Darius. Not for all the men in Brighton."

"It won't be a foursome. You can go off by yourself whenever you want." Jamie rolled over and poked him in the ribs. "My birthday's on the Thursday. That's why Tim picked those dates. You wouldn't miss my birthday, would you?"

Bennet groaned. "Please, Jamie, don't do this to me."

Jamie grinned, knowing he had him. "My twenty-first."

## Chapter Five

"GAY BOY'S BACK," Marlon sneered.

Bennet slung his bag onto a chair. His brother sat slouched on the sofa, watching daytime TV.

The house in Beldon seemed more cramped every time he came home, and his mother, bustling through from the kitchen in her faded apron, looked thinner. Everything seemed smaller except his brother. Marlon was almost nineteen, and his job with a removal firm had built him up in the last few months. The bare arm on the back of the couch was beefy with muscle.

"Now don't you two start, the moment you walk through the door," their mother said.

"I haven't opened my mouth," Bennet said.

"Well, Marlon, don't swear at your brother the minute he comes home."

"I didn't swear," Marlon protested.

"You said the g-word, I heard you," their mother said. *Gay* was an insult, the way Marlon used it, so she didn't allow it in the house.

"I don't care if he says it," Bennet put in. "It wasn't my idea to ban it. I wish we could be open about it."

"You know your dad and I don't mind," his mother said.

"But when you and Marlon talk about it, it causes arguments."

"And what if I said him being straight is what causes the arguments?"

"It's the whole subject," his mother said. "The whole subject is what causes the arguments. Anyway, you two have been fighting since before either of you was anything."

"Exactly," Bennet said. "That's why it's not logical to censor me!"

His mother shook her head and went back into the kitchen.

"What happened to 'Welcome home, Bennet'?" he called after her.

"Sorry, love." She came out and gave him a brief, dry kiss on the cheek, then disappeared again.

"*Welcome home, Bennet*," Marlon mimicked in a high, silly voice. "And eff off again soon."

"I plan to. Is Dad working?"

"Obviously."

Their dad drove airport shuttle coaches between Stansted and London. If he was home he'd either be asleep—and Marlon would be wearing earphones to watch TV—or he'd be sitting on the couch where Marlon sat now.

Bennet grabbed his bag and went upstairs. His room was the smallest in the house, but it had always been big enough for him . . . until now.

Now, the room was dominated by a chrome and white elliptical trainer.

He stared at it in disbelief as Marlon thumped up the

stairs after him. "What happened to my desk?"

Marlon folded his arms in the doorway. "Yeah, I've got my gear in there now. Don't mess with the settings or I'll effing kill you."

"Stuff your settings. Where's my desk?"

"There wasn't room for it, was there? You don't live here any more. You said last time that you won't be moving back after you finish your poncey college course."

"But I haven't finished it yet."

Marlon shrugged. Bennet dropped his bag, pushed past his brother, and started back down the stairs.

"Mum! What have you done with my desk?"

"We gave it to Freecycle. I didn't think you needed it."

She stood in the kitchen doorway, wiping her hands on her apron. He felt sorry for her, not for the first time. What a life she had. But that didn't stop him fighting his corner.

"So where will I study?"

The worry line between her brows deepened. "It's all practical, isn't it, what you do now? Work experience at that hotel?"

"No! That's a weekend job. I have assignments to write, and final exams in June."

"Well, if you've got homework, can't you do it down here?"

*Homework.* As if he were a child. He threw up his hands in frustration. "You know I can't concentrate with the television on. That was why you got me the desk in the first place."

"I thought you'd have grown out of that. I can read my

books in front of the telly."

She could. She treated the TV like any other piece of furniture. She didn't pay it any attention unless *Bridgemaston Days* was on. Then she'd put down her reading material, hush any of her menfolk who were still in the room, and say reverently, "That's Bennet's college!" The rest of the time, she'd settle beside her husband or Marlon on the couch, absorbed in her magazines or a historical romance from the bargain box in the charity shop, oblivious to whatever sport or news or video game blared out from the screen.

"I can't study down here," Bennet said. "I'll have to go to the library. I'm not like you. I'm not like any of you."

She gave him a warning look. That was another subject he wasn't allowed to discuss.

---

MARLON WAS A warped copy of their dad, a big man with fox-brown eyes and a scrunched-up boxer's nose. Even the way they moved, sat, and shovelled food into their mouths was the same. Their dad was easygoing where Marlon was aggressive, but that was the only difference.

Bennet didn't have much in common with them. He was certainly nothing like his younger brother. Marlon had always been big for his age, but Bennet was quicker, able to wriggle out of trouble. Their childhood had been one long fight with no clear winner.

Bennet had felt so out of place in the family that he'd thought he must have been adopted. He saw news reports about abducted babies and imagined he was one of them.

Different versions of the story played through his head on sleepless nights. He couldn't see his Rourke parents as kidnappers, so they were always innocent—the baby-thieves had panicked and abandoned him on one of his dad's buses, or his mum had been asked to babysit by someone who never returned.

His fantasy birth family was prosperous, intelligent, successful. The mother was glamorous, the father wise and generous. They had a new car every two years and a house in the country with dogs and a big garden. One day, they'd find Bennet and take him back.

Soon after his fourteenth birthday, Bennet learned that if he was adopted, he'd have an adoption certificate instead of a birth certificate, so he told his mother he needed his birth certificate for a family history project at school. She said she'd lost it, but she had that pink, flustered look that meant she was lying.

He searched for the document one Sunday when everyone was out, venturing into his parents' room. The silence, the tidiness, and the smell of talcum powder marked it as forbidden territory, making his pulse race. He took off his shoes at the door, and the thick pale carpet embraced his toes as he crept in. His heart beat so loud in his ears, he thought it would rattle the bottles on his mother's glass-topped dressing table.

He looked under the bed, then in the wardrobe. The shoe boxes contained only shoes, and the suitcase on top of the wardrobe was empty. Then he tried the drawers.

This was her hiding place. Behind a folded pile of scarves

and socks, he found packs of tampons and condoms. His parents still had sex? *Eww.*

He slammed that drawer shut and opened the next. There he discovered an old biscuit tin. Jewellery?

He shook the tin, but it didn't rattle. He lifted it out and pulled off the lid. It was full of photographs and papers.

He sat cross-legged on the floor with this treasure chest in front of him. His heart pounded and his fingers trembled. He sorted through snaps of himself and Marlon as little kids, before his parents had a digital camera. He found mortgage documents and his parents' passports (expired). Then something official, headed in red type on cream paper—a birth certificate, Marlon's. Another one, his own. He spread it open on his knees.

*Certificate of Birth*, it said. Not adoption.

So he did belong here. He gazed at it, struggling to take in the few lines of information. He'd been registered as Bennet Jackson, his mother's maiden name, and the date was right. So no other parents were waiting out there to claim him. This family was the only one he'd ever have.

Or was it? Jackson was a common enough name, and this was the short version of the certificate, without the parents' names. He might have been born to some other people called Jackson. He looked again at Marlon's—Marlon Rourke. Yes, something was off.

He dug deeper for the marriage certificate. They'd been married in the middle of the eighteen months between his birth and Marlon's. And there was a document changing his own name to Rourke.

A couple could have a child together and then marry. But his gut told him that wasn't what had happened.

A noise from the doorway made him jump. His mother stood there with her coat on, clutching her handbag over her stomach like a shield.

Bennet's voice didn't sound like his own. "He's not my father, is he?"

"He's your dad. He's been a good dad to you."

"But he's not my biological father."

When he said it out loud, all the implications hit Bennet like a punch to his solar plexus. Half of his family was his by blood and the other half wasn't. Like he was hanging on to his place in the world by one string, while Marlon fit, Marlon had it all.

"Does everybody know—the aunts and uncles and grandparents?"

Stupid question. Of course they'd have known if she already had a baby when she met his dad. And none of them had ever said anything. All of them had betrayed him with their silence, with their lies.

"And *his* parents?" he blurted out. He wished he hadn't, because the answer had to be that his Rourke grandparents weren't his grandparents after all. Somehow he'd failed to consider that in his adoption fantasies.

"They love you," she said helplessly. "They love you just the same."

He didn't believe her. "How can they? It *isn't* the same."

If she replied, he didn't hear. His insides were a hot, sticky mess of loss, anger, and shame.

In his head he knew that the facts were nothing to be ashamed of. Plenty of his classmates had stepparents or single parents or whatever. But he'd had no idea, when everyone else knew his secret—everyone in his parents' generation, anyway. That was the shameful thing. He'd got it all wrong. He'd thought he was adopted. They'd laugh if they knew that. It made him feel stupid, like finding he'd gone around with *idiot* written on his forehead.

And there was still something he needed to know—something massive. His breath came fast and shallow. "Who's my biological father?"

She didn't answer.

"Who?" he insisted, his voice rising. It could be one of his dad's friends—it could be somebody he saw all the time.

"Just a chap I knew."

"What's his name? You may as well tell me, because I'll find out. I can send for a copy of the full version of this." He waved the certificate at her.

Could he apply for the other one before he was eighteen? Maybe not, but she wouldn't know.

She shook her head, though. "It's not on there. I left that box blank."

He stood up, and she took a step back. Was she frightened of him? He was bigger than her, and he was angry enough. He made himself say, "I won't hit you. Just tell me his name."

"Dave. His name was Dave."

"Dave what?"

"I don't know. I don't remember."

"Dave Bennet?"

"No. Like I always told you, I picked your name out of a book. I wanted a different name for you, a special name."

"What did he do?"

She flushed. "You know where babies come from."

The heat rose in Bennet's own face. "I mean what was his job?"

"Oh. He worked at Stansted."

"Doing what?"

"Security, I think. But he left. He'd gone by the time I found I was expecting."

Dull, solid men patrolled the airport halls. They didn't fit the image of his fantasy father any better than coach driver Alan Rourke.

"You must remember his name," he insisted.

"If I was going to remember, I'd've remembered at the time. They were always on at me to tell them."

"Who were?"

"The Child Support people, when I claimed benefits. But then I met your dad, and he said he'd look after us. And he has, hasn't he?"

Bennet still thought she was lying. He'd had romantic ideas about straight relationships in those days. It took him years to realise she probably never knew his biological father's last name.

"Don't tell Marlon," she said.

Give Marlon a reason to bring on a whole new set of insults? Not likely.

"And don't tell your dad you know," she added.

He agreed to that too, in the confusion of the moment. All the pieces of his life had come apart to make a new and monstrous shape, and he couldn't imagine wanting to talk about it, not then.

But later, there were many times when he almost blurted it out. If it wasn't for Marlon, he'd have preferred to have everything in the open. His secret knowledge made him feel as isolated from their family of three as if he *had* been adopted.

---

ON THE LAST night he was home, Bennet met up with Charlotte, whose family lived less than ten miles away. He suggested Checkers, off Beldon High Street, because he didn't think Marlon would go there.

In his school days, Checkers had always been half-empty, a pretentious but unattractive bar with paisley wallpaper and a lot of dark corners, frequented by adulterous couples. But it had been updated, and a younger, livelier crowd was in here now.

He found a table, and Charlotte arrived in a red raincoat over a clinging, low-cut top and short skirt. She kissed his cheek. "So what have you been up to?"

Her breath smelled of tobacco, and a craving prickled his nose. He hadn't had a cigarette since the one she'd given him on the fire escape at Rush, the night he'd first met Darius and Tim—no, make that Tim and Darius. Why had Darius popped into his head first?

He shook off the thought. "Nothing much."

The gin and tonic he'd bought her stood waiting on the table, the ice just beginning to melt. She shrugged out of her coat, hung it on the back of her chair, and sat down. "Did you hear any more from that interview? What's their name, Diverti—"

"Distinctivent. No, the director's still not back. I don't have much hope. I didn't have a chance without her. But the place—it was amazing. Like I fitted right in, and could have sat down and started. It felt so right."

"Your version of The One? Except it's a job instead of true love?"

Someone pushed past, jogging Bennet's chair. He scooted it nearer to the table. "Yeah, like it wasn't possible for me *not* to get that job. But then I did. I mean I didn't. All those open doors slammed in my face."

"Bummer." She wrinkled her nose in sympathy. "Talking of jobs, you know I've resigned from Credlands? I found out they paid me less than everyone else for the property viewings because I'm a student. Can you believe it?"

He took a swig of his pint. "No way. You should look up the employment law on that."

She shrugged. "All it says is that they have to pay minimum wage, which they did. But the other weekend staff had higher basic rates plus bonuses and minimum contracted hours. They said I didn't qualify for any of that because I was an intern, but it was no way related to my course. So I told them where they could stuff their so-called internship."

They discussed internships for a while—exploitation or opportunity?—then Charlotte downed the last of her drink and pushed back her chair. The wooden legs squealed on the tiled floor. "I'll get another in. What's that, Foster's? I'd better switch to plain tonic—I've brought the car."

She went to the bar, and his gaze wandered around the room. A few familiar faces, but none he could put a name to. Weird to think this grim town was once his whole life.

Then one guy turned. Someone he knew only too well. Someone who saw him, looked away, looked back, and came over.

"Bennet?"

"Callum." Bennet flexed his fingers to stop his hand clenching into a fist.

Callum put his pint down on Bennet's table. "How are you doing? On your own?"

Bennet pointed to Charlotte's coat, then to the bar, where she was paying.

"Oh, right!" Callum grinned. "That's a turn-up."

"Just a friend."

"Uh-huh. Mind if I sit down?" He grabbed an empty chair—not Charlotte's—and flopped onto it before Bennet could answer. "So what's happening? Are you living here again now?"

*Never.* "No. Back to Meriton tomorrow."

"Not staying for Easter?"

"No, I've got a part-time job over there. Working Easter weekend."

"That's good. You've got a bit of cash coming in, then."

Meaning Bennet could pay his debts. *Their* debts, which Callum should have shared. It was time they talked about this. But Charlotte was approaching, with a drink in each hand and a packet of nuts gripped between her teeth. He couldn't raise it now. He'd have preferred not to talk to Callum at all with Charlotte listening in, but he didn't have a choice. She stared at Callum with unmasked curiosity and plumped down in her seat, waiting for an introduction.

Callum didn't speak, so Bennet dragged the words out. "This is Callum. And this is Charlotte, a friend from college."

Charlotte's smile was predatory, on the hunt for gossip. "So are you—"

"An electrician," Callum cut in, handing each of them a card. The company, the logo, and Callum's number were the same as Bennet remembered, but the job title had changed.

"You've finished your apprenticeship?" Bennet said.

"Yup. Passed all the exams."

"So *you* must have a bit of cash coming in too," Bennet said. Maybe he'd finally see some of it.

"Not as much as you'd think." Callum pushed his chair back. "I'd best be off."

Charlotte stopped him. "My dad wants some wiring done in his garage. We're in King's Beacham. Do you cover that area?"

"Can do. Give me a call—on the mobile, not the office, then I'll do it as a private job. It'll cost him less. Or do you want to give me your number, and I'll call you?"

She dictated the digits, leaning over to check he had them right. He stood up.

Bennet said, "Wait. We need to talk about the money."

"Sure. Buzz me next time you're back, yeah?" And Callum was gone, across the bar and out into the wet street. Wriggling out of his responsibilities, again.

Charlotte watched Bennet with narrowed eyes. "Who's he?"

"He's an ex."

"Oh yeah? So why was he staring at my tits?"

"He's bi."

"And what was that about money?"

Bennet shook his head. "It's too stupid."

Charlotte said, "You'd better tell me, or I'll ply him with coffee in my dad's garage and get his side of the story."

Bennet could picture it. She'd have the information out of Callum in no time.

He ran a hand through his hair. "We got into debt, okay? We were gambling in online casinos. It was his idea—he had this scheme for betting on the zero in roulette and doubling up. Not every time, we weren't that gullible, but that kind of thing. It never crossed our minds that if schemes like that worked, casinos wouldn't be in business. I'd had my eighteenth birthday and he hadn't, so I applied for four credit cards, and we maxed them all out—in two hours."

In his head, Bennet was back in that hot, sick moment two years ago, looking at the screen with their balance at zero, and all the cards that were supposed to be for backup blocked, and all that money gone. Money they'd never had.

Then Callum had said, "Hey, let's see what would have happened if we'd had another couple of hundred," and Bennet had yelled "No!" but too late, Callum had already started the wheel, and it came in on the zero. Their number. If they'd had the money for one last bet, they'd have won it all back.

But they wouldn't have stopped there. They'd have gone on, and sooner or later they'd have lost it all. A scheme like that always loses in the long run, because of the house edge. He understood the statistics now. He'd had no idea at the time.

"Shit," Charlotte said.

"Yeah. And I was still at school, but he was earning. He had this apprenticeship. So he was supposed to make the payments for the first year, and I'd take it on after that. But he never did. He never paid a penny. The interest mounted up, and it's all in my name, so I'm stuck with the lot."

"Bummer."

Bennet swallowed a mouthful of beer and searched his mind for something else to talk about. They had one shared class—that would do. "How are you getting on with the business plan assignment? I had a go at it, but it's impossible to concentrate at home."

Charlotte grimaced. "I haven't started. I'll do it next week, when I hear you're swanning off to Brighton with a certain lawyer?"

After seeing Callum, Bennet wasn't in the mood to be teased. "I'm not going with *him*. I'm going with Jamie and Tim. The lawyer can tag along, but he'd better not get in my way."

"He's hot, though," Charlotte said.

"So why don't *you* go? Jamie would be as happy to have

you as me."

"He would not. And you don't mean that, anyway. Your little tongue's hanging out at the thought of all that Brighton totty."

"Well, yeah," he admitted. "So many men, so little time. How will I satisfy them all?"

# Chapter Six

B ENNET WAS CHECKING the mail by the window in the hall when Tim's blue Lotus pulled up outside Longbourn Manor.

"You didn't tell me he had a sports car," he said to Jamie. "If this is what he takes you out to dinner in, I begin to see the attraction."

Jamie laughed. "It's not about the car."

Bennet hoisted his bag onto his shoulder and followed his friend out. Jamie had his suitcase, plus a cooler box.

"Does he let you drive it?"

"No, because of the insurance. I've sat in the driving seat, that's all."

"Like a big kid," Tim said, coming up the path. He caught Jamie's wrist, brought it to his lips, and gave it the briefest kiss. Jamie's face lit up for a second, then he pulled away and slung his case in the boot. He stowed the cooler with care, blocking it in to keep it upright.

"Can you manage with yours inside, Bennet?" Tim asked. "This beast isn't big on storage space."

"Sure." Bennet scrambled into the narrow back seat, dragging his bag after him. The beast wasn't big on legroom, either. He twisted round and stretched his legs sideways.

That worked, as long as he'd be alone back here.

"Are we picking up Darius?" If they were, Bennet would get out in central London and go the rest of the way by train. It would be hell sharing this cramped space with somebody he didn't like.

But Tim said, "No, we'll go round the M25. He'll bring his own car. He's going up to Derbyshire on Friday."

Jamie chose the music—something classical. Tim chattered away nonstop and sometimes threw a comment over his shoulder, trying to include Bennet. But the Lotus's low, sporty chassis amplified the road noise, and to follow the conversation Bennet would've had to put his head between the two front seats—not easy, with his legs in their current position and his seat belt pinning him back.

Watching Jamie and Tim, he felt an emptiness deep in his gut, a need for something more than another body to bring to his bed. Would he ever have a relationship like this himself? Callum was the closest he'd come, but he and Callum had never fit together as well as these two, even before the roulette losses had driven a permanent wedge between them.

Where was his guy? He must be out there somewhere in the world now, maybe with someone else, maybe waiting for life to bring them together. It might happen in Bennet's first job after college . . . or even now, in Brighton. He grinned to himself. Not likely. These two days—and nights—were for fun.

Tim turned off the A23 just before they reached Brighton, to give them a view of the sea. Bennet leaned into the gap to stare with them through the windscreen. The sea lay far below them, sparkling in the sun.

Jamie asked, "Where's France?"

"Over the horizon," Tim said.

"The water's like a big blue carpet," Jamie said. "It's hard to believe it's real."

Tim reached over and took his hand, and they sat for a moment staring at the distant water. Then Tim released the handbrake and drove on down through side streets to the seafront.

"It'll seem more real here," Tim said as he slipped the car into a short-stay space just off the King's Road.

Jamie jumped out and stared at the mass of grey and gold pebbles that lay between them and the water. "Where's the sand?"

Bennet dragged his stiff legs out from the back of the car, stretched, and went to lean on the railings overlooking the beach. Jamie headed for the sea. Tim bought the car a parking ticket and went with him, looking back to zap the locks.

The sun had dropped behind a bank of cloud and would soon be setting, but people still crowded the beach. Lots of kids—they were on their Easter break too. Bennet crunched his way over the shingle, his feet sinking into the shifting stones. Ahead of him, Tim had stopped. Jamie was walking on towards the water by himself. Heads turned as he passed, but Jamie took no notice.

Tim turned to Bennet with a worried face. "I think he's disappointed. Apparently there's miles of sand in Merseyside."

Jamie reached the swelling surf and stopped a few yards down from the line of wet seaweed that marked the last high tide.

"He'll handle it," Bennet said. "Brighton has other advantages."

Tim shaded his eyes to watch Jamie. "How long have you known him?"

"About eighteen months. We began our courses at the same time and lived in the same house from the start."

"Where are you from? I assume not Meriton, or you'd be living at home."

"Beldon, on the other side of Hertfordshire. And you're from Derbyshire, is that right?"

"No, it's Darius who's from Derbyshire. I grew up not far from here, in fact. I'm a Sussex boy."

"I thought you two were at school together."

Tim nodded. "It was a boarding school."

"Oh, right." Of course, it would be. A famous one, no doubt—Eton, Winchester, somewhere like that.

Jamie's father had gone to one of those schools. His two older brothers, too. Jamie had escaped by failing the entrance exam. He said he hadn't done it on purpose, but he hadn't been sorry. He'd been happy to stay at home and hang out in the kitchen outside of school hours, finding his vocation as a chef. But after he'd left his local day school, he'd insisted on leaving home to take professional cookery with Philippe Hennice at Meriton. Pictures of the college buildings, looking as old and stately as any boarding school, had won his parents over.

Tim's phone rang. He glanced at the display and took the call. "Yes, we're here. On the beach, near the pier . . . I don't know. It's on our left as you look at the sea." He paused, and mouthed the word *Darius*—as if Bennet hadn't guessed.

Darius found them almost at once. He'd taken off his jacket and tie, but he still wore the rest of his suit. He must have come straight from the office—or did they call it chambers? His trousers followed the line of his hips and thighs perfectly. Could they be tailor-made? Was that still a thing? Whatever, they drew the eye, especially here among the hippies and kids chilling out on the shingle. Bennet had to concentrate to stop his gaze fixing on Darius's lower half.

They didn't stay long on the beach. As soon as Jamie rejoined them, Tim wanted to get back in the car to take the bags to the hotel.

"I'll walk," Bennet said.

Tim insisted on everybody exchanging phone numbers before he and Jamie climbed into the blue Lotus and pulled out into the road.

"Which is yours?" Bennet asked Darius, looking around at the other cars in the roadside spaces. They all seemed too old, too dirty, or too much like family cars for a barrister with an inflated view of his own importance.

"Mine's at the hotel."

Bennet tensed. "So . . . you mean you're on foot too?"

"Yes, why not? It's not far."

Having Darius for company was not part of Bennet's plan. He set off, stiff and uncomfortable with the barrister's silent figure beside him.

But it was awesome to stride along the Brighton seafront breathing the salty air, with evening coming on and two nights of fun ahead of him. Half of the guys he saw checked him out—so different from back home. Anticipation bubbled inside him. All he had to do was get rid of Darius.

He turned to cross the road.

"Where are you going?" Darius asked.

"Through the Lanes."

"It's not that way. It's straight ahead, the other side of the pier—assuming we're all staying in the same hotel."

"Yeah, I know. I fancy exploring. You go on."

Darius hesitated. "Do you know your way around?"

"Yes." It wasn't exactly a lie. He'd spent so much time online in the last few days looking for gay clubs and pubs that he'd memorised most of the city map. Not that it was any of Darius's business.

"I think we should go straight there," Darius said. "Tim will want to make plans for this evening."

Bennet's shoulders stiffened. "Listen, I'm grateful to Tim for bringing me down here, but I don't intend to do everything in a foursome. Do you?"

"Not everything, no." Darius gave a quick laugh that lit his whole face and made him seem almost human.

So he had a sense of humour. Who'd have known? If he would show it more often, they might have a chance of getting through the next two days with no murders.

"But you'll have to check in by seven," Darius added, "or they'll let your room go."

"Jamie will check in for me."

His phone rang—Jamie, saying they'd booked a restaurant table for nine o'clock. Bennet promised to be at the hotel in time to shower and change.

"So I'll see you later," he said to Darius.

"There's enough time? Then I'll come with you. I've already checked in."

Bennet let out a sigh as they crossed the road. He'd thought that maybe, while he wandered through the narrow alleys that made up this oldest part of Brighton—once a fishing village, now a stretch of cafés, boutiques, jewellery shops, and bars—he might meet someone who'd want to hook up later. In a place where one-third of the population identified as something other than straight, it should have been possible.

But Darius's frowning presence put an end to his hopes. He stalked along beside Bennet as if they were a couple who'd had a fight. Pair after pair of eyes met Bennet's, sparking as they connected, then flickered over to Darius and didn't return.

Darius, meanwhile, looked straight ahead, his expression blank. He seemed to have no interest in Bennet, nor in anyone or anything they passed. Why hadn't he gone with Tim and Jamie? Was he doing this on purpose, to mess with Bennet's head?

After ten minutes Bennet gave up and took a direct route to the hotel.

Tim was pulling Bennet's bag from the back seat of the Lotus. "Sorry!" he said, breathless. "We forgot to take this up for you earlier. But it's still here, no harm done."

"No problem." Bennet gripped the bag and set off across the forecourt towards the hotel's main entrance. Tim and Darius followed. Bennet couldn't help hearing what they said.

"Are we clubbing later?" Darius asked Tim.

"How about tomorrow? There's a restaurant Jamie wants to try tonight."

"Clubbing and eating are not mutually exclusive."

"We don't want to have to rush the meal, or spoil it by jigging around on a full stomach. It's his birthday."

"I thought his birthday was tomorrow."

"It's the whole time we're here, as far as I'm concerned. Anyway, one night of clubbing is enough for me."

Darius snorted. "Never thought I'd hear you say that, this side of forty."

A uniformed porter opened the door for them. Inside, plush carpets and dark wood panelling stretched away across the lobby.

Bennet turned back to Darius. "I wouldn't mind grabbing something quick to eat and cruising the clubs, if that's what you plan to do." They could separate inside, and Jamie could have a quiet meal with Tim.

Darius frowned. "Shouldn't you attend your friend's birthday dinner?"

Putting Bennet in the wrong, again. "I only meant—"

But Darius strode across the lobby and took the stairs two at a time.

Bennet's anger simmered in his chest. He said to Tim, "I

just thought you and Jamie might like some space."

"No, no, you don't need to worry about crowding us. Can I be honest with you, Bennet?" Like most people who asked that question, Tim went on without waiting for an answer. "It helps to have you here. It's wonderful for me to have the chance to show Jamie a little more of England, and I think this is the only way we could do it. I respect his principles and I don't want to keep discussing them because it's a little frustrating for me, and I can see my frustration could lead to arguments that I'd prefer not to have."

What a verbal tangle. But Bennet knew what he meant. Arguing with Jamie was pointless. Jamie never preached or judged others, but his rules for his own life weren't flexible.

"At this point we're focusing on getting to know each other," Tim went on, "and we can do that just as well in company as when we're alone—maybe better."

Tim looked so earnest that Bennet couldn't come right out and say he wanted to skip dinner in order to hunt down some willing stranger and get laid. Besides, if this meal was a whole big deal for Jamie's birthday, then Darius was right, and of course Bennet would go. But the first chance he had, he'd be out looking for his share of Brighton's gay men.

# Chapter Seven

"AND WE'LL HAVE a bottle of the Margaux," Darius said.

Bennet raised his eyebrows.

"Problem?" Darius asked.

"I haven't seen the list."

Why did Darius think he was the only one qualified to choose the wine? Okay, based on his selection in the college restaurant he had good taste, but ordering without consulting anyone else . . .

Darius closed the wine list and held it out across the table. That was another thing, the seating. Darius had indicated a chair for Bennet when they first came in, and Bennet had accepted that place without thinking, which had been stupid. He shouldn't have let Darius dictate to him. Darius had gone around the table to take the seat opposite, while Tim and Jamie lagged behind, chatting.

So Tim and Jamie were separated, which maybe Tim didn't mind, going by what he'd said earlier. But it meant every time Bennet looked up, he found Darius's eyes on him across the table. Hadn't Bennet sworn never to put himself under this scrutiny again? And with good reason. It wasn't a comfortable position.

The waiter flicked his pencil from side to side while Bennet studied the wine list. Rushing customers—Bennet would have had something to say about that, if he'd been in charge here. But he had to admit Darius had made a good choice.

"All right, the Margaux."

Jamie leaned over from his place on Bennet's right. "Is it expensive?" he murmured. "Let me see."

Bennet shrugged him off and gave the list back to the waiter. Of course it was expensive. As soon as they'd walked into the restaurant, he'd known this meal would take all the cash he'd brought for the whole of their stay. After tonight he'd have to borrow from Jamie. He had no other option. His account balance was £1.23, his next student loan payment was a week away, and with his history, the bank wouldn't let him overdraw.

Darius said, "I'll cover it. I know you don't drink alcohol, Jamie. What would you like?"

"This is fine." Jamie reached out to touch the condensation on the jug of chilled water in the middle of the table.

Bennet ordered cullen skink to start. It wasn't the cheapest dish, but since this meal would wipe him out anyway, he planned to enjoy it.

The Scottish speciality arrived with a mound of fish and potato in a strong, steaming broth. He sipped at his first spoonful. The flaking texture of the haddock was perfect in the thick potato soup.

"Too much pepper," Darius said. He had the same dish.

"It's fine for me," Bennet said.

"Bennet likes it hot," Tim teased.

Darius shot Bennet a look. Their eyes met, and Darius's seemed full of fire, as they had in that moment on the roof at Rush. Bennet bristled under the remembered insult and held his gaze, defiant.

Just wait till they made it to a club. The first chance he got, Bennet would pick up some gorgeous guy. That would show Darius he was more than *just about fuckable*.

Whatever Darius had said about the soup, he finished every last drop, tipping the bowl to get the dregs. Then he crumpled his napkin into a ball, dropped it on the table, and stalked off to the men's room as if he were entering court to browbeat a witness.

Bennet relaxed. Now he could look straight ahead without risking another encounter with that piercing gaze.

Tim said, "Darius has a mind like a razor."

"Do you mean sharp, or cutting?"

Tim laughed. "And you're not so different, Bennet."

Jamie warned Tim, "Don't tell Bennet he's like Darius, if you want to survive this trip."

"Do you find him brusque, Bennet?" Tim asked. "Some people do, but he's a loyal friend. He'd defend those he loves, whatever it cost. Sometimes it gets him into trouble. I think you're similar in that too."

Bennet didn't answer. Maybe they shared some values, but it didn't mean they had to like each other.

Darius strode back to his seat and tucked his legs under the table. "What were you saying?"

"We were talking about loyalty," Tim said.

"Ah." Darius spread his napkin. "Loyalty is something you can have in excess. Loyalties conflict, and then there is war."

"Which is much what Tim said," Bennet put in.

"Is it?" Tim asked. "I had no idea I was saying anything so clever. I hope your ideal man isn't an intellectual, Jamie."

"No, just a nice guy," Jamie said, smiling.

Tim flushed with pleasure and turned to Bennet. "What do you look for in a man?"

Bennet shrugged. "I don't have a specification."

"As long as he's hot?" Tim said.

"What do you mean by that?" Darius cut in. "We hear that word all the time. Someone says, 'You should meet so-and-so, he's hot,' and then he's nothing more than another handsome face—good for a night, perhaps, but you're itching to get away before dawn. A truly hot guy has more than looks."

Bennet leaned back so the waiter could take his soup plate. "Yeah, everyone *says* that, but when it comes to—"

Darius didn't let him finish. "I'll tell you about my *hot guy*. Yes, he's attractive, but he also has intelligence, wit. He's confident without being arrogant. He's clear about his values, willing to stand up for what he believes in; not afraid of conflict, but able to admit when he's wrong. He knows when to work and when to play. He's comfortable in any social circle. He's open, but he doesn't give his heart too easily. That's what *hot* means to me."

Bennet was sour about being interrupted. "I imagine you're single, with a checklist like that," he muttered.

"You're right," said Tim. "He is picky."

"Because I don't fall in love with every man I meet?" Darius asked.

Tim waved a pointy finger at him. "No, because you don't give anyone a chance. You're introduced to the most gorgeous men, and you find some fault with all of them."

"Sounds like he's a closet straight guy," said Bennet.

Tim laughed. "Yes, with a wife and kids hidden away at Pemberley." He looked across at Jamie. "That's Darius's ancestral home. I'm always telling him that when I make my first billion, I'll buy it."

"It's not for sale," Darius said.

The waiter arrived with huge white dinner plates on his arm. "Casserole of guinea fowl with chestnuts?"

"Mine," Bennet said.

Darius raised an eyebrow. "Chestnuts in April?"

Who was this guy to challenge everything Bennet did? He opened his mouth to snap back, but before he could say anything, Tim held up a hand, making peace. "Bennet has the right to eat chestnuts whenever he likes."

"I'm surprised they're on the menu at this time of year, that's all," Darius said as the waiter slid rib of beef in front of him.

Bennet took a forkful of food. The gravy was good and rich, but the chestnuts were starchy and flavourless. Darius had been right to question his choice.

Bennet didn't plan to admit that out loud, however. Before anybody could ask how his meal was, he turned to Tim. "How's the gallery going?"

"Not badly, considering how new it is," Tim said. "When you count the number of sales and the number of people who come in, there's a high percentage of buyers."

Darius said, "But how many people come in? A hundred percent of one is still only one."

"That's the thing. If I could entice more people through the door, it would make a big difference. Of course, now we're coming into the summer, the visitor numbers will go up. And did I tell you I found someone to cover the time we're down here? I think it's important to be reliable. If people find it closed unexpectedly, they may never come back."

"And how much will your assistant have to sell to cover his wages, given that more than half of the sale price goes to the artists, and you have to cover all of the overheads?" Darius asked.

"*Her* wages. It's a woman." Tim looked around for the waiter. "Do you think they have any horseradish sauce?"

Darius laughed. "Don't change the subject."

Tim fidgeted with the corner of his napkin. "It's bound to make a loss at first. And of course it's a tax thing to some extent—"

Bennet almost choked on his guinea fowl. Did Tim buy the gallery as a tax loss? His private income must be huge.

"But I don't want it to be a complete failure," Tim went on. "The problem is that most people only see what's in the window, and if that doesn't interest them, they'll walk on by. I change the display as often as I can, but with day trippers I only have one shot."

"So you need a way to bring them inside," Darius said.

Bennet said, "How about a few tables? You could do coffee."

"You mean like a café with art on the walls?" asked Tim. "They'd expect food, wouldn't they? I don't see myself doing that. Besides, I think it devalues the artworks."

"If he wanted to run a café, he'd have bought a café," Darius said.

Bennet scowled. "That's not what I meant. Not sandwiches and all that—too messy, and you don't want to fill the place with deadbeat teenagers. You want to attract people who'll buy the paintings. The kind of people who'd stay at the Black Lion or eat in a restaurant like this one. No more than three or four tables, some good-quality coffee and tea—"

Tim's eyes lit up. "An exclusive little *salon de thé*? With macarons and patisserie?"

"Yeah, maybe. It could be the most expensive coffee shop in the town, it wouldn't matter—in fact, it might be good if it was. You'd be bringing the right people inside and making a little money from them while they appreciated the art at their leisure. And you could put something on the tables for them to take away, like a promotional leaflet."

"I can just visualise it!" Tim said, beaming. "Can't you, Darius?"

"It's an idea."

The waiter cleared their plates, dimmed the lights, and glided out with Jamie's birthday cake, a white chocolate mille-feuille gateau with one golden candle flickering in the centre.

"Did they send out for this?" Darius asked Tim. "What about your allergy?"

"We brought it from Meriton. It's made with coconut and almond flour. Isn't it stunning?"

Darius sat back and turned his critical eyes on the cake. "It is. I wouldn't have imagined you could get something like this in such a small town."

"Jamie made it himself," Tim said with pride, as Jamie blew out the candle and began cutting into the layers of white chocolate, pastry, and cream.

Darius frowned. Bennet stared at him. What had rattled the lawyer's cage now? Couldn't he handle anyone having skills he didn't possess?

The cake was good enough to stop conversation—gooey and sweet, with the pastry giving enough crunch to temper it. Almond flour? That must have been why the canapés at Tim's gallery party had tasted so weird. In a sweet cake, with mostly coconut flour, the result was much better.

Darius put down his fork. "I congratulate you, Jamie. It's delicious." But his voice was cold.

Tim asked for the bill. Bennet held his breath, waiting to hear how much he owed. Tim said nothing, dropping a card on the plate. Was he paying it all? No, Darius put his card in for the wine.

They seemed to expect nothing from Bennet and Jamie. Oh, but Jamie had provided the dessert. Only Bennet hadn't contributed. That didn't feel right. He reached into his pocket.

Jamie shook his head at him, and Tim said, "Don't

worry, Bennet. It's covered."

"Let me get the tip, at least."

"Service is included."

Bennet let it go, but he didn't like it. Deep down, he was glad to save the money, but that only made him more uncomfortable. The less he had, the more he cared about paying his way.

As Tim and Jamie headed for the door, Darius turned to Bennet, his face still grim. "So I can guess who'll be selling cakes to Tim for this tea shop you've talked him into running."

Bennet stopped with one arm half into his jacket. His joints stiffened, and his skin bristled. "I didn't talk him into anything. It was an idea, that's all. I don't care if he acts on it or not."

"Tim is easily swayed."

Bennet pulled his jacket on, tugging at it hard enough to strain the seams. "For God's sake. You agreed yourself it might work. You're not telling me *you're* easily swayed, are you?"

Darius smiled for a second, but he didn't answer.

Bennet hurried out of the restaurant, leaving Darius to follow. He didn't want anyone—not the staff, not the strangers at the other tables—thinking they might be together.

Tim hailed a cab. Halfway back to the hotel, Bennet saw a name he recognised: one of the gay clubs.

"Wait!" He tapped on the glass to stop the driver. "I'll see you all tomorrow, okay?"

But as he was opening the cab door to jump out, Darius said, "Do you have ID? You'll need to prove you're over eighteen."

Bennet gave him what he hoped was a withering glare. "Come on. I'm twenty, and I look my age. Nobody ever asks."

But as he said it, he realised he'd been thinking of Rush, where the door staff knew him.

"They check everyone down here," Tim said. "They asked for mine last time, and I'm twenty-seven."

*Shit.* Bennet's ID was in his wallet, and he'd left his wallet at the hotel. He hadn't wanted to explain why he couldn't use a card, so he'd only brought cash and his phone.

Across the street, a vibrant line of people waited to get into the club. He yearned to join them, to be one of a chattering, laughing, dancing crowd.

He could still do it. He could pick up his ID and come back. He pulled the cab door closed, settled back into his seat, and told the driver to go on.

He paid the cab fare. They let him do that, at least. Tim and Jamie went on ahead, into the hotel. Darius waited on the steps. Why? Didn't he think Bennet would have enough money? *Please.* It was less than a tenner.

The taxi pulled away, and he headed up the steps, passing Darius with a quick "Good night."

His wallet lay on the shelf beside his bed. He picked it up and walked to the window, looking down into the street. Two or three noisy, laughing groups went by. If only he was with a posse like that. What did he have in common with

Tim and Darius? Nothing. And Jamie was his best and sweetest friend, but not the one he'd pick for a wild night out. Kofi and Leon would be more fun. Even Charlotte would have been dragging him into the clubs, not trying to hold him back like these guys.

If he went out on his own, it wouldn't be the same. On the two occasions he'd been to a big club in London—once with Callum, and once last year with friends from college—he'd been uncomfortable in the frantic crowd at first. He was still a small-town boy. It had helped having people to hang out with while he acclimatised.

He wasn't shy or scared—of course he wasn't. But he didn't go out again. When he turned away from the window, he threw his wallet onto the bed and headed for the shower. There was always tomorrow.

# Chapter Eight

JAMIE'S BED WAS empty when Bennet woke the next morning. He found Jamie downstairs, having breakfast with Tim and Darius.

Tim was chattering away as usual, and his plate and Jamie's were still half-full. Darius had finished eating. He'd pushed his chair back and was staring out of the window with a scowl. The only remaining place was beside him.

Bennet put his wrapped gift on the table in front of Jamie. "Hey, happy birthday."

Darius looked round to see who'd invaded his space, then turned back to his view of the hotel's garden.

"I told you not to get anything," Jamie said.

"Couldn't resist." Bennet had found the carved wooden box in one of Meriton's charity shops. Jamie unwrapped it, folding the paper as carefully as if he planned to reuse it, and opened the hinged lid.

"A memory box! Perfect, thank you. I can put all my souvenirs in it."

Tim leaned over to admire it. "Pretty. And isn't it a beautiful day? We picked the right time to come here."

Bennet said, "Yeah. Why didn't you wake me, Jamie?"

"I thought I did," his friend said. "I called your name

and you moved."

"That doesn't mean I'm awake."

"Slugs move," Darius said, without turning.

Darius was calling him a slug? *It's Jamie's birthday. Don't rock the boat.* Bennet counted to five, then said, "I'll get some food. Anyone want anything?"

"More coffee," Darius said.

Bennet's patience snapped. "Didn't your expensive education teach you to say 'please'?"

Darius fixed him with a look of mild surprise, and the front feet of his chair came back to the ground with a thump. "Certainly not. 'Please' is an obsequious middle-class convention."

"That's a joke," Tim told Bennet.

Really? Darius didn't appear to have been joking. And he'd said *middle-class* like it was another insult. For Bennet, reaching the middle class would be a big step up. He clenched his teeth.

"Don't take it personally, Bennet," Tim pleaded. "Darius doesn't like the look of the weather."

Bennet stared through the window in disbelief. The sky outside was solid blue. The sun made the white walls shimmer. "What is he—a vampire?"

Darius's mouth flickered. Was that a smile? Yes, Bennet had almost made him laugh—but not quite. God, this guy was hard work.

Bennet strode off to the breakfast bar. Since it was all-you-can-eat, he piled his plate with everything that looked good—bacon, eggs, a folded pancake, baked beans, a croissant, and a banana. When he reached the coffee dispenser, he filled a jug instead of a cup. Back at the table, he pulled his chair a couple of inches away from Darius and sat down.

Tim poured everyone's coffee. Darius took his black. Bennet put his banana on the table and set about tackling his food. Darius stared.

Bennet put down his knife and fork. "What are you looking at?"

"Don't you want a separate plate?" Darius said. "You're getting beans all over your crepe."

"It's all going in the same stomach."

Darius took a clean side plate from the table behind him and set it beside Bennet's place. Controlling, or what?

All the same, Bennet slid the crepe onto the plate with the croissant, scraping off the beans with his knife.

Halfway through his meal he noticed something new on Jamie's wrist—a cool designer bracelet made of black leather and silver, with links that looked a little like clasped hands. Bennet stopped eating, stared at it, and did an exaggerated eyebrow waggle at Jamie.

"Birthday present," Jamie said. He shot a glance at Tim, who was talking to Darius across the table, then leaned forward and whispered, "It's not too BDSM, is it?"

"Ha. Maybe a tad. No, but it's gorgeous. Wish someone would buy me gifts like that."

Not true, of course—if they did, Bennet would be even more uncomfortable than he'd been in the restaurant last night, thinking he should reciprocate and not knowing how—but Jamie didn't call him on it. He laid his forearm along the table to admire his bracelet, while Bennet finished his first plate of food, switched it for the second one, and refilled his coffee cup. He offered the jug around, but no one else wanted more.

"Listen, don't wait for me," he said. "I don't know what you guys are thinking of doing today, but I've made my own plans."

"It's perfect weather for the beach," Tim said. "I thought we'd drive along the coast towards Littlehampton, where it's sandy, and we can do the bucket-and-spade thing and have a picnic in the dunes."

"Okay," Bennet said. "Go ahead. I'll see you later. I'm going climbing."

Darius gave him a sharp look. Tim stood up, brushed the crumbs from his lap, and grabbed Jamie's hand. The two of them made a quick exit. Darius hadn't moved.

"Aren't you going to the beach?" Bennet asked.

"I am, in fact, but not at Littlehampton." Darius took a mouthful of coffee. "Where are you planning to climb?"

"A sports centre on the edge of Brighton. They have a wall with more challenging routes than I've done before, and I can't wait to try them." Bennet checked his watch. Fifteen minutes until the next bus.

"I know the wall at home too well," he went on. "It only goes up to grade six, which isn't much if you get a lot of practice, and I could do all their climbs in my sleep."

"That's in Meriton?"

"No, in my hometown. There's nothing at all in

Meriton. That's why this is such an opportunity. You could say it's the reason I'm here."

"Uh-huh." Darius set down his coffee cup. "Are you meeting someone at this sports centre? A belay partner?"

Bennet froze with a forkful of crepe halfway to his mouth. *Belay?* Who used that word, except climbers?

Derbyshire. Peak District. Rock climbing heaven. And Darius had grown up there. *Shit.*

Darius must have seen the thoughts clicking into place. He gave a wry smile. "Does Tim know you climb? He said nothing to me. If he set this up assuming we'd keep each other company today, it's a pity he didn't tell us. He has no idea how much planning goes into a day's climbing. I'm going along the coast to the cliffs."

Climbing something real, a sheer and crumbling surface exposed to the sun and wind, with the sea pounding below . . . and Bennet had been raving about an indoor wall. All his excitement drained away. He didn't trust himself to speak.

"I haven't done much on chalk," Darius went on, "so I've fixed up a professional, a local guy, to lead. He might not mind an extra one, if you wouldn't be letting anyone down."

Bennet's heart pounded. It would put him in Darius's debt, but to have the chance to climb coastal cliffs . . .

"You look a little apprehensive," Darius said. "If you—"

The words rushed out. "I am *not* apprehensive! It sounds fucking amazing. And I'm not meeting a partner—I'd assumed I could hook up with another random tourist. But I don't have the equipment. You need ice gear for chalk, don't you?"

"Yes, but most of the protection's already in, and he can bring whatever else we want. Shall I give him a call?"

Bennet bit his lip and nodded.

---

ON THE PHONE, Darius described Bennet as "a competent indoor climber, by his own account." Patronising, or what? But Bennet held his tongue, and half an hour later he was in the passenger seat of Darius's black Audi, heading east along the coast. It wasn't a flashy car like Tim's, but it gave a much smoother ride.

"Do you have sun cream?" Darius asked. "You'll need it, in this glare. There's some in my bag."

Bennet reached round to the back seat. The bag was leather, and it bore the initials D.G.D.L. Another sign of Darius's privilege. But being in his powerful car, rummaging in his things, felt weirdly right, as if they'd known each other all their lives.

Climbing did have that effect on him. In Beldon, he used to come down from the wall treating everyone like his best friend—even Marlon. But that was *after* a climb. Being this relaxed before he'd started was new. It must be the prospect of tackling chalk for the first time that was making him feel like he belonged anywhere near Darius.

They left the Audi near the coast and met up with Spider, a thin, ragged guy with dreadlocks, riding a bicycle that he locked to a road sign. Bennet, in his shabby cargo pants and worn grey T-shirt, fit right in with Spider. Darius's clothes seemed brand-new—knee-length dedicated climbing shorts and a burnt-gold shirt, both displaying the logo of the same expensive brand. He looked hot as hell in them, but wouldn't anyone, at the prices that company charged?

They went down steps to the shingle and made their way around the jutting thirty-metre cliffs. They were out of sight of the few early sunbathers when Spider stopped.

"There's seaweed on the cliff face," Bennet said, as Spider handed him a helmet.

"Yeah, this is a tidal bay. The sea comes right up over the beach."

"Lucky for you," Darius told Bennet, "or I'd have been here at dawn and you'd have missed out."

"Lucky for *you*," Bennet retorted, stepping into his harness, "or you wouldn't have my sparkling wit brightening up your day."

Darius's mouth twitched, as though he might be about to laugh.

Spider said, "We go up one at a time here. I'll take you for belayer, Darius, since your friend doesn't have so much outdoor experience. I'll lead with the rope and check the protection, and I'll give you some instruction before you go up. We can't go over the top because there's a nature reserve up there. See that ledge, a couple of metres below? We stop there."

Spider and Darius roped up, then Spider scrambled up the vertical cliff face, hooking into the holds with his axes, gripping with the pointed crampons fixed to his shoes, attaching the rope for them.

"The axes are for support," Darius told Bennet. "You mustn't hack at the cliff like ice, or you'll ruin the route."

"I can see it's not Everest." Not that Bennet would have known what to do if it had been. The closest he'd come to ice climbing was scrambling up a snowy slope in Beldon with his sledge during one unusually cold winter.

Spider reached the ledge, secured the rope, and came back down. He instructed them in the use of the axes and crampons, then nodded to Darius. "You want to go first?"

Darius looked at Bennet. "Perhaps you—"

"No, it's fine. Go ahead."

"Okay. Are you ready to belay?"

"Me?" But that sounded like Bennet didn't know how, and he did, of course. He'd done it hundreds of times. He'd just assumed Spider would do it today. But it made sense this way, when he thought about it. Spider's role was to give the clients as much activity as he could, and Bennet was a client, bizarre as that felt. "Sure," he added hastily.

Spider said, "You want to check each other's knots first?"

Bennet froze, and a sudden stillness at his side told him Darius had done the same. Checking each other's knots meant hands-on contact with the harnesses around their hips. But Spider obviously had no clue that there might be any issue there, and if Darius wasn't going to say anything, then neither was Bennet.

And there wasn't an issue, not really. It was just that Bennet preferred not to get so close to fellow climbers he was . . . *attracted to* was the phrase that had popped into his head. But he wasn't attracted to Darius. No way. Not at all. So, no reason why he should feel weird about touching Darius or having Darius's hands on him, right?

He avoided eye contact as he took hold of Darius's rope, testing the knot. He tried not to look at the bulge in the front of Darius's shorts, either, but he had to see where it was to avoid accidentally touching it, didn't he? And if it appeared to grow while Bennet's hands ran over the harness fastenings, that was nothing to do with him or Darius or any tension that might exist between them. It was just how the male body automatically behaved.

Darius's knots were good. His harness was snug and correctly buckled. "Fine," Bennet said, and they switched.

He kept his eyes on the distant clifftop while Darius's expert hands moved smoothly over his harness and tested the carabiner. *Think of something sad. Drowned kittens. That singer who died.*

"Good." Darius's voice was dry and professional. He stepped away. Bennet let out a long breath and brought his mind back to real life.

Spider gave them a quick double-check, and then Bennet moved into position, took the rope, and cleared his throat. "Belay is on. You can climb."

Darius set off up the cliff. Bennet's role was only to stand at the bottom of the cliff and feed him the rope, but he had to pay attention in case something went wrong. So it was his duty to stare at Darius's arse for the next half hour, or however long it took.

He tried to think of Darius as just another climber—a

good one, Bennet had to admit. Slower than Spider, but Spider was a professional, and this was his home territory.

"He's cautious, isn't he?" Spider said, when Darius was halfway up. "Likes to be sure of his holds."

"He's a lawyer. Born cautious."

Spider kept his eyes on Darius as the barrister tackled a projecting edge. "Strong, though, and knows what he's doing. Look at him haul himself over that arête. He'd make a good instructor, I reckon. But of course there's no money in it, not like lawyering. Do you climb together a lot?"

"Never before," Bennet said. And probably never again—which was a pity, because they might make good climbing partners if they could leave their antagonism on the ground. Bennet could use a little more caution. Instructors always told him he was too impulsive. And if some of his adventurousness rubbed off on Darius, it might loosen up the barrister's style.

Darius reached the ledge that marked the top of their climb, applied more chalk, and started straight back down. Bennet took in the rope, watching for slips, but there were none.

Darius jumped down onto the pebbles, and Bennet rubbed the back of his neck where he'd been staring up for too long. Finally it was his turn.

Spider looked at his watch. "We have to be out of here before the tide comes in. Don't rush, take your time, but come down when I tell you, okay? If we have to leave the rope up there, we leave it, and I'll come back for it tonight."

"Okay." Bennet didn't waste time protesting. If Spider

didn't trust him to follow orders, he might not let him go up at all.

Spider turned to Darius. "And you'll belay him, will you? You won't need me till it's time to go, but I'll stick around." He took out his phone and went to sit on a rock.

Bennet started up, gripping his axes, digging in with the spikes on his feet. He didn't like relying on the axes. He was used to closer contact, to feeling his way with his fingers. But when he tried that, his hands scrabbled and slipped on the chalk, finding nothing solid.

Darius fed the rope well, paying attention to Bennet, always giving him the right amount of slack. Nothing to worry about there. But the surface was soft, treacherous, taking Bennet's full concentration. He couldn't escape the sun overhead, and after a few metres his scalp was sweating under the borrowed helmet. He had to keep reaching down to chalk his slick hands. But as he climbed higher, a breeze ruffled his shirt and seemed to clean out his head at the same time.

He was in sight of the upper ledge when Spider yelled, "Break! Start coming down now."

He didn't want to stop. He looked around. The sea was still well clear of their route around the rocks. In another five minutes he could have reached the top.

But he called back, "Break, okay," and started back down. He landed on the shingle with a satisfying crunch.

"You're off belay," Darius said. "Nice technique."

Bennet shook his arms to free up the lactic acid. "Thanks." He bent to take off the crampons, then untied his rope.

"Leave the harness on, we need to move fast," Spider said.

"But the sea's not up yet."

"It's the next bay we have to worry about."

And sure enough, when they ran around the first corner, surf already lapped at the edge of the next jutting cliff. Bennet pulled off his climbing shoes and splashed his way through in bare feet.

When they reached the safety of the beach beyond, Darius stopped and looked back. "He cut it fine," he said in a low voice.

"Perfect timing," Bennet said.

"If you hadn't come straight down—"

"But I did. He trusted me, and he was right to. Anyway, how bad would it have been if we'd been trapped? We could have gone over the top and invaded the nature reserve in an emergency, or roped ourselves to the cliff. We wouldn't have drowned."

"Unless we'd fallen."

"We have phones." Bennet dug his toes into the sun-baked pebbles. "He may take more risks than you would, but he's a good instructor. And it's fucking amazing here."

Darius's mouth curved up. "Glad I brought you?"

"Well, yeah. Of course."

Spider left them at a café near the car. "I need to nip home, check on the kids. I'll see you guys in an hour, okay?" He unlocked his bicycle, swung his leg over, and pedalled off up the road.

"What do you fancy eating?" Darius asked.

"I brought sandwiches."

"You bought a sandwich in Brighton?"

Bennet reached into his bag and held up a thick foil-wrapped packet. "I said *brought*, not *bought*. I know the difference."

"You didn't buy them?"

"I made them."

He slid onto a wooden bench at a shaded table and unwrapped his lunch while Darius went into the café, coming out almost at once with two packaged sandwiches, an apple, a banana, and juice.

"What's in yours?" Darius asked.

"Peanut butter and cucumber."

"Intriguing. Do you want to exchange one, so I can taste?"

"What are those?"

"Chicken or ham salad. They didn't have a huge selection." Darius turned them so the open sides faced Bennet. The meat looked plastic and the bread was dry at the edges.

Bennet wrinkled his nose. "No thanks, but I'll swap you this small one for the apple."

"Deal."

Darius pushed the apple across the table, and Bennet passed him a sandwich.

Darius said, "I was planning to offer you one of the pieces of fruit anyway."

Bennet scowled. "What? You mean I lost a sandwich for nothing? So let me have the banana, or give me my sandwich back."

"No way. We made a contract."

"Huh. Bastard."

Darius's eyes crinkled with amusement. "Legal training. Negotiating deals is my speciality."

He pushed up a corner of Bennet's sandwich to peek inside, took a bite, chewed, and swallowed. "This is all right. Pretty good, in fact."

"They're kind of my favourite thing," Bennet admitted.

"They must be, if you can't live without them for two days. And you bought all the makings in Brighton? I'd call that obsession. What about the foil?"

"The hotel." Bennet hadn't bought anything in Brighton. His water bottle was refilled. The peanut butter and half a cucumber had come with him from Longbourn, and he'd begged the bread from the hotel staff after breakfast. When they'd heard why he wanted it, they'd offered the aluminium foil wrap.

But Darius didn't need to know that buying lunch was a stretch for his finances. Time to talk about something else.

"So where are we going this afternoon?"

"Another cliff. Away from the sun, and not cut off at high tide."

"And clubbing tonight?"

"If you still have the energy."

"Oh, I will," Bennet said. "Never doubt it."

# Chapter Nine

AT 1 A.M., Bennet was a mass of sparks, energy bubbling in him as if he'd never want to sleep again. He'd danced for hours drinking only water, riding the energy that buzzed from the undulating mass of bodies. This was nothing like Rush. This was a real rush.

He met a stranger's appraising glance with a grin. In front of him, a glistening dark neck smelled of sweat and pheromones. Bennet wanted to lick that neck. Then his bare upper arm brushed against the shoulder of the man on his other side. A jolt went through his whole body, and he wanted that guy instead.

A big drunk came galumphing by, and Bennet shifted away. The crowd swelled and heaved like the sea. He lost the dark-skinned guy and the arm-brushing guy, but the waves brought him new flotsam.

Ahead, a strong bare back rippled with the music—a body moving with his own rhythm. If he could get over there and press right up against him, they'd be one form, pulsing together. Sex right here without even seeing his face. That man had a mark on his left shoulder—a tattoo.

Then someone bumped the guy, and he turned.

Darius.

Darius had a tattoo?

Their eyes met, and Bennet winked. He didn't mean anything by it—or did he? No, it was like a reflex, shock that the guy he'd been lusting after could turn out to be Darius, and recognition that they were both on the prowl.

But Darius apparently took it for more. One side of his mouth flickered up, and he started in Bennet's direction. Within seconds he'd cleaved a way through the pack and was right up close in front of Bennet.

Bennet's shoulders tensed. What now? This was not in any plan he'd made. Darius wasn't looking at him, so he stared away over Darius's shoulder. His body went on dancing in time with Darius, together in rhythm but not touching. How could he get out of this?

The pressure of the crowd should have pushed them together, but some force in the space between them seemed to keep them apart, as if the air was solid there, or as if they were magnets brought pole to pole, holding each other off with such strength that they kept a few inches of distance between them all the way down, however much the crowd surged. When one moved forward the other moved back. He could bump anyone else but not Darius. They mustn't touch.

He wanted to see the tattoo, but the light was too dim and the angle wrong, and he couldn't make it out. Some kind of geometric design. A Celtic knot?

He let it go, and his mind seemed to flip over and settle. His shoulders relaxed. It was a dance, and then it was more than a dance. A game. A tease. More even than that—

something real. Life itself.

The space between them prickled with static. He stole a glance at Darius's face. Beads of sweat glistened around the stubble on his upper lip. His eyes were hooded, staring blankly at Bennet's shoulder as if his whole being was concentrated on the music.

The sound changed. In a jarring beat between two tracks, their arms touched. Bennet jerked sideways, but that brought him up against Darius's other arm. This time he stayed, and Darius's hand came to rest on his lower back.

Darius slid two fingers under the edge of Bennet's top and rucked it up. He mouthed something that could have been "Off." Bennet pulled the damp shirt over his head and scrunched it in one hand.

Darius put one palm flat on Bennet's sweating back and stroked the knuckles of the other hand over Bennet's sparse chest hairs. Bennet was so caught up in the urgency of his desire, it didn't feel weird having Darius's hands on him, not here. They seemed to fit together. All he wanted was to get closer.

He gripped Darius's hips. They drew nearer with each beat as if linked by an invisible charge, although their torsos still didn't touch. The desire he'd felt for all those other guys came together and blossomed into the heat and need for this one guy, now. It had to be this one. Nobody else would do.

The music changed again, and this time their thighs bumped. Something long and hot and hard pressed against him. A shiver shot through him. Then the pressure was gone, and Darius's breath was in his ear.

"Let's take this back to the hotel."

Bennet nodded. Of course. No other man meant anything to him now. He only wanted to be out of there, to get physical with Darius.

Darius grabbed his hand, then dropped it as if he'd remembered Tim and Jamie, somewhere in this crowd. Bennet headed for the doors, pushing through the mass of bodies with Darius close behind him, fingers resting low on Bennet's bare back.

The lights in the lobby made Bennet blink. He shivered, shook out his sweat-soaked top, and put it on. He pushed at the door, wanting to be outside, to breathe the night air with its tang of the sea, but Darius took out his phone and asked the doorman for the number of a cab firm.

Bennet would have walked. Paying a driver was not something anybody ever did in his small-town existence, unless they'd booked a cheap flight to Spain or Greece and needed to be at the airport in the middle of the night. Darius was from a different world. But Bennet's antagonism was gone, transformed into desire. Doing things Darius's way was okay now, because Darius had set him on fire. As soon as they were alone—

The padded doors swung open. Jamie and Tim.

Bennet shifted to hide the erection that had barely started to soften. Darius had moved away to make the call. It wouldn't look like they were together. Good. He didn't want to explain this to Jamie right now.

Tim looked from Bennet to Darius. "You were leaving without saying anything?"

Darius held up his phone. "I'd have texted you. Why don't you two stay? You looked like you could dance all night."

"No, no. We're ready to go. Is this your cab?"

A big London-style five-seater had pulled up outside. Bennet climbed in first, half hoping to be pressed against Darius and half hoping not to be, because how would it look if he was still hard when they arrived at the glaring lights of the hotel? But Darius stood back, and Jamie and then Tim came in to fill the other two places on the bench seat. Darius took the pull-down seat by the door, facing Tim—as far from Bennet as he could be.

Tim kept up a stream of cheerful chatter as they drove the short distance to the hotel. Out on the street, the paths were populated with tipsy groups on hen and stag weekends and couples, gay and straight, touching and laughing, heading for bed . . . as Bennet and Darius could have been, if Darius had been willing to walk.

The taxi pulled into the hotel's driveway. Bennet fumbled in his pocket for money to pay his share. Jamie turned to him and said in a low voice, "Can you put something in for me? I'm out of cash, but I have some in our room."

He hadn't kept his voice low enough. Darius heard. "*Our* room?" he said to Tim, with raised eyebrows and a half smile. "I thought you were in singles."

"Jamie and Bennet are sharing."

The smile vanished. "Jamie and *Bennet*?"

"Separate beds, of course," said Jamie.

"To save money, Darius," Tim added.

"I see." Darius stared out of the window. His foot tapped on the floor. He didn't look at Bennet.

"Anyway, I'll get the cab fare," Tim added.

"I called it." Darius handed a banknote to the driver and stepped out, waving away the change.

Tim and Jamie were slow getting out, and Bennet was trapped behind them. Darius stalked into the hotel and was starting up the stairs by the time Bennet made it into the lobby.

Now what? Darius hadn't glanced back. Did he expect Bennet to follow right away? No, it would be crass to make things so obvious to Jamie and Tim, when they were holding back on sex themselves. Bennet had better hang around here for a couple of minutes, then go up.

And he had to think of something to tell Jamie, to explain his absence from their room tonight. If they'd got away from the club without being seen, he could have texted that he'd gone with some guy he wouldn't have needed to name, but now . . .

He went over to the watercooler, where Jamie was filling two cups. "You want one?" Jamie asked. "We're going to sit in the bar for a while."

"No, thanks. Listen, I'm nipping upstairs for something, and then I'll be off again to hook up with someone I met." True enough.

Jamie straightened up and looked him in the eye. "You're going out again? You won't do anything unsafe?"

"Of course not." Bennet retreated towards the stairs.

"Text me the guy's address," Jamie called after him.

Bennet went on walking, pretending he hadn't heard.

He took the stairs two at a time, shivering in his thin damp top in the temperature-controlled chill. Then he thought of Darius and the things they could do together, and a flutter of excitement started in his belly and spread out in a flush of warmth to the skin.

Darius's and Tim's rooms were on the third floor, as far as he knew. He went up, expecting to find Darius waiting by the stairs, but there was nobody on the landing. He pushed at the heavy fire door and slipped through. The corridor twisted away in both directions. He turned right and padded along the thick carpet until he could see the last bedroom doors. Nothing stirred, and every door was closed. He went back, past the fire door, to the end of the corridor on the other side. The same.

Could he have the wrong floor? He and Jamie were on the second, and Tim and Darius were definitely above them. They'd always gone on up the stairs when they all came in together. Maybe the fourth? He went on up, but the fourth floor corridor was the same—a little narrower, a little shorter, but equally silent and empty. And that was it. There was no fifth floor.

Darius had disappeared on him. Unbelievable. Wasn't it the golden rule of dating that you never led a guy on and then failed to deliver?

But wait. They'd all exchanged phone numbers their first day in Brighton. Maybe Darius had texted him the room number. Bennet hadn't felt his phone vibrate, but he pulled it out of his pocket. Nothing.

He found Darius in his contacts and called. His fingers were shaking. The call went straight to voice mail.

The flutter in his stomach turned to a tangle of anger and frustration. This was so typical of Darius! How could Bennet have forgotten how rude he'd been at Rush that first night, blanking anyone who asked him to dance, insulting Bennet on the roof? Dating etiquette did not apply.

He went back to the third floor. Still nobody there. He felt like banging on all the doors, but 2 a.m. was not a great time to be thrown out of a hotel.

What made Darius think he was so special? Okay, he had a hot body, and he knew how to make a guy want him, but the first was achieved by putting in time at the gym and the second was a technique anybody could learn. There must have been fifty guys in that club who'd looked as good.

And looks weren't even that important to Bennet. What mattered to him was the connection they'd made, first at the cliffs, then on the dance floor—or the connection he'd thought they'd made. Had it all been endorphins, after all?

He didn't give up easily. He checked the second floor, then the first, and the main lobby again. He glanced into the darkened lounge bar where Tim and Jamie were talking, too wrapped up in each other to notice him. Darius was not with them.

Darius was nowhere. Darius had dumped him.

Bennet banged his shoulder against the main hotel doors and shoved his way out. He'd told Jamie he was going out again, so he would.

He wove through the parked cars. He wanted to take a

hammer to Darius's black Audi because it was Darius's, but he couldn't because it was gorgeous, and it wasn't the car's fault its owner was such a bastard. Besides, it was parked by a security camera . . . and he didn't have a hammer.

Next up was Tim's Lotus. Bennet would be squashed in that rear seat again tomorrow for the trip back to Meriton. This was his last night in Brighton, and Darius had fucked it up for him. Why?

The answer came to him before he reached the street. The conversation in the cab, when Darius had found out Bennet and Jamie were sharing—that was when his mood had changed. Did he think they were more than just friends, or was it the money? The money, most likely. The snob thought Bennet was too far beneath him to take to bed, because he couldn't afford his own hotel room.

"*Just about fuckable, I suppose, but hardly up to* my *standards.*" And not even fuckable, now that Darius knew he was skint. Well, Darius could go fuck himself for the rest of his life, since nobody else was good enough for him.

The sea smelled the same but sounded louder without the daytime rumble of traffic. The shouts and shrieks of late-night revellers cut through the air like a devilish echo of the daytime cries of gulls. Bennet's limbs felt stiff and heavy, as if his blood had transformed to mud. His steps slowed.

Maybe he was doing a stupid thing, coming out like this. What kind of guy would he meet at this time of night? Was he desperate enough to hook up with whatever dregs and drunks remained on the dance floor? In Meriton, he wouldn't go home with just anybody. How was this different?

And would the club let him back in? He pulled out his phone and found their website. *No readmissions.* He'd have to pay again.

*Fuck it.* He turned around and walked back to the hotel.

They should go down in the record books. Four gay men under thirty spending two nights in Brighton without any of them having sex with anybody the whole time? It had to be a first.

Unless Darius had gone out again after they came back from the restaurant last night—or was out there somewhere now, hooking up with someone else. That would be so fucking ironic. And just like the bastard.

# Chapter Ten

WHEN JAMIE CAME into their room, Bennet was standing by the window, tossing and catching his phone. He'd showered and worked off his frustration with a soapy hand—but even that had been infuriating, because in the last seconds he'd lost control of his mind, so when he'd come, he was wrestling with Darius's sweating body on the floor of the nightclub in a whirlwind of passion and release.

The anger unfurled and sent out a rush of words. "I hate that guy."

Jamie sat down on the edge of his bed. "The guy you were planning to meet? He's let you down?"

"That's one way to put it." Bennet dropped the phone onto his sheets.

"Why didn't you go home with him from the club? What were you doing with Darius? We didn't get that."

"Darius fucked it up for me. I could have had anyone tonight, if it wasn't for him. He's fucked up my whole time here."

"He took you climbing."

Bennet dropped down onto his bed. "Yeah, that was sneaky. He was fine at the cliffs, so I started to think he was all right. But he's a complete bastard the rest of the time."

"Tim has so much respect for him, I'm sure he can't be a bad person."

"You don't think *anyone*'s a bad person."

Jamie shrugged. "Everyone has a spark of pure goodness at their core, whatever bad things they might do."

"Not Darius. He's evil through and through."

Jamie laughed. "You sound about ten years old. Whatever he's done, let it go now."

But Bennet couldn't. "He'd better not come near me tomorrow."

"He's going to Derbyshire, remember? I expect he'll leave early, before we get up."

Bennet let out a deep breath. "I hope you're right. And you'd better let me know when he comes to Meriton again so I can keep out of his way, or blood will be shed. That town is not big enough for the two of us."

"All right. You won't have to see him again if you don't want to."

"Except at your wedding," Bennet said. "I'm not missing your wedding."

Jamie looked away. "We don't have any marriage plans."

"Not yet, maybe. But that bracelet is a love token if ever I saw one. I bet he's only waiting to be sure you'll say yes."

---

AS JAMIE HAD predicted, Darius was gone by the time they made it to breakfast next morning. No craggy, handsome face at the table, no black Audi parked outside—Bennet had checked. It should have been a relief. It *was* a relief. Yet he was still jumpy, looking around as if something was missing.

He had to eat fast, to pack and clear the room before the hotel's 11 a.m. deadline. They made one last visit to the beach, with Bennet dragging behind because Brighton was so over for him now. Then they crammed into the sun-blasted Lotus for the trip north.

"Best moment?" Tim asked as they hit the main road and the car started to gather some speed.

"Swimming in the sea at Littlehampton," Jamie said. "Yours, Tim?"

"All of our wonderful day in the dunes." Tim's hand left the wheel to clasp Jamie's for a moment, and his soppy smile filled the mirror. "Other than that, the birthday cake! I never tasted a wheat-free cake that was so delicious. Bennet?"

"Climbing the cliffs." No question. It was all he could look back on without rancour or regret. Darius hadn't managed to spoil that.

Tim dropped them back at Longbourn Manor and went straight on to the gallery. Nigel hummed happily to himself as he made them coffee and listened to Jamie's impressions of Brighton. Even Nigel's been getting some, Bennet thought sourly.

He caught Monsieur Philippe outside his office one day in the first week of the new term. The college was quiet, in the middle of the last morning teaching hour, and Bennet was on his way to the restaurant for lunchtime duty. Outside on the back lawn, through the screened-off windows that the students weren't supposed to approach, the production team had set up tea in the shade of the cedar tree for the characters of *Bridgemaston Days*.

The head of department was wearing what his students called his "penguin," an impeccable black three-piece suit with a white shirt beneath. But he moved like a much statelier bird, gliding through the corridors of the college. Where other men of his age might have a belly hanging like a beach ball below a scrawny chest, Philippe had kept his figure. It must take some work, Bennet thought.

"I need to talk to you about jobs," Bennet said. "Can you spare five minutes?"

"Yes, I want you. Come in." Philippe waved him to a seat. "How serious is this affair with the gallery owner?"

Bennet hadn't even sat down yet. "Huh?"

"James Kershaw and Tim Wilson. I heard you went to Brighton with them over Easter, hmm?"

"I can't speak for Jamie." What business was it of Philippe's? Nigel must have been gossiping.

"Is he thinking of staying in Meriton?"

"I don't know. Possibly." Bennet hadn't come here to talk about his friend.

Monsieur Philippe went on, "I can't imagine him in London, can you? He'd be swamped, poor boy. He needs a good country house hotel. Perhaps even the Black Lion? I could offer him some hours as a teaching assistant if he stays here. Let him know, will you?"

So Philippe wanted to recruit Jamie to his private army of part-time college staff. "Okay," Bennet said. "Now if I could ask—"

"As for you, why haven't I been writing references for

you? Haven't you been looking at the ads that my secretary pins on the noticeboard?"

Bennet shook his head. "I don't want to work in a hotel chain. I was thinking of events management."

"Ah." Philippe sat back and made a steeple with his hands. "I might be able to get you in at Pemberley Hall. How about that?"

"What is it?" Bennet asked. Philippe was smirking as if this was a big deal, but the name made Bennet uncomfortable, and he couldn't remember why. "I think I've heard of it, but—"

"Of course you have. They host all the celebrity weddings. They had a footballer last week. You didn't see it? It made the television news. But it's not only weddings. Conferences, shows, the occasional opera. The managing director, Catherine Brackenbrough, is an old friend of mine. I'll set you up with an interview."

"But I don't know if—"

There was a knock at the door. Without waiting for an answer, the department secretary put her head round. "Sorry to interrupt, Monsieur Philippe, but they're asking for you in the restaurant."

"All right." Philippe sprang to his feet.

"But could we just—" Bennet began.

"Send Catherine your CV, mention my name, and I'll give her a call in the next day or two. Aren't you on the restaurant rota this lunchtime, anyway? Come along."

Bennet stood up to follow him, and his memory kicked in. Pemberley... didn't Darius have a house there that Tim had joked about wanting to buy? And at Tim's opening party, hadn't Philippe claimed his old friend Catherine was related to Darius in some way?

Philippe was striding down the corridor. Bennet trotted to catch up with him. "Monsieur Philippe? Pemberley Hall—is it in Derbyshire?"

"That's right."

So it *was* Darius's family home. "That's not where I want to be."

"It's not far from Manchester. Plenty of life up there. Plenty of *scene*, as you call it. I think you'll find it's the kind of thing you're after, if Catherine will have you. Not another word now, Bennet. Look at this—what a shower of incompetents!"

A puddle of lentil salad lay like vomit on the restaurant floor, right by the entrance where the students would soon be pouring in for their lunch. An argument was raging between Richard Jones and one of the first-year students about whose fault it was. Like the incident between Richard and Leon last term, except now there was also an abject but cute-looking man in his late twenties, shifting his weight from foot to foot with his face screwed up in apology, claiming all the blame for himself.

It was the guy from Rush last month—the one Darius hadn't been able to face. Interesting. His gaze slid over Bennet and away, then back with a little twitch of a smile as if he remembered him. Even more interesting.

Richard and the other student fell silent at the sight of Monsieur Philippe, and then they and the guy from the film crew all started talking at once.

"She was carrying way too much."

"He barged straight into me!"

"I'm so sorry, I'm afraid I—"

"Stop!" Philippe cried. "How many times do I have to tell you? Cleanup first, recriminations later." He turned to another student who'd brought a broom but couldn't use it because of the three standing around the mess. "Not a brush! There's oil everywhere. Get another dustpan, scrape up the food, and then wash and dry the floor, or people will slip. And has anyone given the kitchen the glad news? They'll have to rustle up another pièce de résistance for the salad bar."

The students scattered to obey him, and the filming guy stepped forward. His light-brown hair flopped over one eye.

"Are you Philippe Hennice?" He looked earnest and eager, like a spaniel.

"I am indeed, sir. And who are you?"

The guy mumbled his name too fast for Bennet to catch. "From the *Bridgemaston Days* camera crew. I was looking for you, actually. We need your permission—"

"If it's anything to do with the location agreement, you'll have to see the principal."

"I know that's the usual procedure, but he's out all day, and we need permission for a scene at the side door—the one that leads to your storage room? It's our servants' entrance. Of course the actors don't really go in, but this time we need someone to stand in the doorway. Only just inside, but technically she'll be in the college, so it's not covered by the—"

"Wherever it is, it's not up to me," Philippe interrupted. "Try the vice principal."

"He's out too. And I was told you're next in seniority?"

The VP was female, and all the department heads were of equal status, in theory, but Philippe didn't correct the guy. "All right. Wait outside, and I'll see to it when we've cleaned up this mess."

The guy smiled and tilted his head. "It's urgent, that's the thing, because the light is only right at noon. So if you wouldn't mind initialling each page—" He produced two copies of a folded document, several pages long.

Philippe threw up his hands. "I don't have time to read all this!"

The guy's eyes went big, pleading, and he hopped from one foot to the other. "It's a standard filming waiver, but I can explain it to you. This section sets out the parties to the instrument, and here's the reference to the original agreement, and—"

"Yes, yes." Philippe took the papers from him and glanced at the first page, then back at the students. The girl who'd dropped the dish was scraping up the food, and another student had brought a bucket of water. Bennet dropped to his knees to help wash the floor.

"Is that water hot?" Philippe said.

Richard, carrying a mop, skidded on the oily patch and hit the bucket, splashing soapy water over Bennet's arms. Bennet glared. He'd bet Richard had done that on purpose.

Philippe stepped away, tutting. "We'll have to do this in my office," he said to the cameraman.

"I don't need to take up any more of your time, if you could just—"

With an impatient "*Pfah!*" Philippe took the pen the guy was offering and signed. "Is one of these copies for me?"

"For the college, yes, but I'll need to get it countersigned from our side. Then we usually take the paperwork to the principal's office, I think."

"All right, give it to his PA." Philippe waved the guy away. "Now, has someone told the chef what's happened to his lentils?"

Bennet looked up from his cleaning to watch the cute cameraman leave. The guy glanced back at him before he disappeared through the double doors.

Nice mover and plenty of charm. Bennet hoped he'd be seeing that smile again before filming ended.

---

*Pemberley Hall—Where Your Dreams Will Come True*

LYING ON HIS bed at Longbourn, Bennet browsed the website. Weddings, celebrations, conferences. The location was stunning. A massive country house of grey stone, set in the Derbyshire hills, with a stream running through the grounds. Trees everywhere, formal gardens . . . even a lake graced the approach to the house.

Someone was coming up the stairs—Jamie. Each person's tread on the creaking wood was different. Bennet went to the door.

"Jamie, do you have a minute?"

"Sure, what is it?"

Bennet put the computer on his desk, gathered up all the clothes that lay on his two chairs, threw them on the bed, and drew the chairs up to the desk.

"Monsieur Philippe thinks I should apply to this place, Pemberley Hall, but doesn't Darius have some property called Pemberley? They've talked about it."

Jamie settled in one of the chairs. "Wow, it's huge."

"Yeah. I thought there'd be a village called Pemberley, and Darius might have a house there, but no. Pemberley is just this place, as far as I can see. The nearest town is called Lambton. So is Darius involved in this events business?"

"I don't think so. He works in London." Jamie peered at the blue and gold website. His big hazel eyes were a little shortsighted.

"Tim said Pemberley was Darius's ancestral home. Do his parents live there?"

"I think his parents are dead. Couldn't 'ancestral home' mean his family used to own it, but not any more?"

"That's what I'm hoping. But then why does he still go up there? He went from Brighton."

Jamie pointed to the screen. "Look at *About Us*."

"I already did. It has photographs of the company directors and some of the staff. Darius isn't mentioned." Bennet brought up the page. "This is Philippe's old college friend, Catherine Brackenbrough, the managing director."

She was blonde, with sharp eyes and a brittle smile. "She's well preserved if she's the same age as Philippe," Jamie said.

"Airbrushed, I think."

Jamie pulled his chair in closer, squeaking the legs against the floorboards. "Who's this Annabel Brackenbrough? A sister?"

"Daughter, maybe? I think she's younger, but her photo hasn't had the same treatment."

"Is there nobody called Lanniker?"

"No. But if he's some kind of sleeping partner, I don't want anything to do with it. There's no way I could work for that—"

Jamie held up a hand to stop him. Swear words seemed to give Jamie a physical pain. "I know how you feel. I can ask Tim."

"He'll wonder why you're interested."

"I'll tell him I saw the website. Did you look at this page—the history of the house?"

Bennet clicked on it. "The present house was built by the Darcy family in the eighteenth century . . . the last male heir died in the First World War . . . wait, here's a Lanniker. 'Their daughter, Elizabeth, married her brother's commanding officer, Colonel G. J. Lanniker.' But that's a hundred years ago. Nothing about the current owners. How has it ended up with these Brackenbrough people?"

"They might rent it from Darius's family."

"Or they're all related, and he has a share in the business. That's what I'm afraid of." Bennet clicked back to the home page. "Okay, ask Tim—but be careful what you say. Don't mention me or jobs. This looks like the kind of thing I might want to do, but I need to be sure it's Lanniker-free."

# Chapter Eleven

WHEN BENNET WALKED into Rush that Friday, the brown-haired guy was already there, with the same two older men from the crew and two young women. He saw Bennet at once and shot him a quick smile. Perfect. A night with someone like him would wipe out all trace of the humiliation Bennet had suffered in Brighton. If it involved digging up some dirt on Darius too, all the better.

He didn't want to seem desperate, but he didn't want to wait too long, either. He gave it five minutes, then went over and yelled, "Hi, I'm Bennet."

The guy said his name, but it was a blur of syllables, even though the music was quieter than usual tonight. Bennet shook his head. The guy laughed and fished a card out of his pocket. He moved in so close that their shoulders touched as he handed it over.

*Wyndham Moorhouse, Camera Operator, Bridgemaston Productions Ltd.*

Wyndham. Interesting name. Bennet slipped the card into his pocket. "Can I get you a drink?"

Term had started and he had the last instalment of his student loan, so he could afford to offer. All the same, he wasn't sorry when Wyndham answered, "Just water, thanks."

When Bennet came back with two glasses, Wyndham said, "I've seen you at the college, haven't I? What are you studying?"

"Hospitality management."

"That gent in the waistcoat seemed quite a character. Your tutor, or whoever he is."

"Head of department."

"You get on with him?"

Bennet shrugged. "He's okay."

"Thought he might be difficult. Pernickety."

"If you stay on the right side of him, he's fine."

"What do you have to do to stay on the right side of him?" Wyndham winked. He seemed different from the way he'd been in the training restaurant. Less apologetic, more hyped up.

Bennet laughed. "Nothing like what you're thinking." Bizarre conversation, and yet he felt a buzz. "You want to dance?"

They made their way onto the floor. Dancing at Rush was not like being one of the mass of sweaty, exciting bodies in the packed club in Brighton. Maybe that was why dancing with Wyndham, cute as he was, was not like dancing with Darius. None of the heat and tension. No rhythm, either. Was Wyndham even paying attention to the music? Bennet kept having to adjust his own position to avoid bumping knees or elbows.

But hey, the guy couldn't help it if he wasn't a great dancer. He was still the best-looking man in the place, except for Jamie, who came in a few minutes later, holding hands with Tim.

Only the two of them, thank the stars. No Darius trailing along behind.

Wyndham turned to see what he was looking at. "Nice arse—the younger one, I mean. Not bad from the front, either."

Bennet winced. "That's my best friend."

"Sorry. Looks like he's taken, right?"

"Yeah. You don't know Tim?"

"His boyfriend? I don't think so. Should I?"

"His name's Tim Wilson." Wyndham's eyes narrowed. Bennet added, "He owns a gallery in the town. He has a friend, Darius Lanniker—"

Wyndham stopped dancing.

"You know Darius, don't you?" Bennet said. "I thought, last time you were here, he was afraid of you, or something. Like, he left as soon as he saw you."

"You saw that? Are you—Do you know him well?"

Bennet shook his head. "Only through those two."

Wyndham nodded. "Do me a favour, okay? Don't introduce me to them. Nothing against Wilson, but he'll report back."

Jamie and Tim headed towards them. Wyndham snaked away and Bennet followed, but there wasn't a massive crowd. It was hard to put more than five people between them and the other couple.

They were right under the speaker now. Bennet had to yell. "So what's going on?"

Wyndham shook his head. "Long story. Not the place or

time."

They danced. Bennet put his hands on Wyndham's hips, and Wyndham seemed fine with that, though his gaze dodged around the room. Tim looked over once, with a smile for Bennet. No reaction to Wyndham. Not like Darius. What was the deal there?

Around midnight, Wyndham said, "I'm working tomorrow. We should go . . . I mean, if you want to."

"Sure, yeah." Bennet didn't plan to turn down his one chance of action in what felt like forever.

They went through the lobby, out into the night—a soft, moonlit night, with the smell of summer in the air. Neither of them had a jacket.

"Do you live with your parents?" Wyndham asked.

"No, I rent a room in a shared house."

"Cool. Part of the college?"

"No, it's a private house. In fact, it's owned by the partner of our head of department that you met. But it's a bit of a walk, on the edge of the town. How about you? Where are you staying?"

Wyndham grimaced. "I can't take you back there. Some of the production team are in hotels, but not me. All I get is a crappy mobile home with another guy, a straight guy." His puppy-dog expression reappeared. "Can I walk you home? A mile doesn't sound that far. We can get to know each other on the way."

"I'd like that." *That and more.* Bennet's blood zinged at the thought of having Wyndham in his bed.

A big, noisy group had gathered in the middle of the

marketplace, and Bennet steered Wyndham away down a side street. His bicycle was chained up nearby, but he could pick it up tomorrow. He didn't want it to make a barrier between them.

"So what's the story about Darius Lanniker?" he asked.

"Oh, Darius and I go way back—but not in a good way."

They stopped to cross the road outside a row of Georgian houses that opened straight onto the pavement. One car came roaring by, then all was quiet. "Is he an ex?" Bennet asked.

"God, no. Heaven preserve me." Wyndham gave a short laugh. "I couldn't believe it when I saw him here last month. Quite a coincidence."

"It's not entirely coincidental. He's here because of Monsieur Philippe—Philippe Hennice, our head of department. Tim Wilson was looking to buy an art gallery, and Philippe has a friend who... Well, she runs Pemberley Hall. The wedding place. So she knows Darius and Tim."

He hadn't put it well, but Wyndham seemed to follow. "Your Monsieur Philippe has his finger in every pie, doesn't he? I've heard he's a bit of a tyrant—is that right?"

"No, really, he's fine. What's Darius's connection with Pemberley Hall, exactly? Do you know?"

Wyndham nodded. "He owns the place."

"Darius owns that huge house? And the events business?"

"He doesn't own the business. Just the property. Yeah, I wasn't specific. There's a difference between Pemberley Hall Limited, the wedding business, which is the tenant of the house, and the house itself, which is part of the Pemberley estate, which Darius owns. The house was never called Pemberley Hall. They added *Hall* for the name of the company. He's, like, their landlord."

"He isn't a partner in the business?"

"No." Wyndham sounded certain, and some of Bennet's tension drained away.

"Up here." Bennet indicated the shortcut, a path through an old archway at the side of the health centre.

"Why do you want to know about Lanniker?" Wyndham asked.

"I might have a chance to work there, but I don't like the guy. I don't want to end up with him for a boss."

Wyndham's shoulders relaxed, and he laughed. "Oh, right. Okay, I get where you're coming from. You're right to steer clear, that man is poisonous. But no, you'd be fine working there. You might see him passing through from time to time, but he's not involved in the business, except for taking Catherine's rent money."

"You know her?"

"She's my aunt. My father's sister." They emerged from the archway into the looming shadow of a brick building dotted with small windows. Wyndham looked around. "What's this place? Looks like a prison."

"It's actually a care home, I think," Bennet said. "But isn't Catherine Brackenbrough Darius's aunt too? So you're his cousin?"

"No. I'm not related to him by blood, thank God. She's... What would she be? His step-aunt, I suppose. His mother's second husband's sister."

Okay. So Bennet might be able to work at Pemberley Hall and never see Darius. And even if their paths crossed occasionally, Darius would have no power over him. That was what mattered.

But Bennet was still curious. "Why did Darius walk out of Rush last month when he saw you?"

"I shouldn't really say. It's family stuff."

"Something to do with Catherine Brackenbrough?"

"No, no. From when we were kids." Wyndham took a small stone from the top of somebody's garden wall and sent it skimming across the road. "It's kind of personal. But if he's prowling around here, perhaps you should know."

He didn't say any more for a moment. They'd reached Longbourn Lane, a quiet road of detached houses in big, well-tended gardens. It was lit, but not brightly, and Wyndham took Bennet's hand.

Bennet's arm tensed. Hand-holding was for relationships, wasn't it? Not for someone he'd just met. But Wyndham's easy affection was appealing, so he let Wyndham interlace their fingers, and it was okay. Hot, when he thought about what else that hand might do for him, later.

"We're stepbrothers, Darius and me," Wyndham said. "His mother married my father when we were both nine years old. They lived at Pemberley—none of it was let, back then, and his mother had the place and plenty of money. I lived with my mother most of the time, but I used to visit my dad up there sometimes, in the school holidays. I never felt welcome. My stepmother was okay, but a little distant.

She never tried to be a mother to me. My dad was in her shadow. And Darius resented me."

So Wyndham was the outsider in the family. Bennet knew how that felt. He tightened his grip on Wyndham's hand but didn't interrupt.

"He made it clear he considered himself vastly superior to me and my father," Wyndham said. "He must have been furious about their marriage. He was possessive, controlling—didn't want to share the place with anybody he hadn't invited himself. Sometimes he'd have school friends staying. Tim Wilson was one of them, I think, but I wouldn't have recognised him if you hadn't pointed him out. He was chubbier back then. They'd do things I'd never had a chance to learn, like horse riding or rock climbing—things Darius was good at, so he could show off and exclude me."

It all fit. Darius couldn't do anything by halves. He had to excel.

"Soon there was a baby," Wyndham went on, "a child of this second marriage, a boy, a cute little thing. They named him Giorgio—they'd been to Italy for their honeymoon. You can imagine how jealous Darius was of him. He despised me, but I was only a hanger-on. I wasn't a real threat to him. I had no claim on his mother or the estate, like Giorgio did. When I look back, I'm surprised Giorgio lived to grow up—Darius hated him that much."

Bennet shivered. Yes, he could imagine Darius not wanting to share. He'd disappeared without a word when he'd found out Bennet had no money—had he thought Bennet was after his wealth?

They passed Longbourn church, so small that the yews in its graveyard hid it from sight. Wyndham continued his story.

"Fast-forward ten or twelve years, and my stepmother, their mother, died. Cancer. Sad for Giorgio, he was still so young. And Darius was studying law, so he knew all the legal tricks to stop Giorgio inheriting anything. My father got a small house in Sheffield and a little cash, but he should have had a lot more. And Giorgio should have had a share in Pemberley, and he got nothing at all. Darius would have had to sell Pemberley then, you see, and he didn't want to."

"I thought those places always went to the eldest son anyway," Bennet said.

"Not any more. You're thinking of the old days when estates were entailed, but that was abolished in the 1920s. That's why there are so few big country estates now. Most of them have been sold or split between several children. But Darius wasn't going to let that happen to Pemberley."

They weren't far from Nigel's. Bennet slowed his steps so they wouldn't arrive before Wyndham finished. He wanted to hear the end of this.

"Then couldn't your father have taken it to court? Aren't there rules for dividing an estate?"

"Only when somebody doesn't leave a will. She did leave a will, that's the thing, and she left enough to my father to make it hard to challenge. Darius knew how sick she was, even before my father did. He had plenty of time to work on her. She'd have signed anything he gave her, by the end. And my father—well, he's a lovely man, but he's not exactly assertive."

Wyndham took after his father, then. Easygoing, eager to please.

"So Darius got the whole of Pemberley," Wyndham went on. "And to make sure there was no trouble, he took Giorgio out of school, found him a private tutor, kicked my father off the premises, and made the kid a virtual prisoner. When he let the place to Catherine, he kept one old cottage—a hovel, run-down and damp—and put Giorgio in it. The kid's still stuck there, all alone."

Wyndham's voice caught, as if this was hard for him to talk about. Bennet gripped his hand but didn't interrupt.

"He's seventeen now, so his tutor's been fired. I can never see him—Darius and I have had some furious arguments, as you can imagine, so I'm banned from the place—but my father gets through the gates from time to time, and he says Giorgio's become neurotic. My father wants him to live in Sheffield, of course, but Giorgio doesn't dare go anywhere or do anything for himself in case Darius wouldn't like it."

What a story. Hard to believe it could happen in the twenty-first century. But social equality was a myth to some people—people like Darius. Men of his class might not be the celebrities they used to be, but they still existed. And if one of them had grown up expecting to be master of a place like Pemberley, and someone threatened to break it up and take half away, he might feel entitled to use underhand tactics.

"It's like something out of *Bridgemaston Days*," Bennet

said.

Wyndham kicked at a lump of mud on the grass verge. "Let's change the subject, okay? I don't want to think about Darius any more. He's blighted enough of my life."

Bennet squeezed his hand. "Sure. This is it, anyway."

They'd reached Nigel's gate. Wyndham's eyes widened as he looked at the moonlit weathered stone walls, the sash windows, the well-kept garden. "You're renting a room here? You must be doing well."

Bennet shook his head. "He doesn't charge much. Less than some places, because it's on the wrong side of the town for the college. There are five of us, so it adds up for him. Do you want to come in for coffee?"

Wyndham looked up at the house again. "How do you get on with the others? Will they mind you bringing a man home?"

Bennet laughed. "No, it's fine. You saw Jamie at Rush—he's an amazing cook. And Leon, the blond guy? He was chatting to one of your mates."

Wyndham broke into a smile. "You mean you're all gay?"

"Except Charlotte."

"Aha! So your landlord and his partner pick out all the best-looking gay students for eye candy around the house."

Bennet laughed. "I'll take that as a compliment. Do you want to come in?"

---

HE LED WYNDHAM up the stairs, coffee in hand. The house

was dark except for the low landing light, left on all night. Most of his housemates were at Rush. Kofi had stayed home with a cold, and he snuffled as they passed his door, always open a crack. Nigel slept on the next floor.

Bennet turned on a lamp in his room, but Wyndham wanted the strong overhead light—"To see you better," he said.

"Like the big bad wolf," Bennet said.

"Huh?"

"In Red Riding Hood?"

Wyndham's mouth turned down. "My childhood wasn't big on fairy tales."

*No more family stuff, please*, Bennet thought. He didn't want Darius barging in on this, even in their minds. Things were tense enough already. The overhead light was too bright, clinical. How could he move this onto a physical—preferably horizontal—level?

He put a hand on Wyndham's shoulder. Wyndham's eyes crinkled in a smile. Bennet brushed Wyndham's cheek with his lips and pressed forward.

But Wyndham broke away. "I'll just deal with this," he said, taking his phone out of his pocket.

What was he doing—checking his messages? No, a couple of taps and he was smiling back at Bennet.

Bennet moved closer again. "You want to . . ."

"Sure."

They met between the desk and the bed. Bennet put his hands on Wyndham's back—warm flesh through a thin shirt—and bent his head for a kiss. His cock pulsed with hunger. He closed his eyes against the light and moved one hand up to push his fingers into Wyndham's hair, the other down to knead Wyndham's arse. Oh yes. This was what he needed.

He pulled Wyndham in closer so their hips bumped and their cocks rubbed together through their clothing. With his eyes closed, his mouth on Wyndham's, and the contact lower down, Bennet started to lose himself.

Wyndham plucked at Bennet's top. Bennet broke away from the kiss and stripped it off over his head. Wyndham nipped at Bennet's shoulder with his teeth, then fumbled at Bennet's belt. Bennet took over, undoing the button and pushing his trousers down. He ached to be touched there, but Wyndham was taking off his own shirt.

Bennet drew him nearer again. Their bare chests came together, and Bennet's cock found the crease at Wyndham's thigh. Wyndham's jeans provided extra friction. Bennet rubbed, sending a hot current jolting through his limbs.

He'd missed this. It had been way too long. Wyndham's mouth explored his neck. Bennet sucked at Wyndham's earlobe and manoeuvred his hips to where he wanted them.

Wyndham pulled down Bennet's underpants and gripped his arse. "I want to fuck you," Wyndham said.

"Okay." Bennet had imagined it the other way around, but whatever. He didn't want to mess this up.

He opened the drawer beside the bed and offered Wyndham a condom, but Wyndham pushed it away. "I'm allergic to latex."

"So . . . do you have special ones?"

"Yeah." Wyndham felt in his pockets. He was still holding his phone and wearing his jeans. The apologetic puppy-dog look was back. "They must be in my jacket."

"Where's your jacket?"

"Back at the crappy mobile home. Bummer."

"And I suppose if you're allergic it doesn't make a difference who's wearing it? It would still irritate you if it was on me?"

"Yes."

Bennet dropped the condom. "No problem. We can do other stuff. We have hands and mouths, right?"

He put his palms flat on Wyndham's shoulders, moving back into a kiss. He reached down to ease Wyndham's jeans off. He hadn't done this in way too long. Their mouths bumped, then locked. He slid one hand down Wyndham's smooth, warm back to the swell of his arse. Pity he couldn't—but he couldn't. He'd take whatever else was offered.

Wyndham broke the kiss but kept his lips on Bennet's cheek. Was he going down? No, only over to his ear. That was hot, but Bennet wanted more.

"I want to fuck you," Wyndham whispered. "Fuck you hard and hot and long."

That kind of talk would have been fine if they could do it. But since they couldn't, Bennet preferred to think about lips and tongues and throats and having his mouth filled with thick, throbbing meat. He let his underpants drop to the floor and tried to push Wyndham's down, but Wyndham began moving towards the bed. Maybe he'd sit on the edge and Bennet could—but no. Wyndham was clambering onto the bed, pulling Bennet with him.

Fine. He gripped Wyndham's shoulder, ready to twist around, but again Wyndham seemed to be going in another direction. He wanted Bennet face down on the bed.

"Listen, let's do something else," Bennet said. "I don't fuck without a condom."

Wyndham's soft brown eyes gazed into Bennet's. "Come on, you can't let me down now. I know you want it."

"I want something, but not that."

Wyndham gave him a broad, dimpled smile. "I don't have any diseases."

"It's still a no. I might have an infection myself and not know it." That was bullshit—Bennet hadn't had sex since his last screening—but it was simpler than arguing about Wyndham's possible status.

His cock was turning sulky and soft. Wyndham rolled on top of him and moved in for another kiss.

"I'll take the risk," Wyndham whispered.

"What, you mean you'd let me fuck you bare?" Not that Bennet planned to do it.

"No, I mean I'll take the risk of catching something from your hot little arse. These things aren't dangerous, not any more."

"But I don't want the responsibility of maybe passing something on to you." Bennet eased his body out from under Wyndham's. "There's so much else we can do. Why don't we play around and go with what feels good?"

Wyndham's face fell. "I wanted so much to fuck you."

He looked cute when he was disappointed, but Bennet wouldn't give in. He reached out a finger and stroked Wyndham's nipple.

Wyndham shrank away. "I'll go, then."

"Go? What the—" Bennet remembered Kofi, sleeping in the next room, and lowered his voice. "This is crazy. There's tons we can do."

Wyndham rolled onto his back and looked down at his groin. Inside his underpants, his cock seemed to have shrivelled to nothing. "I think I've lost it for tonight, with all this talk. Maybe another time?"

Bennet sat up and ran a hand through his hair. This could not be happening. "You're joking. I'll find some porn."

"I have to work in the morning, anyway. You've got my card, right? Let's get together in the next few days. What's your number?"

A cute guy, naked in his bedroom, and he still couldn't get any action. Unbelievable.

"We'll see each other again," Wyndham said, stepping into his jeans and picking up his shirt.

Bennet watched, powerless, as Wyndham slipped out through the bedroom door. The stairs creaked as he walked down, and the front door closed with a bang.

After a moment, Bennet got up and shut his door. He turned out the too-bright overhead light and switched on his computer.

Porn alone, then. Again.

# Chapter Twelve

"Darius is coming through tonight," Jamie called from his room as Bennet clattered down the stairs the next day for a shift at the Black Lion.

Bennet halted four steps from the bottom, with one foot in midair. "No way. I thought we'd have at least one more weekend."

Jamie came out onto the landing. "You won't see him. He's coming for dinner, staying with Tim, and then we're going to an auction preview tomorrow morning. But I promised I'd warn you when he was in town."

"Yeah, thanks."

"Tim invited him for last night, but I don't think Darius wanted to go to Rush," Jamie said.

"No, I don't suppose he did. He'd want to avoid Wyndham—the guy I was with. He had stories about Darius you wouldn't believe. But I'll have to tell you another time."

Outside, Bennet's bicycle wasn't in its usual place. Of course, he'd left it in town to walk with Wyndham.

He couldn't afford to be late. He crashed back into the house. "Jamie! Can I borrow your bike?"

"Yes. You know the combination for the lock?"

"Sure." Not difficult—Jamie's birthday. Which brought

back recollections of a black and silver bracelet on Jamie's arm at the hotel breakfast, long legs in climbing shoes and— No, his mind was not going anywhere near that Brighton club. Maybe he'd call Wyndham later, see if he wanted to bring his special condoms over. Bennet needed a focus for his desires.

He'd got over his annoyance at the way Wyndham had bailed on him last night. Maybe he had an erection problem, who knew? Bennet would be happy to help with that, if he could.

But the summer rush was on, the Black Lion was busy, and the weekend passed without Bennet finding the right time to call. Never mind. Next week might be better. He didn't want to seem desperate . . . even if he was.

He kept his eyes open for Darius all weekend, but Jamie was right. Bennet didn't see him.

Everything seemed fine until Tuesday night. Then Bennet came home late from college, tired after an evening in the training restaurant, to find Jamie pacing his room with the door open.

"What's wrong?" Bennet asked.

"Tim went to London with Darius on Sunday, and he hasn't come back. I don't know what's happened. He's not answering my calls."

Bennet slung his bag on the floor of Jamie's room. Jamie usually kept it immaculate, but tonight things were out of place—laundry on the floor, dirty mugs on the desk.

"When were you expecting him?"

"This morning, at the latest. He should have been there

to open the gallery. He always keeps to the advertised hours. You remember, he talked about that in Brighton."

"You've been to the gallery?"

"Yes, after college. It was closed. I saw mail on the floor inside that nobody had picked up, and no sign of his car. I didn't know he was even taking his car. I thought he'd go with Darius and come back on the train." Jamie ran a hand over his face. "Do you think he could have had an accident?"

Bennet sat down on the bed. "Anything could have delayed him. Maybe the car's broken down."

"But he'd have told me. I've phoned, I've texted—"

"He lost his phone? Or forgot it, left it in London, and the engine died on his way back. So he's stuck in a hotel somewhere, waiting for it to be repaired."

"For twenty-four hours? He'd have hired another car."

"Or he's sick. Flu can knock you out."

"He'd be able to send me a text. Unless it's something serious—and then I should be there." Jamie began swiping the screen on his phone.

"What are you doing?"

"Maybe he's badly hurt. I'm looking for hospitals near his flat."

"You mean in London? He still has a flat there?"

"Of course."

*Of course.* As if everybody had a London pad as well as a bijou art gallery in a country town.

"And I've rung the landline," Jamie added.

"Have you tried that prick he calls a friend?"

"Darius? Yes, voice mail and text. No answer from him,

either."

"And you've looked online? Has Tim posted anything in the last couple of days?"

"Nothing. The gallery website's been updated, but I don't think he's doing it. He hired someone for that."

"Darius would have told you if he was in hospital," Bennet said.

"Not if they went together and had an accident on the road."

Bennet pictured the black Audi, crumpled, overturned, bursting into flames. An icy claw of dread clutched at his chest. Where did that come from? He was letting Jamie's stress get to him.

He shook himself. "That's not possible. You said Tim's car wasn't there, so they went separately. Let's think this through." He took off his shoes and brought his feet up onto the bed. "Did something happen at the weekend? Why was he going to London?"

Jamie pulled out the chair by the desk and sat sideways on it. "I don't know . . . just for a visit, I think. We went to the preview on Sunday, but there was nothing that interested him, so instead of staying here for the auction on Monday, he went back with Darius. Or that's what I thought. But he's taken his own car."

So maybe he hadn't gone to London at all, Bennet thought. He could be anywhere. "How far did you go with him last weekend?"

"Not far. The preview was at a big house a few miles away."

Bennet would have laughed if Jamie hadn't looked so pale. "No, I mean sex. Did you do more than you—" But Jamie was shaking his head. "Or did Tim try something and get annoyed when you said no?"

"No. Darius stayed on Saturday night, so there was no opportunity. Tim was joking that I'd have sex with him if I loved him . . . like boys used to tell girls in the 1950s. 'Dear Agony Aunt, my boyfriend says if I really loved him, I would sleep with him.' So I told him what the agony aunt would say—if he loved me, he'd marry me. We laughed about it."

Maybe that was it, Bennet thought. The idea of marriage had scared him off, even if it was a joke.

The door swung wide and Leon stood there, blinking at the light. "What's all the noise, guys? Not interrupting anything, am I? No, I can see I'm not. Shit. I thought someone had corrupted you, Jamie."

"Go back to sleep," Bennet said.

"Sorry we woke you," Jamie added. "It's late. You go too, Bennet. Maybe in the morning there'll be some news."

"News about what?" Leon said.

Bennet shepherded him out and closed the door behind them. "Nothing you need to worry about."

He woke in the night to hear Jamie's low voice in the room next door, talking on the phone. Good. It must be Tim. He rolled over and went back to sleep.

But in the kitchen in the morning, Jamie's face was grey and lined, as if he hadn't slept. He had a steaming mug of coffee, but he wasn't eating.

Bennet dropped a couple of pieces of bread into the

toaster. "Wasn't that Tim I heard you talking to?"

"No. I called some hospitals, but I didn't find him. Not in London, or here, or anywhere between."

"Well, that's good, I suppose. Are you going by the gallery on your way to college? I'll come with you. Here, eat this." He took a piece of hot toast by its corner and dropped it on the counter in front of Jamie.

They left earlier than usual, looping through the town. As they slowed outside the gallery, a postwoman pushed a handful of envelopes through the slot beside the door to join the scattered pile on the tiled floor below.

Bennet followed Jamie down a lane to the back of the building, their bicycles bumping over cobblestones. Jamie pointed out the empty space where Tim normally parked his car.

At college, Bennet was first to arrive in the management studies seminar room, upstairs at the back of the main building. He walked to the window. What the hell was Tim thinking? Jamie shouldn't be left to worry like this.

The film crew were working on the lawn below, shooting a knee-high layer of mist that stretched over the park between the ha-ha and the river. Wyndham's toned figure was pushing a camera into position in the shade of the cedar. Maybe he'd give Wyndham a call in the next few days . . . if Tim came back.

"Move away from the window, Bennet. You know the rules." The management studies lecturer had arrived to connect her computer for a presentation.

"The cameras are pointing the other way," Bennet argued,

but he left Wyndham to his work and slung his books onto a table near the middle of the room.

Charlotte came in late, red-faced from running up the stairs. She flopped into the seat next to Bennet, seconds before the lecturer finished fiddling with her cables and turned to face the class.

"Why didn't you wake me?" she whispered.

Because he'd temporarily forgotten she existed. Fortunately, she didn't expect an answer.

---

HE'D STILL HEARD nothing from Distinctivent, so he called them again. He asked for Donna Clare, and this time he was transferred to her. His heart thumped.

"Bennet Rourke? I do remember the name," she said.

"I had an interview, but you weren't there." In case that sounded whiny or accusing, he added, "They said it was a crisis. I hope everything was okay."

"My son had an accident, but he's on the mend. I'm sorry, we've filled the position you applied for."

He'd been expecting it, but his shoulders slumped, all the same. He kicked at the leg of his desk. "Is there anything else coming up? I know I'd be an asset to you."

"You're at Meriton?" She was typing as she talked—he could hear the keys clacking. "I'll keep you in mind, but I doubt we'll be taking on anyone else straight from college this year. We're not that busy."

Bennet ended the call and sighed. Okay. Pemberley Hall, then. Wyndham had seemed certain that Darius wasn't involved in the business, and it might be the kind of thing Bennet would enjoy. The place was well-located in prime rock climbing country. The nearest city was Sheffield, the birthplace of indoor climbing walls. To the west was Manchester, with its huge gay scene. He'd have no trouble filling his free time—assuming they gave him some.

He fired off an email to Catherine Brackenbrough, attaching his CV, with a copy to Monsieur Philippe.

---

THE WEEK WORE on, and Tim didn't come back. Jamie sent him another text and messaged him online—no response. Jamie wasn't the type to have public crying jags or meltdowns, but Bennet had to grit his teeth every time he saw the hurt in his friend's eyes.

Bennet brainstormed ideas that didn't involve a dead or dying Tim, and he came up with a few scenarios: a bereavement, a major hangover, bankruptcy—

"And he's in endless meetings with bank managers, or whatever. And his phone and computer have been repossessed to pay the debts, so he can't contact you. Or he's been arrested."

Jamie didn't move from the window, where he was gazing out at the cloudy sky. "Arrested for what? He's not a criminal."

"A case of mistaken identity."

"Darius would get him out of jail."

"Tim's the double of an international terrorist. There's no way they'd let a suspected terrorist out on bail."

"Why wouldn't Darius tell me?"

"He's afraid you'll be arrested too, if the police get hold of your name as one of Tim's suspicious contacts."

Jamie laughed. Finally.

But on Friday, Bennet went down to the college kitchen where Jamie was supposed to be cooking lunch, and he wasn't there. He'd called in a favour, and someone was covering for him—the classmate who'd cut herself on the night of his first date with Tim. "He looked like he'd had bad news," she said.

"So where is he?" Bennet asked. None of them knew.

He called Jamie's phone—no answer. Maybe Tim was back in Meriton, and Jamie had gone to him at the gallery? It wasn't like Jamie to cut classes, but if Tim was in some kind of trouble . . .

Bennet checked the bike shed. Jamie's bicycle was still there, chained up next to his own. So he must be somewhere on the college premises.

Bennet found him at last under a tree on a raised piece of ground to one side of the college, outside the fence that marked the limits of the no-go area where the TV cameras reigned. Jamie sat on dry earth strewn with pine needles, gazing over fields where the morning mist had given way to a hot, still, cloudless day.

He didn't move as Bennet approached. His face could have been carved in stone. But his eyes were red-veined, and his cheeks glistened where tears had dried.

Was Tim dead, after all? Bennet sat down beside Jamie without speaking, and waited.

"I called Darius again, but his phone was switched off." Jamie's voice was shaky. "Then I remembered that cousin of Tim's who came for dinner—Quentin. I thought since he's family, he'd know if something had happened. So I found him online."

He passed his phone across for Bennet to read the message thread.

**Jamie Kershaw:** *Hi, we met once in the restaurant at Meriton College with Tim and Darius? Just checking if Tim's ok? He's not at his gallery here.*

**Quentin Wilson:** *he's fine but I don't think he'll be back with you anytime soon*

**Jamie Kershaw:** *Why?*

**Quentin Wilson:** *moved on*

Bennet read it twice. He'd disliked Quentin on sight, and this stoked the fire. He felt like throwing the phone against the tree, but destroying Jamie's phone wouldn't solve anything.

"This makes no sense. Tim was crazy about you."

Jamie took back the phone. "*Was*, past tense. Feelings change."

"Not that much, that fast."

Jamie's voice was dull. "Perhaps he's met someone else. We never made any promises. I must have misunderstood. Maybe it was nothing serious for him."

"Bullshit. He was all over you. If he wasn't serious about it, he should be on the stage, because he'd make a bloody convincing actor."

But what about Darius—all over Bennet in the

nightclub, disappearing without a word at the hotel? Same attitude. Did they learn that behaviour at their boarding school, along with not saying *please*?

"What will you do from here?" Bennet asked. "Try to contact him again? Tell him you've been in touch with Quentin?"

"I expect Quentin will tell him. I think I should give him some space."

"Space? Fuck that. I'd be in London banging on his door if I knew his address."

Jamie's brow creased with distress. "Bennet, please don't go anywhere near Tim. It won't help."

Bennet had meant *if I were you*, but it was an idea. He didn't answer.

"No calling, or texting, or banging on the gallery door if he comes back," Jamie went on.

Bennet said nothing.

"Bennet . . ."

He only gave in because Jamie looked so upset. "All right, I promise I won't bother him. If I see the worm, I'll turn my back and walk away."

"And don't call him a worm, please. Tim's a good man. He'll be trying to do the right thing, as he sees it."

"The right thing? Wouldn't that at least include a text to say sorry?"

Jamie didn't answer that. He stood up and brushed the dust and pine needles from his clothes. "I must go back. And don't you have an assessment?"

He was acting his usual calm self, accepting everything,

going with the flow. But there was a crease between his brows and a dead look in his eyes that Bennet had never seen before.

# Chapter Thirteen

THE GALLERY STAYED closed all weekend. Bennet could have said a few things to Tim about that, too. It made no sense in business terms. With summer coming on, Meriton had more and more visitors.

Cycling to and from the Black Lion, Bennet often saw people looking at the art works in the window—the well-heeled thirty- and fortysomethings that Darius had said made up the ideal market for art. He slowed down to peer around them each time. No sign of Tim, and the heap of unopened letters kept growing.

Jamie stopped wearing the bracelet Tim had given him in Brighton. Bennet tried to protect him from the torture of questions at Longbourn Manor. Charlotte was not known for her tact, so he told her, as casually as he could, that Tim was away for a while. But he could have saved his breath. She had other things on her mind and wouldn't tell him what. She'd driven off on Friday night, saying she was going home to King's Beacham—but she said that every weekend. He didn't believe it. She wasn't that devoted to her family.

He caught Kofi and Leon together in Kofi's room, and made them promise not to mention Tim in front of Jamie.

"Have they broken up?" Leon asked, eager for gossip.

"I don't know. Maybe. Jamie doesn't want to talk about it."

Bennet had most of that Sunday free, working only breakfast and dinner at the Black Lion. So he was home for the communal Sunday lunch, the one meal they ate together. It was Nigel's turn to cook, and he'd spent the morning shut in the kitchen with a saddle of lamb.

Towards midday, Bennet glanced through the open door of Jamie's room. Before he'd met Tim, Jamie would always be in the kitchen on Sundays, helping whoever was cooking. But today he lay on his bed with his hands behind his head, blank-faced and silent, like the phone on the bedcover beside him.

"Anything new?" Bennet asked.

"No."

"Can I bring my computer in?"

"If you like."

He went in and sat at one side of Jamie's big desk. The other side was stacked with textbooks and cookery books, but the lined pad beside them was blank.

Bennet clicked through a website and made a few notes. After a while Jamie asked, "What are you working on?"

"An assignment on the entertainment industry."

"You mean television?"

"No, nightclubs and theatres. Live entertainment."

"Due tomorrow?"

"Tuesday."

"Uh-huh." Jamie subsided back into silence. Bennet went on taking notes. He filled one page, turned it, and half filled the other side. Then Jamie said, "I think he'll be back then. Tuesday, I mean."

Bennet put down his pen. "Yeah, maybe."

"He won't want the gallery to stay closed another week. Do you still have a free period midmorning on Tuesdays? I have assessed practicals all day, and then I'm in the kitchen for dinner."

Bennet nodded, guessing what was coming. "You want me to go into town and look?"

"Will you? Don't talk to him. Don't even let him see you. Just check if it's open and if his car's there, and text me."

"Okay." After a moment Bennet added, "Jamie, you won't fail this assessment on Tuesday, will you?"

"I don't think so."

"If you're thinking about him all day instead of—"

"I'll need to know if he's back. If you won't find out for me, I'll have to take a chance and go myself, and then I might fail."

Bennet blew out a breath. "I said I would, didn't I?"

"Yes. Thank you. Knowing that, I can keep my mind clear." Jamie sat up and pushed his feet into his sandals. "It must be nearly lunchtime. We should go down, or Nigel will be flustered."

---

NIGEL WAS ALREADY flustered, and not only because he was cooking. He'd laid the usual six places in the dining room, even though Charlotte was away. And on the other side of the hall, the door to the room Nigel called his parlour stood open, and an unexpected guest was sampling aperitifs—Wyndham Moorhouse.

Bennet stared. Wyndham glanced round and gave him a smile but stayed where he was, chatting to Kofi, bringing him out of his shell. Way out of his shell. Kofi shook with giggles.

Leon was opening a bottle of wine in the dining room—the kind with a real cork. His face was pink.

"Who invited Wyndham?" Bennet asked.

"Not guilty. Or perhaps just slightly guilty." Leon shrugged one shoulder. "I was chatting with some of the crew the other day—I'm sure they'll find me a spot as an extra, it's just a question of not giving up—and he recognised me from Rush. And he somehow knew I lived here, and he'd heard about Jamie's cooking, and he was, like, salivating all over me, dropping heavy hints about how he's been living on spaghetti hoops or whatever in some horrendous caravan."

He wrestled the cork out and held up the bottle to offer Bennet a glass. Bennet shook his head.

"So I told him he could come," Leon said. "I forgot it was Nigel's week, not Jamie's. Oops. But Wyndham doesn't seem to mind. I'm not sure if it's the food he's really after, or something else." He winked, nudging Bennet's arm. "Looked like you two were getting on swimmingly at Rush."

"You might have warned me."

"I thought it would be a nice surprise. But I do see what you mean." Leon tipped his head to give Bennet's creased shirt and loose jeans a critical appraisal. "Never mind, you still have time to dash up and change into something gorgeous and flirty."

But gorgeous and flirty was not how Bennet felt today—not with Jamie so unhappy. If Wyndham was the kind of guy Bennet needed, he'd appreciate that.

He went back over to the parlour. Wyndham gave him a broad grin and disentangled himself from Kofi.

"Hope you don't mind me crashing this? I couldn't pass up the opportunity to sample one of your amazing Sunday lunches."

He did have the cutest smile. "Nothing to do with me," Bennet said. "I'll only be handing round the carrots."

"And perhaps later...?" Wyndham opened his eyes wide.

Bennet bit his lip. He didn't want to make that kind of noise in his room this afternoon, with a heartbroken Jamie next door. "I don't know. Not here—things are awkward. Maybe we could go for a walk?"

"Oh." Wyndham's face fell. Like, really. Every inch of it seemed to drop. "I never have any luck."

Bennet could have said the same. "I don't mean we can't—"

But Wyndham had turned away. And Nigel crossed the hall, his face bright red from the heat of the oven, to demand Bennet's services as a waiter.

In the kitchen, Bennet held the serving dishes while Nigel spooned vegetables into them.

"Your new friend's been taking photographs of these

rooms," Nigel said. "He knows a magazine editor who's doing a series on alternative rural homes."

"What's alternative about Longbourn Manor?"

"We're hardly the average husband, wife, and kids, are we?"

Nigel followed Bennet into the dining room. Wyndham brought in a big black bag on a long strap, hooked onto his shoulder. Nigel reached out his hands. "Let me take that for you."

"Don't trouble, it'll be fine here." Wyndham put it down on the sideboard behind him, next to the silver tray where Leon had left the wine bottle.

"What's inside?" Leon asked.

"Ah, that's a secret. Maybe it's a camera." Wyndham laughed and winked at Bennet, who'd taken a seat at one end of the table, on Wyndham's right. "I might get it out later and give you a screen test. You could all be appearing in *Bridgemaston Days*. Anybody object to that?"

"*Object*?" Leon squeaked. "Oh my God. Do we get costumes for this screen test? I want to be a footman in livery."

"He's joking, Leon," Bennet said.

"They wouldn't want *me*," Kofi said, wrinkling his nose unhappily. He was on Wyndham's other side, with Jamie opposite and Nigel on his left. Jamie and Nigel always liked to be near the kitchen door.

"Oh, they might," Wyndham said. "Victorian England wasn't one hundred percent white. It's just a question of whether the camera likes you. And with some faces, it's pretty much a certainty."

Wyndham's eyes lingered on Jamie as he spoke. Any other time, it would have made Jamie uncomfortable, but today he didn't seem to have heard.

They passed dishes around and began to eat. Wyndham chatted about the script, the actors, and the hassles they'd had with scenery. So different from how Darius would be if he came here. He'd be silent and critical, judging them all. But he had never come to Longbourn and surely never would now.

"Seriously, can you get me in?" Leon asked. "I'd do anything. I've been asking everybody." He grabbed the wine bottle from the sideboard and served himself. Bennet took the bottle from him and went round refilling the other glasses, pouring more mineral water for Jamie.

"I'll see what I can do," Wyndham said.

It was kind of him, Bennet thought. Darius would have stomped on Leon, seeing him as a pest and nothing more. He wouldn't have realised how vulnerable Leon was, underneath.

Jamie ate slowly, chewing without expression, as if everything on his plate tasted the same.

"What's wrong with it, Jamie?" Nigel asked sharply. "Not on a diet, are you?" He looked pointedly at Jamie, who still didn't raise his eyes from his plate. Nigel turned to Wyndham. "Excuse Jamie, he's in love. It's supposed to make people glow with charm, but it seems to have the opposite effect in his case."

If Bennet could have kicked Nigel, he would have, but he was at the other end of the table. Kofi leaned over and whispered in Nigel's ear.

"Oh, poor boy." Nigel patted Jamie's hand. "But it happens to us all, you know. You'll get over it."

Jamie put down his fork.

Wyndham sent the two of them a quick, interested glance, then said, "So I've heard all of you are gay? You must have lots of fun here." He winked at Leon.

"Oh, you wouldn't believe," Leon said. "Cavorting naked, orgies every night—if you want group sex on the table after lunch, I'm sure it can be arranged."

"Leon!" Nigel looked horrified.

Wyndham laughed. "If you have a spare room, let me know, Nigel. I wouldn't mind moving in!"

"Dear boy, it would be a delight, but sadly all the beds are occupied."

"You could share one, though." Leon took another slurp of wine, spilling a couple of drops on the tablecloth. "Any one, take your pick. Oh, wait, not Jamie's. He doesn't do sex. Jamie doesn't do sex, and the rest of us don't do relationships. Except Nigel, he does relationships. I bet he'd still let you in his bed, though. Just don't tell Monsieur Philippe." Leon reached for the bottle again, but Bennet moved it away. "Fuck off, Bennet, you're not my mum."

Wyndham said, "Oh, you have a partner, Nigel?"

"I don't think I—"

"He's been fucking Philippe Hennice for years," Leon said. "They don't live together, and it's supposed to be a big secret, but everyone knows."

"Please, Leon," Nigel said, but his eyes sparkled as if he

was enjoying the attention.

"There's only one rule here!" Leon cried. "Rent reduction if you have sex downstairs where everyone can watch!"

Wyndham laughed. "Seems like a fun house."

Nigel got up and went to fetch the ice cream. His flushed face wore a little smile. Bennet collected the glasses and followed him into the kitchen, pouring the dregs into the sink.

"There's a bottle of Sauternes cooling in the fridge," Nigel told him.

Bennet shook his head.

"Perhaps you're right," said Nigel. "This deserves to be served alone."

"And Leon's had more than enough already."

"Oh, but there's no harm in him. Doesn't he make you laugh? I was the same at his age."

Bennet tried to picture Nigel at eighteen or nineteen, but failed. "I'll put the coffee on."

According to the rota, when Nigel cooked, Jamie was on cleanup. If Bennet wasn't working, he'd help stack the dishwasher, leaving Jamie to wash the heavy pans and the glasses that Nigel wouldn't put in the machine. Today, when the dishwasher spurted into action, Bennet told Jamie, "You look like you've had enough. I'll do the rest, if you could check whether they want more coffee."

"Don't you want to talk to your guest?"

"Later. This won't take long."

"Thank you."

Jamie left the pans soaking in the sink and went out,

wiping his hands. He came back with a couple of coffee cups and refilled them. A few minutes later his heavy tread mounted the stairs.

Alone in the kitchen, Bennet whistled under his breath as he worked. Sunlight blazed in through the window. A rain shower had come and gone while they'd been eating, and drops sparkled on the leaves of the nearest plants. Life outside chirped and buzzed, and the breeze brought in warm, scented air.

A good day for a walk. He and Wyndham could head away from town, avoiding the popular beauty spots. They could take something waterproof to lie on and look for a place on the edge of a field, with a few trees to hide them from view.

He'd thought Wyndham might come and help, giving Bennet a chance to explain why he didn't want to take him upstairs, but it didn't happen. Never mind. There wasn't much to do. He scrubbed the last of the fat from the roasting tin and rinsed out the sink.

When he went out to the hall, the house seemed empty—cool, dark, and silent. Where were Kofi and Leon? They weren't entertaining Wyndham in the parlour, as Bennet expected. And Wyndham's bag was gone from the dining room.

Had Wyndham left? Had Bennet had missed his chance again? *Shit.* And it was odd that Wyndham hadn't said goodbye. Or could he be waiting upstairs in Bennet's room?

Bennet went up, avoiding the worst of the creaking treads. As usual, Kofi's door hadn't closed, and muffled giggles came through the crack. Kofi and Leon were in there, doing whatever they did—everything they could think of, no doubt.

Then someone spoke low inside the room. Bennet couldn't make out the words, but he knew the voice. Wyndham was with them.

A flash of resentment and jealousy passed through him and was gone. To his surprise, he found he didn't much care.

They took what they wanted so easily. If only he could do the same.

He went into his room and opened his HR textbook at the section on zero-hour contracts. He read the first paragraph three times without taking anything in. Then he went to the drawer beside his bed and took out the pack of latex-free condoms he'd bought the previous weekend. Wyndham's card was underneath it, but he let that lie. He went out onto the landing, pushed Kofi's door wide enough to get his hand inside, and tossed the condoms in. Then he closed the door and pulled hard on the knob until he felt it catch.

Let them have their fun . . . but don't let it hurt them.

# Chapter Fourteen

BENNET TOOK HIS assignment into the department secretary's office on Tuesday. No electronic submission for Monsieur Philippe—he expected everything on paper.

Bennet glanced at the clock while the secretary wrote his receipt. Eleven fifteen. The gallery should have opened at ten.

He hurried outside, unlocked his bike, and manoeuvred it out of the crowded shed. He pulled up his hood against the drizzle and headed down the cycle path that crossed the river outside the college grounds, the quickest way into town.

He stopped at the corner of the marketplace. The gallery door was shut, but the sign had been turned to *Open*, and a figure was sitting at the counter inside. He assumed it was Tim. Good. Jamie might have another chance with him or at least get closure.

But when Bennet went down the lane to check on the car, he saw neither Tim's blue beast nor Darius's black Audi—only a green VW Polo with a local registration. A rental car, maybe? Had Tim been in an accident after all?

He'd promised Jamie he wouldn't let Tim see him, so he crept up to the side of the gallery window and peeked in.

The person inside wasn't Tim, but a woman in a trouser suit and a fedora. Tim had hired a woman to open the gallery when they went to Brighton. This could be the same person, back for another few days. The Polo was probably her car.

So where was Tim?

Jamie hadn't banned him from talking to anyone else, only Tim, so after thinking for a minute, he walked up to the gallery door and pushed it open, jangling the bell.

"Can I help you?" the woman asked.

Her lavender scent permeated the gallery. She had an accent he associated with horses, tweeds, and muddy Land Rovers, but her smile was friendly enough.

Bennet held the door open, in case he had to make a quick exit. "Is Mr. Wilson here?"

"No, sorry."

He went further in, letting the door close. "Can you tell me when he'll be back?"

"I'm afraid I can't. May I take a message?"

"Will you be seeing him?"

"He's abroad, I think, but I'll be speaking to him on the telephone."

Tim had left the country? "Has he gone on a buying trip?"

She pressed her lips together, as if he was asking too many questions. "What was your interest? Are you an artist? I'm the manager here. Perhaps I can help?"

The manager. Temporary or permanent? Bennet couldn't think of a way to ask without sounding like he was poking his nose into her terms of employment. He fell back on the question he'd prepared.

"It was about the flat—the flat upstairs. I saw nobody had been here for a week or two and I thought maybe he'd left, and it might be available? To rent, I mean?"

She shook her head. "He hasn't given me any instructions about that."

The bell clanged and a guy in a brown courier uniform came in. Bennet moved out of the way. The gallery manager pointed to a pile of boxes near the counter—two big cartons and a suitcase.

This didn't look good.

"Is he moving out?" Bennet edged closer, trying to see the address on the labels, but the courier was in the way.

The manager said, "I don't know what plans he has for the flat. If you'd like to leave your name and number, I could ask next time I speak to him. But if he does put it on the market, I imagine he'll want to use an agent."

In other words, it wouldn't go to the first person who walked through the door. Bennet didn't care. He only wanted to know if Tim was still living here, and it looked like he wasn't. And Bennet didn't want to leave his number, even with a false name. What if she gave it to Tim? He might recognise it if it was still stored in his phone from Brighton.

He said, "Okay, thanks. I expect he'd go through Credlands? I'll keep an eye on their website."

Outside, he texted Jamie. He didn't want to upset him in the middle of assessed practicals, so he didn't mention the manager or the boxes. He simply said Tim wasn't there.

But when Jamie came home that night, he'd been past the gallery and seen the pile of mail gone from inside the door. Bennet had to tell him it wasn't Tim who'd picked it up.

When Jamie heard about the manager, he sat down heavily on Bennet's bed. "Was there no sign of him at all?"

"She said he'd gone abroad. He could be buying pictures."

"Abroad? Where? Somewhere in Europe?"

"She wouldn't tell me. I'm not sure if she knew."

"When is he coming back?"

"She didn't seem to know that, either."

Jamie sat still for a moment, his hands clasped on his knees. Then he said, "There's something you're not telling me. I need to hear everything, please."

Bennet got up from the swivel chair at his desk and sat beside Jamie on the bed. This was tough. He hated to see Jamie hurting, and now he had to make it worse. He told him about the courier and described the packages.

Jamie said, "So those were his clothes and things from upstairs. He must have come to pack them without even telling me he was here."

"Not necessarily. She might have done the packing."

Jamie turned away. "Whatever. He's gone. He's moved out."

"But if it was permanent, he'd rent out the flat, and he's not doing that."

"Yet," Jamie said, with the first hint of bitterness.

Bennet reached for Jamie's hand. It was as unresponsive as dough, but he took it and pressed it between his. "There'll be other guys."

Jamie's whole body jerked. He pulled his hand away. "No. You don't understand."

"I've been in love, Jamie. Everybody's been in love."

Jamie got up off the bed and walked over to Bennet's desk. "No, you've had crushes, or you've fallen in love in the way that's all hormones and desperation. That's nothing like knowing somebody is the right one, the perfect fit, the one who supports and challenges and completes you—the one who makes you a better person. The one you want to spend your life with."

Bennet couldn't argue with that. Jamie was right—he'd never felt it.

He clenched his fists. He could have killed Tim with those bare hands at that moment. If he was so perfect, where was he?

---

JAMIE'S LIFE DIDN'T stop. He didn't lie in bed all day. He went to college and followed his routine. But his eyes were bleak, empty, as if his soul had shrivelled up and retreated into a deep, dark cave. He didn't seem to be there, in his body, any more.

This explained why Tim and Darius were friends, Bennet thought. It wasn't a case of nice guy and nasty guy, opposites attracting. There was no nice guy. Tim had put on an act to get into Jamie's pants, and when he'd understood that it wouldn't happen without a major commitment, he'd walked away. By now he'd have picked up someone else, someone easier, someone less special.

Jamie was better off without him, if only he could see it. The whole of Meriton was better off without Tim and Darius.

Way better. So why did the town seemed smaller and emptier? And why did Bennet's pulse beat loud in his ears every time a slim stranger in a suit walked into the Black Lion?

He wasn't sorry to leave Meriton for Beldon that Saturday. He'd promised his mother he'd be home once in each term, and he wouldn't be able to go in the middle of the reading week as he'd originally planned because his parents had booked a holiday in Spain. So he cancelled a couple of shifts at the Black Lion and went.

The first thing his mother said was, "How long can you stay?"

He put down his bag, avoiding her eyes. "I need to go back tomorrow."

"Only one night?" She deflated like a balloon. "Couldn't you have taken Monday off from college?"

Maybe he could have, but he hadn't wanted to leave Jamie alone for too long. Feeling guilty, he said, "The exams are coming up—my final exams. They could make all the difference to my career prospects. I'm aiming for a distinction."

"That's good, is it, a distinction?"

"It's the highest possible grade."

She clutched her hands together, all her disappointment gone. "The highest possible! Oh, Bennet, I'm so proud of you."

"I haven't got it yet." But her faith in him, so nakedly exposed, tugged at his heart and made him blurt out something he hadn't meant to let her know. "I have a job interview at Pemberley Hall. The email came this morning."

Her eyes sparkled. "I never dreamed you might work there! When is it?"

"Next Friday."

"Imagine! You'll see all the celebrities. It was on the news again last week—that pop star with the red hair and his boyfriend, they got married there. Think of being there for that! Could your dad and I come and visit, do you think? Sometime in the winter, when you're not busy?"

This was why he hadn't planned to tell her. "Mum, it's only an interview. Nothing's decided. I might not get the job."

"But they want to meet you, don't they? They must be keen if they want you to go all that way. Oh, it must be such a beautiful place. Even prettier than Bridgemaston House—I mean, your college. And the gardens! You'll take photos to show us, won't you? Alan, did you hear that? Marlon? Bennet might be working at Pemberley Hall, where all the famous people get married!"

His dad and Marlon were on the couch, watching horse racing. His dad grunted. Marlon said, "For eff's sake. It's bad enough having a brother who tells the whole town about his orien-effing-tation, without him working at Namby-pamberly Hall to top it off."

But nothing took the stars out of his mother's eyes.

Restless that evening, Bennet walked around the town. He'd called a couple of his school friends, but one was away at university and the other had left Beldon to work. Marlon would be in one of the pubs, but if they ever got together over a brotherly pint, it wouldn't be this decade, and Marlon wouldn't let it happen in front of his mates.

He peered into Checkers. He hadn't phoned Callum—he didn't want to sound like he was asking for a date when he wasn't—but if Callum happened to be in there, Bennet wouldn't mind a chat.

He saw his ex almost at once, sitting in a quiet corner with a girl, laughing at something she'd said.

A girl with a red coat slung over the back of her chair.

Charlotte.

They hadn't noticed Bennet. He slipped out and let the heavy wooden door fall shut. Then he stood looking at it. Why not go in and say hello? They must have met by chance, and they'd both be glad to see him. But something in their postures made him hesitate. He went around the corner and texted Charlotte.

*I'm in Beldon, want to meet up?*

Nothing about having seen her. He'd leave it up to her to tell him where she was.

But the reply, when it came, said, *Busy 2nite. Lunch 2moro?*

---

HE MET HER in a café near the station. He was on his way back to Meriton. His mother had offered to drive him, to get another look at the college, but she was a nervous driver, and Bennet wasn't sorry when his dad gave him the train fare and took the car to work.

In the café, he bought coffee and nothing else. Charlotte came in while he was being served, and they settled at a table in the window. He took his sandwiches from his bag and unwrapped them on his knees, out of sight of the staff at the counter. His mother had made them—peanut butter and cucumber, of course. Weird how hers always tasted better.

"So you were busy last night, huh?" Bennet asked.

Charlotte had bought lentils and grated carrot in a plastic bowl, a chocolate bar, and a bottle of water. She pulled the top off her salad, poured dressing over it, and licked her fingers.

Then she gave him a sidelong glance. "What's that smirk for?"

"What are you looking guilty for?"

She erased all expression from her face and met his gaze with wide, innocent eyes. "Guilty?"

"I saw you in Checkers with Callum. What was that about?"

"Ah." She stirred her salad with a fork, giving it all her attention. "I was going to tell you, honest. I hadn't got around to it yet, that's all."

"Tell me what?"

"I've kind of been seeing him."

Bennet almost choked on his sandwich. "You mean last night wasn't the first time?"

"He came over to do my dad's wiring at Easter, and we

chatted a bit, and we've met up a few times since then."

"Is this why you've been home every weekend this term—to see *him*?"

Charlotte said, "What else could I do? He wouldn't come to Meriton. He didn't think you'd appreciate it."

"Appreciate it? I don't fucking believe it!" His voice rose. How could she be so stupid?

"Shh. He said you'd be like this. But come on, you guys split up two years ago or more, and you were the one who ended it."

"Yes, because he screwed me over with his get-rich-quick scheme! I'm not jealous, for God's sake—I'm trying to make you see sense. He's a bastard. He stuck me with a huge dungpile of debt and never paid a penny of his share."

"From your perspective, yes, but there are other ways of seeing it. It's not like he conned you or forged your signature. You signed all the card applications, you registered with the casino. You were eighteen and he wasn't. You were a responsible adult, in theory."

"He's only three weeks younger."

"So you could have told him to wait for his birthday. But you didn't, because you were just as stupid and greedy, and you thought you'd make a fortune."

"Which I would have split with him, fifty-fifty."

She unwrapped the chocolate bar, though she hadn't finished the lentils. "Maybe, but you wouldn't have had to, by law. You took the risk, and you could have kept the money."

"He told me we'd share the risk."

She shrugged. Callum had got to her. She was blind to Bennet's perspective. He tried another angle.

"I thought you were going to be a tour guide when you leave college. What happens then?"

"I'll mostly be training for the first few months. I'll only be in London, so I can come home at weekends, if this lasts. Look how often that friend of Tim's used to come up."

Bennet didn't want to think about that. "It still leaves Callum free all week."

Charlotte frowned. "What are you implying? Why would I worry about that? Did he play around when he was with you?"

"Not as far as I know," Bennet admitted.

She pushed her bowl away and bit into the chocolate. "So what's your point, then? Why do you look so pissed off if you're not jealous and you don't think he's going to break my heart or whatever?"

"I just think you could do better for yourself."

"Snob."

"It's not snobbery. He dragged me down, and I don't want the same thing happening to you, that's all."

But maybe it was none of his business. It was her life, and it wasn't like she was committed to anything.

Bennet had finished his sandwich. He reached for her lentils. "Can I have the rest of this, if you don't want it?"

"Sure."

She'd soon see. When she went to London and started meeting other guys, she'd realise Callum wasn't such a great catch.

# Chapter Fifteen

BENNET STEPPED OFF a bus in the wilds of Derbyshire on the evening of the first Thursday in June. His interview was the next day, but when they'd offered to put him up the night before, he'd jumped at the chance. It was a long journey by bus and train, and he'd see more of the place this way.

Pemberley Hall had its own bus stop, outside a pair of huge iron gates with gilded spikes. The little town of Lambton was a few miles down the road. Across the valley, sheep dotted the hills like lumps of dirty cotton. Further north lay the gritstone edges he hoped one day to climb.

Inside the gates, a big board on the left bore the slogan he'd seen on the website: *Pemberley Hall—Where Your Dreams Will Come True*. To the right, a smaller, shabbier sign, *Strictly Private: Peak Lodge and Home Farm ONLY*, pointed up a pitted lane that disappeared into the trees.

He went left, up the winding, tree-lined drive to Pemberley, with his bag slung over his shoulder. The house sprang into view as he emerged from the trees after the last turn. He'd seen pictures, of course, but the huge mansion of weathered grey stone in its lush, rolling park still took his breath away. The old bridge, the distant woods, the stream cascading into the lake below . . . nature herself might have been posing for the photographers.

The receptionist directed him to a cramped room on the top floor. His window looked out to the back, where the land sloped up to a triangular copse thick with green leaf. The glass roof of the vast orangery, used for weddings and parties, covered most of the ground to his left. To the right of the copse, the pitched slate roof and tall chimneys of a smaller building peeked out between the treetops. What was that? The old stables, maybe?

In bed that night, his brain raced, rehearsing the answers he'd prepared for the interview. He kept switching on the bedside light to note down what seemed, in his dozing state, to be unbeatable lines. Later, Darius and Wyndham drifted into his half-awake mind as children, ghosts almost—Darius a young emperor on horseback, patrolling his domain; Wyndham lost and alone, banished to an attic like this one. When dawn crept through the gap between the curtains, Bennet fell into a fitful sleep.

Then, of course, he slept through his alarm. He'd planned to take a good look around in the morning, but when he woke to the sound of rain beating against the window he had no time for anything but a quick shower and a rushed breakfast to silence his growling stomach.

Ten or twelve other candidates waited in the intimate Club Room on the ground floor, drinking coffee and making cautious small talk. That was a blow. Bennet had thought today was a special arrangement for him alone. And why were they so much older? None of them looked under thirty.

No way could he compete with the experience they must have.

"What job are you here for?" he asked the woman next to him in the queue for hot drinks.

"The events coordinator. Why, is there more than one?"

"I hope so," Bennet said.

She peered at him through weak blue eyes. "You do seem young for it."

A woman with a clipboard came in before he'd taken three sips of his coffee, marshalling them into a group for a tour of the building. The interior design was nothing special. It was clean, it was smart, but it could have been any hotel, anywhere, if it hadn't been in this high-ceilinged mansion, in this amazing setting—and if Catherine Brackenbrough hadn't had such a talent for planning and marketing standout events.

In front of a door marked *Private* on the top floor, their guide said, "This is the Brackenbroughs' apartment. Catherine's the managing director, as I'm sure you know, and her daughter Annabel is our head of human resources. You'll meet them both later."

"Where do the other staff live?" somebody asked.

"In Sheffield or Lambton, mostly. Some people commute from this side of Manchester. It's a nice drive in summer, but not much fun in snow or ice."

Manchester was tempting, with its Canal Street scene, but Bennet didn't have a driving licence. He'd have to settle for Sheffield, less than an hour away by bus. He'd always imagined himself in London, but there was life in smaller cities too. He could go climbing and clubbing, pay off his debts, save for driving lessons.

If he got the job. Right now it didn't seem likely. Events coordinator? Straight from college, against these experienced candidates, he didn't have a chance. Either they had something else in mind for him, or he'd been invited out of politeness to Monsieur Philippe.

Catherine Brackenbrough was the centre of attention at lunch. She was still stunning, though Bennet guessed she was in her fifties. She dressed with panache—a fuchsia suit, including hat, which she didn't take off to eat. She kept up a stream of conversation through the meal, while her eyes darted from one candidate to the next.

Annabel, by contrast, hardly spoke. Pale and thin, she looked like a dulled-down version of her mother.

They interviewed Bennet soon after lunch. He wasn't at his best—he'd gorged on the free food and, after his disturbed night, he'd have loved a siesta. But the interview wasn't challenging.

Annabel invited him to sit down. A guy she introduced as the facilities manager asked what he'd covered in his college course, and Bennet went through the list he'd already sent them. Then Catherine said, "How's Fifi?" and Bennet's mind went blank.

"We've been emailing a lot lately," Catherine went on. "About you, of course—he recommends you highly." She meant Monsieur Philippe. *Phiphi*. Ha. "And before that, about a sweet little gallery in Meriton that a connection of ours wanted to buy."

"I thought he did buy it," Annabel said.

The feather on the fuchsia hat bobbed as Catherine turned to her daughter. "He did, but it's gone horribly wrong. Tim was full of enthusiasm—he was there virtually twenty-four hours a day, devoting himself to running the place. But some dreadful boy got his hooks in and was taking advantage."

Bennet's shoulders jerked, as if he were a puppet on a string. *Some dreadful boy*? Could she mean Jamie? But how had he ever taken advantage of Tim?

"Darius had to extricate him," Catherine went on. "He got him out of this boy's clutches and found some local woman who could look after the gallery. And then Tim was feeling bereft, so Darius packed him off to America. And hopefully he'll find something else to do there."

*Darius* had made Tim leave? Bennet's blood turned to porridge, congealing in his veins. He sat motionless, as if any movement might shatter him.

The facilities manager coughed discreetly. Catherine turned away from Annabel and flashed a smile at Bennet.

"Oh, Bennet, I'm sorry, we've drifted a long way from your application, haven't we? The fact is, we don't have a specific job description to discuss with you today. We're interviewing for something more senior, as you must have gathered. But we're planning some restructuring before the new events coordinator starts, so we wanted to meet you and chat about a possible position in that area."

They "chatted" for another ten minutes, but Bennet had trouble concentrating (Darius packed Tim off to America?), and they were vague about the job he might or might not be offered. The wedding planner was in charge of weddings, the events coordinator organised conferences, Annabel covered HR, and the facilities manager seemed to do everything else. Maybe Bennet would liaise between them?

"And the salary?" he asked.

"We'll include that in any offer we send you," Annabel said. "It would be in line with other trainee positions."

Not much, in other words. A first job never paid well in this industry.

"Bennet, we'll be in touch," Catherine said, gathering her papers together. "Thank you so much for coming. You know Annabel's arranged transport back to Sheffield station later? Have a good look round in the meantime. Go anywhere you want. And give my love to Phiphi."

With that, he was dismissed.

He went outside. The rain had stopped, the sky had cleared, and the smell of wet earth was refreshing after Catherine's perfume.

His mind spun with what he'd heard—not about the job, but about Tim. Darius had somehow made him leave Meriton, leave Jamie? Why?

Wyndham had said Darius was possessive and jealous. This sounded like proof of it.

Bennet walked down to the old bridge over the stream and looked back at Pemberley, glowing in the golden light of the late-afternoon sun. It looked so peaceful, and yet there must often be mayhem in the kitchen and passion in the bedrooms, just like any hotel.

As for the owner of the estate, who knew what went on under his aloof exterior? Could Darius have an unrequited love for Tim? If so, he hid it well. Or maybe Tim was his only friend (hard to imagine Darius having many), and he didn't want Tim settling in Meriton with a partner because he'd have no one to go out with in London.

But then why send Tim to America? He wouldn't do that if he wanted Tim's company. Not if he was in love with Tim, either.

No, Catherine must have got the story wrong. What would she know about it, anyway?

He wouldn't tell Jamie—not even if he found out it was true. He didn't want to destroy his friend's faith in human nature by telling him somebody had schemed to take away the love of his life. The idea was messing with Bennet's head badly enough, sending pulses of anger through his limbs. What would it do to Jamie? Less painful to believe Tim had drifted off for some flaky reason of his own.

Bennet walked faster, looping around the side of the house. Pemberley towered over him, peering down as if every window were a disapproving eye, built on purpose to make him feel insignificant.

It must have been overwhelming to Wyndham as a child. Imagine being driven up through the trees for the first time, nine years old, and finding that Dad's new home was this mansion, as big as a palace. What if Bennet had traced his own biological father and found he was the owner of a huge estate like this, with another child who belonged there and didn't want Bennet around? He'd have felt lost, worthless—

an easy victim for a bully like Darius.

Behind Pemberley, where the ground sloped up the wooded hill, he glimpsed the other building whose chimneys he'd seen from his room. It wasn't the old stables, but a smaller stone house. Another setting for romantic photos?

He moved closer. A thick yew hedge blocked his way, but he found a gap. He took off his jacket to avoid catching its threads on the sharp twigs, and squeezed through.

He was in a garden. There was no sound but birdsong. Insects hovered over a pond crowded with lily leaves, and tall, ragged flowers made a patchwork of colour in the borders. The grass was longer here, and the flowers mingled with no apparent plan, yet it didn't look abandoned.

This house was nothing like the main Pemberley building. That great mansion was symmetrical, even at the back. The windows stood in regimented lines like soldiers on parade. This other place was odd, misshapen—beautiful, in a haphazard way. Its windows were narrow and placed at random, its chimneys tall and thin, its stone darker, dirtier looking. It didn't seem to fit with Pemberley, as if it had been slapped down as an afterthought, out of sight . . . or as if it had grown here. If Pemberley had been a fairy-tale castle, this would have been the witch's house, or the poor woodcutter's.

On the other side of the pond, through another gap in the tall hedge—an intended one, three feet wide—a sandy gravel path led into deep shadow. What was down there?

Nobody seemed to be around. Bennet brushed off his trousers, put his jacket back on, and started towards the path.

"If you go in there, you won't come out."

Bennet jumped. The voice was young and clear, and it came from close by. He looked around, but the garden was empty. He didn't believe in ghosts or in magic, but here...

Then he spotted the boy. Shirtless and barefoot, he was sitting motionless on the thick, knotted branch of a tree about three feet above the ground on the other side of the pond. The light glinting on the water had dazzled Bennet and stopped him seeing into the leafy shadows.

"You're trespassing," the boy said.

Bennet's mouth was dry, as if he'd been caught stealing. He kept his voice level, but it was an effort. "Sorry. I'm here for an interview. I was told I could go anywhere."

"Who told you?"

"Catherine Brackenbrough."

"She shouldn't have. This part's private. And that's our maze." He nodded at the gap in the hedge that Bennet had been heading for.

The boy jumped down onto the grass. He was taller and older than Bennet had thought. Not a child—in his midteens, maybe. A pendant hung on his pale, hairless chest. He was slim and delicate-featured, and he moved with the precision and grace of a cat. But his angular shoulders were tense, as if he were the one being challenged.

"I didn't know there was a maze," Bennet said. "It isn't on the website."

"It's our secret. Our trespasser-trap. You'll be lost forever if you step in there."

Bennet looked back at the house. "Do your parents work here?"

"No. Guess again. You can have three guesses—two more wrong, and you have to leave. And I get to ask you a question between each guess. First question—what's your name?"

"Bennet Rourke."

The boy repeated it, drawing out the syllables. "I like it. It has a good sound." He smiled, a wide grin with a dimple. "Next guess?"

That smile! It was just like Wyndham's. Could he be Wyndham's half brother, the boy who'd been cheated out of his inheritance? Wyndham had said he was here, living in a hovel—not a word Bennet would use for this weirdly compelling house, but maybe it was a mess inside.

His name, what was his name? Something unusual. His parents had been to Italy for their honeymoon . . . "Giorgio. You're Giorgio Moorhouse."

The boy's mouth dropped open. "Who told you that?"

Bennet laughed. "Guess."

"Ha. No, you're the trespasser. You have to answer my question."

"Okay. Your brother told me."

Giorgio's face lit up. "Is he here? Did he bring you?"

Bennet wished he could have said yes. Not because of any feelings he had for Wyndham—he just hated to disappoint the kid. "No, I've come for a job interview."

Giorgio's shoulders sagged. "I haven't seen him in ages. But he talked about me? What did he tell you?"

"Not much. Just that you lived here."

Giorgio put his head on one side and looked Bennet up and down. "Are you his boyfriend?"

Bennet laughed, thinking of the last time he'd seen Wyndham—walking away from Longbourn after an afternoon in bed with Kofi and Leon. "No, I wouldn't say that."

"Maybe one day? I can picture it. You'd be good together."

Would they? Maybe. He could contact Wyndham again. Finding out what went on with Tim could be the excuse. Wyndham might know if what Catherine had said was true.

"I hope you get the job," Giorgio added, with a wistful smile. "If you're working here, he might come and see me more often."

Poor kid, he must be lonely. Bennet could offer him a change of scene, at least. He glanced at his watch. "I'm getting a lift into Sheffield with the other candidates in half an hour. Why don't you come along for the ride? We can have something to eat before my train, and you can get the bus back."

Giorgio took a step back towards the tree. "No. No, thank you. I have my dinner here."

He sounded defensive, almost frightened. Then his head jerked—he'd seen something over Bennet's shoulder. Bennet turned. A woman in an apron stood in the doorway of the stone house.

"I have to go in now." Giorgio walked past him and went inside. The woman scowled at Bennet, waving her hands as if to shoo him away.

He didn't want to force his way back through the hedge, so he headed for a gate in the wall on the other side of the garden and found himself out in a lane, a back road to Pemberley. According to a sign on the gate, this was Peak Lodge.

Why wouldn't Giorgio come to Sheffield? Wyndham had said he was a virtual prisoner. Was it possible he wasn't allowed to leave Pemberley?

# Chapter Sixteen

BENNET CAUGHT THE same London-bound train as three other interview candidates, but by unspoken agreement they all headed for different carriages. Bennet took out his books and focused on exams. He'd better forget about Pemberley Hall for now.

It wasn't easy. He needed that job. But on Saturday night, just after nine, something happened that put the Brackenbroughs right out of his mind.

Darius showed up at the Black Lion.

Bennet nearly dropped the full plates he was carrying. Darius—the bastard who'd separated Tim and Jamie, if Catherine was right. That man had some nerve, coming here.

Unless Tim was back? Bennet's heart beat fast, full of hope. Darius stood there alone, but Tim could be with Jamie, making his peace. All the same, the Black Lion was a surprising place for Darius to choose to eat, after what had happened in Brighton.

Maybe he'd forgotten Bennet worked there. Bennet delivered dinner to his table of four, choosing a route that would take him through Darius's field of vision. When he looked up, Darius was still there. Their eyes met, and the fire that flashed between them made Bennet stumble.

Okay, Darius had seen him, so now he'd definitely leave.

But no, he came on into the dining room, as if looking for a table. Someone should go and welcome him. The maître d' was talking to a diner at a table by the window, so someone else would have to do it. Bennet hurried back into the kitchen so the task couldn't fall to him.

When he came out again, Darius wasn't in the archway. Had he gone? No, he'd parked himself at an empty table— one of Bennet's.

The maître d' caught Bennet's eye and waggled his head in Darius's direction. *You have a customer.*

There was no escaping him now. Bennet froze his face into a bland expression and walked up to the table, notebook poised.

"Good evening, Bennet." Darius looked uncomfortable, and no wonder.

"Is Tim with you?" Bennet blurted.

Darius frowned. "Tim? No. He's in America. I'm here on my own account."

Bennet's shoulders sank as if his arms were made of lead. So Tim wasn't at Longbourn, mending Jamie's heart.

"I thought you'd be in the bar," Darius added.

So he'd expected the restaurant to be a Bennet-free zone? Too bad.

"I'm more often working in here, in fact." Bennet managed to speak in the friendly but professional voice he'd use for any other customer, though his throat was tight with resentment. "If you sit here, you'll have to put up with me serving you. Two tables to your left, and you'll be in someone else's area."

Darius didn't take the hint. "I'm here now," he said stiffly, opening the menu. "What do you recommend?"

He was staying? Okay, Bennet would show him he could handle it. Darius had ordered cullen skink in Brighton—he must like fish. "The sea bass is good and fresh."

"I'd prefer a starter."

"Then how about the mackerel terrine or the roast artichoke heart—oh, but that's in peppercorn vinaigrette. I could ask them to use a plain vinaigrette?"

Darius's shoulders relaxed, and he settled into the seat. He looked up with something close to a smile on his lips. "You remembered I don't like a lot of pepper."

Bennet didn't want him thinking there was anything personal in that. "It's my job. What else can I get you?"

Darius's eyes flicked back down to the menu. "Does the artichoke come with bread?"

"No, but I can bring you a bread basket."

"Fine." Darius closed the menu.

"No main course?"

"Nothing else. Except a glass of white wine—whatever it was I had in the bar last time I was here."

He glanced up again with a mischievous expression. The last time he was here . . . that was months ago, with Tim, right after Tim had first met Jamie. A hell of a test for anyone's memory.

Bennet side-stepped it. "I don't think I served you on that occasion."

"Ah, no, perhaps you didn't."

Bennet offered the wine list, but Darius waved it away. "A good white. You can choose it. Will you have a glass yourself?"

Bennet gave a sharp laugh. "Are you trying to get me sacked?"

Darius looked surprised. *Yes, play innocent*, Bennet thought. He hardened his guard. Whatever Darius was doing here alone, it couldn't be good.

He took Darius's order to the kitchen, fetched a glass of white Rioja from the bar—there wasn't much choice without buying a whole bottle, but this one was drinkable—and took it to the table at a moment when Darius was checking his phone. He approached from behind, put the glass down, and moved away before Darius had time to shift his focus.

The kitchen was busy, so the food took a while. Bennet half expected Darius to call him over with a complaint about the delay, but no. He even said a distant "Thank you," when Bennet put the plate and the bread basket in front of him.

From time to time, as he glided between his busy tables, Bennet's neck prickled, as if someone was watching him. But when he turned, Darius always had his eyes on his phone, his plate, or the other diners. Bennet longed to whip the plate away and slap down the bill in its place, but Darius hadn't finished, and the hotel's policy was never to rush a guest. He could sit until closing time with his starter and his wine if he liked.

He certainly ate slowly—as if he was spinning it out to pass the time. Around ten thirty, Bennet lost patience and went over.

"Can I get you anything else?"

"No. What time do you finish?"

"Whenever the last people leave." Five or six other tables were still occupied. "I'm not throwing you out. I came to check everything was okay."

"My room number's 227."

"You're staying here in the hotel?"

"On the second floor." Darius met Bennet's eyes, as if the second floor was significant.

What was his point? Bennet needed the room number to charge his meal to it, but it didn't matter what floor it was on. If Darius wanted something taken up there, he could call room service or ask a porter. He needn't think Bennet would run up and down stairs to wait on him . . . or waste brainpower trying to figure him out.

"I'll fetch your bill."

Everything was still done on paper here. Bennet had to go to the cash till to print it. He wrote *227* on the bottom and took it back to Darius on the standard silver tray with two chocolates.

"You need to sign, please."

Darius picked up the slip with a frown. Checking it, Bennet thought, until he said, "This wasn't why I gave you the room number."

"You'd rather pay now? Okay, I'll fetch the card reader."

"No, this is fine. It can go on my bill." Darius took the pen and signed.

*Then what the fuck are you talking about?* Bennet didn't

have time for this. His stress levels had been way up all evening because of Darius sitting here like a vulture with his beady eyes on him, and now the man was fussing about how to pay for one starter and one glass of wine that probably cost no more than the lunches he had every day in London.

Darius broke into his thoughts. "I gave you the number so you could come up when you finish your shift."

Bennet straightened, stared. "To your room? Why?"

Darius furrowed his brow. "Why do you think? I know we're not well matched, but there was some chemistry between us, wasn't there, in Brighton? I can't seem to shake it off. I thought if you felt the same way, we could get it out of our systems."

Bennet's mouth dropped open. Darius wanted him to go upstairs for sex? Now, tonight, in the Black Lion? Just like that?

"Is this a joke?"

Darius's eyes widened. "Not at all."

Across the dining room, one of Bennet's colleagues was wiping a table. Two middle-aged women stood up and gathered their things together, preparing to leave. Everything seemed exactly as usual. It didn't look like Bennet had been teleported into an alternate universe. Unbelievable as it seemed, this was happening for real.

And the worst thing was, the idea of sneaking up to Darius's room sent desire twanging through his body. If he just said yes . . .

But he couldn't. No way. He had plenty of reasons not to, and he wasn't afraid to tell Darius what they were.

"I was at Pemberley yesterday, for an interview," he began.

"At *Pemberley*? You're going to work for Catherine?"

"I don't know yet. Maybe."

Darius threw an arm over the back of his chair. "You won't see much of me if you do. I don't get up there more than once a month, at the most."

That did it. Temptation gone. Bennet let his anger bubble up and explode. "It all has to be about you, doesn't it? You think I'd apply for a job there because you own the fucking place? Well, let me tell you, the less I see of you, the better. I'm not going anywhere near your room tonight or any other night. I won't be used, just so you can get something out of your system."

Darius went pale. His upper lip trembled, then stiffened, as if he was struggling for control.

"I've found out a few things about you," Bennet added. "I've met that kid you keep locked up there, for a start."

"Kid? You mean Giorgio? He's not locked up. If he gave you that impression, either he was playing games, or you misunderstood."

"*He* didn't tell me. He didn't say anything about it. It was someone else, but I could see for myself. He was terrified of leaving the place."

"Yes, because—" Darius stopped. His focus shifted to something behind Bennet. Bennet turned his head—the maître d'.

"Everything all right, sir?"

"Perfect, thank you." A muscle twitched in Darius's

cheek. He spoke in a strained, clipped voice. "Your staff member was helping me with some information."

The maître d' looked down at the signed bill. "Well, if everything's in order . . . enjoy your stay." He moved away to straighten a nearby table, keeping one eye on Bennet.

Bennet picked up the bill, leaving the chocolates on the tray. Darius took one. Bennet went to the cash desk and stabbed the bill down onto the spike so hard that the paper tore halfway across.

When he went back out, Darius was still sitting there. He summoned Bennet with a motion of his head. His eyes were hooded, his face like ice, except for two smudges of red on his cheekbones.

Controlling his own simmering resentment, Bennet went over. His limbs felt stiff as he picked up Darius's empty glass. The chocolate lay untouched on its open wrapper.

Darius said, "There must be somewhere we can talk."

Bennet didn't look at him. "Not here. I need this job."

"All right, I'll wait for you outside." Darius stood, threw his crumpled napkin on the table, and stalked out of the restaurant.

Bennet cleared tables and straightened chairs until he was told he could go. He went out of the kitchen door and unlocked his bicycle from the railings at the side of the delivery yard.

He didn't look for Darius. He didn't want to continue the conversation. No point asking about Tim, because Darius would deny everything, just like he had with Giorgio. And he didn't care if Darius waited in the lobby, or wherever he was, all night. It would pay him back for the trick he pulled in Brighton.

But as Bennet slowed to turn out of the marketplace, he saw a familiar figure on the footpath near the nightclub. He squeezed the brakes and stopped beside Darius with a sigh.

"I'll walk you home," Darius said.

Home? Where Jamie might see him? "No, thanks."

"Or buy you a drink somewhere?"

"Don't bother. You can say whatever you want to say, right here."

"Very well." Darius took a step forward. "You accused me of imprisoning Giorgio at Pemberley. I've done nothing of the sort. He has agoraphobia. He won't leave Pemberley because he doesn't like being where strangers will see him. He gets panic attacks."

Bennet wasn't expecting that, but it fit. "That must have made it easy for you to cheat him out of his inheritance."

Darius drew in his chin. "What? Who's been telling you this? It can't have been Catherine or Annabel. Do their staff come out with this nonsense?"

His bewilderment looked genuine, but barristers were like actors, weren't they? They had to convince judges and juries that day was night.

"It wasn't anybody at Pemberley," Bennet said.

"Then how . . ." Darius focused on the nightclub, and his eyes narrowed. "Wait, I saw Wyndham here. Was it him?"

Bennet didn't answer. He watched as a group of young people went into the club. One of them waved, and he returned the greeting. Students from the college.

"Bennet, you're not involved with Wyndham, are you? I thought you had better taste."

Bennet turned back to look him straight in the face. "You mean you thought *you* might be more to my taste?"

"Wyndham is pure poison."

"Funny, that's what he says about you."

Darius made an impatient gesture. "It sounds like he's been spinning you a web of lies, which is his usual pattern. Giorgio lives in an old estate lodge I kept for myself when the main house was let, because that's where he wants to be. I didn't cheat him out of anything. He had nothing to inherit."

"What about his share of Pemberley?"

"There was never any question of Giorgio having a share in Pemberley."

"No, because you dictated your mother's will."

"I did nothing of the kind."

Bennet shrugged. They could go on like this all night—did, didn't, did. What was the point? This wasn't what Bennet cared about.

"I'll tell you something else I heard up there—and this didn't come from Wyndham, so don't try to wriggle out of it by claiming he's a liar. I heard it was you who talked Tim into leaving Jamie without a word."

He watched Darius's face. The tic was back in his cheek. Was he thinking up a story? It had better be a good one.

But after a moment, Darius nodded. "There's some truth in that."

Heat rushed to Bennet's head. "You screwed up my best friend's life?"

"That's an exaggeration, isn't it? I had my reasons."

"Which were what, exactly?"

"Quentin and I got Tim out of that situation because he was falling head over heels way too fast. He didn't want to listen, and he was very upset when he finally saw that Jamie was not that into him."

"*Not that into him*?"

"Playing hard to get. Stringing Tim along."

Bennet gripped the bicycle hard. "Because he wouldn't jump into bed? That's a matter of principle for him. He was crazy about Tim. Deeply in love."

"He didn't show it. I spent more time with them than you did, and I didn't see him give Tim many signs of affection. It looked to me like he was using Tim."

"For what?"

"Perhaps Tim's money attracted him? He was pushing Tim to marry him. That was what convinced Tim I was right."

Pushing Tim to marry him? That didn't sound like Jamie. Unless . . .

A line was forming outside the nightclub. It must be coming up to eleven, when they raised the prices. Some of the people were looking their way. Bennet lowered his voice.

"You mean the day you went to the auction? The last time he saw Tim? That was a joke, what Jamie said about marriage that day. He doesn't need money. Did you think because he's got a northern accent, he's poor? Well, think again. His extended family owns half of Liverpool."

"I doubt that. He's never made any such claim to me or Tim."

Why did Darius have to take him so literally? "Okay, not half of Liverpool, but they're rich. He just doesn't boast about it like some people."

Darius shook his head. "If he's so well off, why were you two sharing a room in Brighton? Wasn't that to save money?"

"Yes, for me!" Bennet's voice rose. "It's me that doesn't have any fucking money!" People stared, but he turned his back on them, not caring now. He had no more thought for anything except the man standing in front of him and what he'd done. "Is that why you disappeared on me at the hotel, because you thought we were after your cash?"

Darius's jaw was set hard, his features tight and pale. "*You* never showed any sign of being after anything, other than my body. But yes, when I heard you were sharing, I thought Jamie wasn't well off and might have ulterior motives. It didn't seem right to get involved with you when I was about to suggest to Tim that he should detach from your friend, so I put my own feelings aside and went upstairs alone."

And *my* feelings, Bennet thought—the humiliation and the frustration and the dull disappointment?

"So now you've split them up, you thought you could come here and indulge your little itch for me? No, thanks. The idea leaves me cold."

Darius inclined his head. He looked as stiff as a clockwork toy. "So you've said. I apologise for taking your time.

I'll let you get home."

He took a step back, but Bennet still had plenty to say. He was furious now, his heart pounding, his palms on the handlebars slippery with sweat.

"Don't walk away from me. You've treated me and my friends like shit—like toys you could pick up and play with or shove in the back of a cupboard and ignore, just as it suits you. You dumped me without a word in Brighton, and now you barge into my workplace with no apology and no explanation, assuming I'll fall at your feet and slobber with gratitude at being offered a quick fuck with the amazing Darius Lanniker."

Darius stood as if frozen in a pool of light from a streetlamp, his face drained of all colour. Bennet might have been talking to a statue, but that didn't stop him.

"You told me earlier that we're 'not well matched,'" he went on. "What does that mean? Do you think you're superior to me because I have no money, speak with the wrong accent, live in a small town, work in a hotel, and don't move in your sophisticated circles? Is that what matters to you? Then I agree, we're *not* well matched, because I judge people on very different criteria."

He brought his foot up onto the pedal of his bicycle. "What you've done to Jamie is unforgiveable, and what you've proposed to me is degrading. I can't order you out of this town, but you'd better stay away from me. I never want to see you again."

He swung his other leg over the crossbar and rode away without looking back.

# Chapter Seventeen

So he'd broken with Darius. Not that there'd been anything to break. But it felt like something had shattered, all the same.

And Bennet felt out of place in Meriton the following week, as if he didn't belong there any more. He'd only missed a day and a half of college for his interview at Pemberley, but after that and the thing with Darius, he seemed to have become a different person. He had secrets now, things he couldn't tell anyone, not even Jamie.

He heard nothing from Catherine or Annabel, but Monsieur Philippe did. He summoned Bennet to his office after classes on Wednesday.

"They liked you," he said. "They want to get to know you better, see you in action. They've asked if you could go up in your reading week, all expenses paid."

"For another interview?"

"To work there." Philippe straightened a pile of papers on his desk. "Well?"

Philippe clearly expected him to jump at the chance, but Bennet had barely processed his last visit to Pemberley. He wasn't sure he was ready for another. He'd have said no right away if it had meant leaving Jamie alone with his books, but

Jamie was going home. Still, there were other considerations.

"You know I work weekends at the hotel here? I couldn't go for a full week. I'd have to travel up there on Monday and back on Friday. And I wouldn't have any study time at all. The reading week's supposed to be for revision."

Monsieur Philippe frowned. "You'll have some free time up there. You'll breeze through your exams, and you can't throw away the chance of a real job for a few shifts at the Black Lion. Ask them for those two weekends off."

It wasn't long since Bennet had taken time to visit his parents. Two more weekends away, and he wouldn't be able to cover the next credit card payments. "Would they pay me, or just give me bed and board?"

"Bed and board and your fares." Philippe stood up, closed his office window, and took his jacket from a hanger on the back of the door. "Think about it, but don't take too long—unless you have another job offer?"

Bennet shook his head. He had no hope of anything else, and Philippe's meaning was clear—if he didn't go, he'd lose any chance of a job at Pemberley Hall. He wasn't crazy about the idea of working there, with its connection to Darius. But Darius had said he hardly ever went back. And Bennet couldn't afford to turn down the opportunity.

He called the manager at the Black Lion and negotiated with her and with Monsieur Philippe. He'd go to Pemberley for the week, but only Monday to Sunday. He'd work the first weekend in Meriton as usual.

ON SATURDAY HE swung into the kitchen at the Black Lion in the middle of his lunchtime shift, slid dirty plates into the dishwashing area, and checked the hatch for any of his tickets. The hotel was full, with the bedrooms booked solid and the dining room a mass of clattering cutlery and chattering voices.

The meals for his table eight were ready—one sausage and mash, one chicken and bacon salad, two child portions of fish fingers, peas, and chips. Awesome. He balanced the kids' plates on his arm and—No, wait.

"Excuse me! I said no red onions in this salad."

One of the kitchen hands came over, examined the order ticket, and looked at Bennet with a scowl. He hadn't been in the country long and his English wasn't great, so maybe he hadn't understood.

"No onions," Bennet said, pointing to them in the bowl as he offloaded the other meals back onto the counter.

"Okay, okay." With an exaggerated sigh, the guy took the hot meals away to keep warm and began extracting the unwanted pink and white rings from the salad with a fork and spoon.

Bennet leaned back against the tiled wall and pulled out his phone to check his messages while he waited. The missed call and voice mail icons flashed up.

He swiped through to see who it was. Three missed calls. The first was from Darius. The second was from . . . Darius. The third . . . What the fuck? They were *all* from Darius.

He'd told Darius to back off. What was wrong with the guy? Hadn't Bennet made himself clear?

His feelings hadn't faded since they'd last met. If anything, his anger was stronger, a permanent ache in his chest. So Darius had wanted to get Bennet out of his system, had he? Not half as much as Bennet wanted Darius out of his. He couldn't stop thinking about what Darius had done to Jamie—and the worst part was not being able to tell anyone. He wouldn't say anything to Jamie, obviously, because it would break his heart all over again, and he couldn't tell anyone else because it wasn't their business.

At home he would stare at his books, taking nothing in. Last night he'd prowled around the town to distract himself, but it had seemed dead and empty. He'd had a beer with some students from his class, feeling disconnected from them all. Nobody who mattered to him had been there.

No Jamie, who'd said he needed to study. No Tim or Darius, of course. No Wyndham, gone with the rest of the crew now that filming had finished in this location. Leon had been on duty at the training restaurant. Kofi had joined a choir. And Charlotte had gone away for yet another weekend, seeing Callum.

He'd gone home early, and then he'd been unable to study or sleep. He'd tossed and turned in frustrated fury, going over every moment of every encounter he'd had with Darius, imagining revenge he knew he'd never take—tipping paint on the Audi, disrupting his court appearances, setting fire to Pemberley.

Now he stared at the voice mail icon. What could Darius have to say to him? Did Bennet even want to hear it? No, but he had to listen, in case it was something about Tim.

The kitchen assistant was still turning the salad, looking for onions. *Okay, let's get this over*, Bennet thought. He called his voice mail, gripping the phone tight against his ear.

"You have three messages," the automated response told him.

Three calls—three messages. Maybe the first one would be blank. That sometimes happened. The caller would hesitate, it would start to record, then they'd hang up and call back when they'd decided what to say.

But no. A short silence, then "Bennet. I hope you'll hear me out. I won't try to change your mind about seeing me, but I've been thinking about our conversation, and I may have been too cautious. There's more I need to tell you, for your own sake as much as mine. I'll try to keep it short." Darius's voice sounded clipped and distant.

"First, I apologise if I was wrong about your friend, but I don't think I'd have done things differently if I'd known he had plenty of money. I'd have thought he was only spending time with Tim for lack of anything else to do. He didn't act like a man in love, in my experience. He appeared lukewarm at best. And ultimately I acted the way I did because I have great difficulty watching anyone I care about get hurt when I could prevent it, for reasons I'll explain in a moment."

Plates thumped back onto the counter in front of Bennet.

"However, you say I misjudged him, and I don't doubt your sincerity. You know him better than I do. Perhaps he was only shy. If we've caused him any pain, I regret it."

There was a brief silence. Then Darius went on, "I need

to tell you more about Giorgio and Wyndham. I have no idea—"

"Hey, boy! Go." The kitchen assistant waved a hand, shooing Bennet away.

Bennet ended the call and put the phone away. He picked up the plates, headed out into the dining room, and delivered the onion-free salad along with the other meals.

Darius had regrets? What use was that, with Tim gone to America... no doubt with instructions to forget Jamie in the arms of as many other guys as he could find?

At the end of the lunch shift, Bennet had an hour's break. He didn't intend to waste it listening to whatever Darius had to say. He was not in the mood for a long justification of whatever Darius had done to his little brother. He gulped down some food in the hotel kitchen, then looked for a quiet place to study. The laundry room was too hot, and the garden was full of screaming kids, so he took his books and went to sit in the churchyard.

But even there, he couldn't concentrate. People kept walking by. Okay, they had a right to, but all those wiggling arses were distracting—like the memory of a half-heard voice mail, burning a hole in his pocket.

Bennet took out his phone.

# Chapter Eighteen

H E CALLED AND let the first message start playing.
"... I have no idea what Wyndham's said, but I do know he's a creative and convincing liar. As I told you, there's no question of Giorgio having any claim on Pemberley. He's my mother's son but not my father's. My father died when I was a child and left Pemberley to me—not to my mother, for the very reason that he didn't want it going to her second husband or other children if she remarried. He was determined it should stay in his family, and I've done my best to make sure that happens."

Bennet packed his books away, stood up, and began walking between the graves. This made sense—but of course it would. If Darius lied, he'd do it well.

"The property was held in trust until I came of age, and my mother had a generous allowance as long she continued to live at Pemberley—too generous, perhaps, because by the time I'd grown up, all the money was gone. What she had, she left to John Moorhouse, her second husband. So it's true that Giorgio inherited nothing from her, but nor did I.

"You can check all this. Wills are public documents, after they've been through probate. You can request copies online. You'll need my parents' full names and their dates of death—I'll give you those in a moment."

Bennet stopped before a flaking, weathered gravestone sacred to the memory of William George Long of this parish, who departed this life on the eighth day of August 1887. Darius's voice continued in his ear.

"Wyndham is John's son by his first marriage. He lived with his mother in term time but came to Pemberley for long visits in the school holidays. We were the same age, and we disliked each other on sight. I'd started at boarding school around the time my mother remarried, and I didn't like having to share my mother and my home with another boy in the holidays, which always seemed too short. He must have been angry about his parents' divorce and his father moving away. We fought, and I usually won. He got his revenge by damaging things I loved—including Giorgio."

Goose bumps rose on Bennet's arms, though he was in full sunlight. Could Wyndham have hurt that sweet and slightly whacky kid? No, Darius must be lying—or stretching the truth, at least.

Darius had stopped talking, right when Bennet wanted to hear more. He moved into the shade of the trees that lined the churchyard wall.

Darius came back on, his voice short with frustration. "Ten seconds left, it's telling me. I'll call again."

The automated voice ran through Bennet's options. His finger hovered over the key to delete, but he changed his mind and let it save.

The second message began playing.

"Bennet. Where was I?"

Bennet smiled to himself. It was cute how flustered Darius sounded. Then he remembered how Darius expected to get what he wanted when he wanted it, with no thought for anybody else. Wasn't this frustration with technology just another example?

Darius said, "I didn't plan to tell anyone the details of what happened to Giorgio, but if Wyndham's prowling around Meriton, I think you need to know. I trust you not to harm Giorgio any further by making his story public."

Bennet remembered the boy's quick smile and the flash of fear that had crossed his face when Bennet suggested going to Sheffield. "I won't hurt him," he said aloud, as if Darius were talking in real time.

"Giorgio is the son of my mother and Wyndham's father. He was always an unusual child—sensitive, charming, but subject to unpredictable moods and rages. He didn't get on with other children and hated going to school. By the time he was seven, the local primary couldn't handle him, the nearest private day schools wouldn't take him, and my mother didn't want him to go to the special school suggested by the education authority. So she and John found a retired teacher who lived nearby and was willing to tutor him at Pemberley."

Wyndham had told Bennet that Darius had taken Giorgio out of school and found him a tutor. Now Darius was saying the same thing happened, but earlier, and it was the boy's parents' decision.

"Giorgio was twelve when my mother died. I'd come of age and Pemberley was mine without strings, but there was no more money—nowhere near enough to maintain it as a private home. Rather than split it up or sell it, I let the house and most of the gardens to Catherine Brackenbrough, John's sister.

"I kept a cottage in the grounds and would have been glad for John and Giorgio to live there, but John decided to move to Sheffield, and Giorgio had to go with him. He was supposed to go to school in the city but he kept skipping classes and cycling or hitchhiking into the national park. Sometimes he made it as far as Pemberley, and John had to fetch him back."

Bennet grinned, picturing Giorgio heading for the hills like a homing pigeon.

"His old tutor recommended a boarding school for gifted and creative children, and we decided to give it a try, with some of Catherine's rent paying the fees. He ran away once in his first term, but I explained his options—the boarding school or Sheffield—and he chose to go back to the school.

"What Giorgio didn't tell me was that Wyndham was visiting him there once or twice a term. In March of last year, Giorgio turned sixteen, and Wyndham took him out the next weekend. They went to Wyndham's flat in London."

Bennet had wandered into the deepest, darkest part of the churchyard. He leaned against the old stone wall and let his bag fall on the grass.

"Giorgio and Wyndham have different versions of the story from here. Giorgio says Wyndham gave him champagne to celebrate his birthday, deliberately getting him drunk. Wyndham asked him to sign something and then said he had to go out, leaving Giorgio with a 'friend' who introduced him to anal sex. Giorgio did consent, but it was painful, and he changed his mind halfway through. The man wouldn't stop."

Darius's voice was harsh and uneven, as if the pain had been his own—as if he were walking over knives as he spoke. Bennet's fingernails dug into his palm. He didn't want to hear this, but he felt compelled to go on listening.

"After the man left, Giorgio found a hidden camera. He guessed at once that Wyndham had set him up to appear in a porn movie. He looks younger than he is, as you'll know, and the younger a teenager appears, the more valuable the footage—especially if it seems like rape."

The churchyard wall was damp. Bennet took a step away, scuffing at the bare ground with his shoes. Could anyone do this to such a charming kid? Bennet's skin crawled at the thought. Paedophiles did, of course—but could *Wyndham* use his own brother his way? Wyndham with his easy, puppy-dog grin?

"Giorgio had a meltdown, throwing everything he could find at the camera. Wyndham rushed in and stopped him destroying the place. He must have been watching on a linkup from the next room.

"Giorgio ran into the street and hitchhiked to Derbyshire. His former tutor, out walking her dog, saw him on the road to Pemberley and called me, thinking he'd run away from school again. I drove up and found him hiding under a blanket inside a wardrobe in Peak Lodge. He was curled up tight, and he flinched away when I touched him. He wouldn't move or speak, so in the end I called a doctor, and Giorgio was admitted to a psychiatric hospital. The school . . .

"Oh, the damn thing's out of time again. I'll have to call you back. I wish you'd get a better—"

The automated voice announced the third message.

"Bennet . . . God, you're driving me crazy." Darius spoke so fast and low that Bennet wasn't sure he'd heard right. He hit Replay. Yes, that was it.

Darius must have been talking to the phone, or literally to God. He couldn't mean Bennet was driving him crazy, because none of this was Bennet's fault.

"I'll keep it short," Darius said. "I went to see Wyndham. Giorgio still wasn't talking, but his school told me who'd picked him up. Wyndham claimed Giorgio had agreed to have sex on camera. He showed me the form Giorgio signed, which mentioned acting in a faked nonconsensual sex scene. He told me Giorgio had been fine with everything until they had champagne—which Wyndham said they drank after the scene had been filmed, not before—and the alcohol had made him paranoid and violent.

"Wyndham offered to sell me the rights to the film, at a high price. It was blackmail, in my view. I refused. Wyndham must have been new to the porn industry, because he didn't know that although the age of consent for sex in this country is sixteen, a person has to be eighteen to act in adult movies. I threatened him with the police, and he wiped the unedited film in my presence. Perhaps I was wrong not to have him prosecuted, but I didn't want to put Giorgio through the stress of a criminal investigation."

Of course not. Jesus. If this was true, Giorgio had been through enough. Bennet felt dizzy and sick.

But was it true? If the film had been wiped, there'd be no evidence. Darius had had a week to make up this story or decide how to tell it. Maybe it all happened as he said, maybe it was a lie, maybe something in between. Bennet would probably never know.

He looked at his watch. He should have been back at the Black Lion five minutes ago. He hitched his bag onto his shoulder and started walking.

"Giorgio spent some weeks in the hospital and only went back to school to take his GCSE exams. After that, he persuaded us to let him live at Peak Lodge. His father has a new partner, and Giorgio didn't want to be with them. So he shares the house with two of Catherine's staff, who make sure he eats and takes his medication. His father visits often, and I go up when I can."

Bennet took the steps out of the churchyard at a jump and hurried around the corner to the hotel. Darius had paused, and for a moment Bennet thought that was the end of it. But then the voice came back on.

"Bennet, I know you're not a vulnerable sixteen-year-old and your relationships are your own business, but it worries me that you know Wyndham well enough to have heard his stories. I hate to think you might have been used as Giorgio was. If you've done anything with Wyndham or his friends that might have been filmed, with or without your consent, let me know, and I'll do everything I can to track it down and get it offline. You won't have to see me. Just call or send me a text."

He used his fingers to comb his hair in the mirror in the lobby, while Darius reeled off his parents' names and dates in case Bennet wanted to look up their wills. He didn't.

"End of messages. To replay this message—"

He ended the call and walked into the dining room. The woman he was replacing briefed him on the current state of her orders, but he didn't take in what she said.

He hadn't had sex with Wyndham, so no worries there. Not bringing his latex-free condoms—had he hoped Bennet would let him fuck bareback? As porn, it wasn't in the virgin-schoolboy bracket, but it might have a market. But they'd done nothing worth filming in the end.

And he still didn't know if he believed Darius. The barrister told a convincing story, and Bennet had been caught up in it at the time. But when he thought about it, this version of events didn't fit with his impressions of Giorgio.

The teenager was vulnerable and frightened, yes, but he and Bennet had talked about Wyndham, and Giorgio hadn't acted like someone who'd been betrayed and exploited by his brother. In fact, he'd said he wished Wyndham would visit more often.

Which was weird, thinking about it, because Wyndham had said he wasn't allowed to visit at all.

But wait—Giorgio had *two* half brothers. Had Bennet mentioned Wyndham's name, or had he just said he'd met Giorgio's brother? Giorgio might have thought he was talking about Darius. Then he'd have meant he wanted *Darius* to visit more often.

*You'd be good together*, Giorgio had said. Bennet and Darius? No, not possible. Giorgio wouldn't have put the high and mighty Darius with a guy who was applying to be an underling at Pemberley Hall. He must have meant Wyndham.

It made Bennet's head spin all through the evening. He took orders, served meals, cleared away dishes on autopilot. He delivered the right food to the right people and matched up the customers with their bills. But he wasn't concentrating.

He went off duty at ten and checked his phone. A text from Darius—as if three voice mails weren't enough. Would this guy never leave him alone?

*I find I need to know if you received my message. A simple yes or no is fine.*

Bennet typed *Yes*. He added, *I did not have sex with W*, because if Darius was telling the truth, he had a good reason for wanting to know what Bennet and Wyndham had done or not done.

Darius texted straight back: *Thank you for letting me know. Enjoy the rest of your weekend.*

Bennet unlocked his bike and started to cycle home. Enjoy the weekend? How was he supposed to do that, with this on his mind and exam revision to pack in between shifts at the Black Lion? Meanwhile, where was Darius? On his way out to some fancy restaurant followed by one of the massive London clubs, no doubt. Who would he take home tonight?

And who cared? *Not me.* Because whatever had happened with Giorgio, Darius had still broken Jamie's heart, and he only gave it a couple of sentences in his super-long three-volume voice mail epic. The rest was all about him and his family and his precious estate. The whole message could be summed up as: *I ruined your best friend's life? Oops. But hey, let's talk about me.*

Wyndham might be the bigger bastard, but even if everything Darius said about him was true, Wyndham hadn't done Bennet or his friends any harm.

Bennet swung round the corner into Longbourn Lane and hit a pothole. A shudder went through the bike, jolting his memory.

What about Kofi and Leon?

---

THEY WERE IN the living room, leaning shoulder to shoulder on the couch. Kofi was watching TV. Leon appeared to be studying at first glance, but he held up his reading matter as Bennet walked in—a magazine.

"Check out the Hottie of the Month, Bennet. Don't you think he looks like what's-his-name, that friend of Tim Wilson's?"

The model wore dove-grey underpants and nothing else, and he had one elbow leaning on the white marble mantelpiece of a big old fireplace in an oak-panelled room. It could have been at Pemberley, and the guy did have a look of Darius, though his body didn't have the solid strength that

Darius had displayed on the cliffs. It was something in his face, in the arrogance of the unsmiling pose.

Bennet wished he hadn't looked. More fuel for the unwelcome fantasies.

"There's something I need to talk to you about," he said.

Leon put down the magazine, leaving it open on the couch, and they both gazed at him with wide, expectant eyes.

"Could we have the TV off? Or the volume down, at least?" Bennet asked.

Leon reached for the remote with an exaggerated gesture, and switched it off.

Kofi said, "What have we done?"

Leon gave him a little slap. "Haven't I told you, don't go looking for trouble?"

"It's about Wyndham Moorhouse," Bennet said, settling into a chair.

Kofi opened his mouth to speak, but Leon gripped his arm.

"I've heard he's been making secret videos," Bennet went on. "Remember when he came to lunch—he had that big bag, and we were joking about how it might have a camera inside?"

Leon, still all innocence, said, "Uh-huh?"

"I wondered what he did with the bag when you took him upstairs," Bennet said.

Kofi bit his lip. "You know about that?"

Leon shushed him. "We were only showing him Kofi's photos from Ghana."

Bennet reached out to the magazine and flipped it closed.

That model was too distracting. "I was in the next room—I heard you. I threw in some condoms for you. I hope you used them."

"He had his own." Kofi's mouth dropped as he realised what he'd said. He covered it with his hand.

Leon gave him another light slap on the arm. "But honestly, Bennet, if you didn't want us to have a go with him, you should have said. You took no notice of him at lunch and went off to wash up like you weren't interested, so we thought you'd had your turn and that was it."

Bennet sighed. "Yeah, that's fine. I don't care what you got up to. But he might have filmed you, that's the thing."

They both sat up straight as if electrified. Leon said, "You mean we're in one of his secret porn movies? Awesome! Where is it?"

Bennet rolled his eyes. He'd wasted his time trying to break it to them gently.

Leon jigged up and down on the couch. "Get online, Ko. What's the name of the site, Bennet? You have to see it—it was such a hot session."

Kofi giggled, picked up a phone from the seat beside him, and swiped the screen.

"I don't believe you two," Bennet said. "Don't you even care about him filming you without your consent? What if your families see it? Your grandmother, Kofi?"

Kofi looked up at Bennet in surprise. "Nothing shocks my gran. She nicks my DVDs and has her friends round to watch them. They sit there hooting with laughter over their tea and biscuits. So what's the website?"

"I don't know. It could be anywhere or nowhere."

"What?" Leon protested. "You get us all worked up and then—"

"He's like that, though, isn't he?" said Kofi. "No fun."

"I'm not even sure he made a video," Bennet said. "I heard sometimes he does, that's all."

Kofi said, "He did, I swear. He put the bag on the desk, in the perfect position to film the bed, and he opened it up and fiddled around inside, didn't he?"

"He fiddled around inside, did he?" Leon snickered.

Kofi elbowed him. "Yes, when he got that mask out."

Leon's eyes brightened. "Oh God, yes. It still gets me hard thinking about that. He said he wanted to watch us playing first, because we looked so cute together with Kofi so dark and me so fair, so we got naked and got on the bed and started doing stuff, and after a while he put on this mask—"

"A stocking mask," Kofi said.

"Yeah, like a bank robber, over his whole head. He looked all weird and scary. It was unbelievably horny."

The rape theme again? Or was it for anonymity?

"And he came over and fucked me," Leon went on, "and I lasted, like, ten seconds because of the bank-robber thing and because of having my cock in Kofi's mouth at the same time, and then he fucked Kofi, but slow, so he'd last longer—"

"So slow it was almost *unbearable.*"

"Yeah, he was squealing and squirming and begging Wyndham to go faster, and it was so hot to watch, by the time they finished I was hard again, and Kofi was so sweet, he let me fuck him too, even though he'd just come."

Leon stroked Kofi's head. The two of them exchanged a smile of perfect understanding and started to kiss.

Bennet shrugged and stood up. "You guys are going to fall in love with each other if you're not careful."

Kofi pulled away. "No way. We don't believe in it. Look what it's done to Jamie—you'd think he had a terminal disease. Best friends forever, that's us."

"BFFs with benefits," Leon added.

"Okay, if you don't care if your arses are all over the internet, I'll leave you to your benefits."

Leon spun round when Bennet was halfway to the door. "Wait, how will we find this video? The crew have gone, and we don't have his number. We have to see it—our own personal porn movie!"

Bennet shook his head and left them discussing how to track Wyndham down. Upstairs, he took Wyndham's card from his bedside drawer and tore it into tiny pieces, so that if they asked him, he wouldn't have to lie.

# Chapter Nineteen

GIORGIO JUMPED OUT from behind a tree and threw out his thin arms in a big gesture of welcome. "Bennet! You're back."

Bennet held back a sigh. His first chance to get outside and breathe since he'd arrived at Pemberley yesterday, and here was somebody else demanding his attention. But he liked Giorgio, and he hated whatever had happened to the boy on his sixteenth birthday, so he forced himself to smile. "Yup."

"You got the job?" Giorgio asked.

"Not yet. Just up here for a few days—work experience or extended interview, I don't know exactly."

"Catherine must like you, though."

"Maybe." Or she and Annabel wanted some cheap—no, free—labour. They had a busy weekend coming up, with two weddings and the reunion of a group of women who'd known each other since their days at a boarding school on the moors. Catherine had him running here, there, and everywhere with messages or vases or instructions to change the layout of a room. Finally she'd given him an hour off in the lull between lunch and dinner, and he'd been hoping to relax.

Giorgio hadn't moved since he'd appeared on the path, blocking Bennet's way. His outspread arms now looked stiff and posed. His smile had tensed up, as if he'd pasted it onto his face consciously. Some therapist must have told him all he had to do was smile and his interactions with other people would go better. But above the wide, friendly mouth with its straight white teeth, his eyes were big and anxious.

"Maybe you can help me," Bennet said. "I want to get away for a few minutes. Where's a good place to go?"

The tension washed out of Giorgio's face, and he let his arms drop. "Follow me."

He walked away down the path, his back straight, arms crooked at the elbow, feet in blue tennis shoes moving with swift precision. Where the path looped around to head back to the house, he turned off through a gap between two trees and went straight on, up the rising slope, until the trees parted. He stood in a shaft of sunlight, waiting for Bennet to catch up.

Ahead was a rocky edge, challenging but not so high that a climber would need ropes. Bennet walked up to it, putting his hands flat on the sun-warmed gritstone. Before he'd even thought about it, his fingers were gripping two projections, his right foot was in a cleft eighteen inches from the ground, and his left was searching for the next foothold.

Wait, his shoes—he hadn't changed them before he came out, and he couldn't afford to wreck these, his only smart pair. He jumped down and rubbed at the leather over his toes. No permanent damage.

Giorgio laughed. "There's an easier way around the

side." He pointed to the left.

Bennet started in that direction but stopped when Giorgio didn't move. "Aren't you coming?"

Giorgio shook his head. "I don't like heights. How long are you staying? Will you still be here at the weekend?"

"Yeah." Bennet was itching to get to the top of the bluff.

"Go on, then."

He found the other route easily—a scramble rather than a climb, a mossy path. It was steep enough that he had to go on all fours in places, but no harm was done to his shoes.

At the top he came out into sunlight. Dandelions and daisies dotted the grass, and bumblebees buzzed around a small patch of clover. He walked to the edge. Giorgio had gone.

It was a good place. He lay down and closed his eyes, hearing nothing but a wood pigeon cooing in the trees behind him. He could have been a hundred miles from the madness that was Pemberley Hall. He exhaled and felt his shoulders relax into the welcoming ground.

---

"THERE YOU ARE. What are you doing?"

Catherine's voice cut into the stillness of the lobby outside the Bleaklow room, where the school reunion was meeting. Bennet jolted, and coffee splashed into his saucer. This carpet was treacherously thick. He hadn't heard her approach.

He put his cup down behind two tall vacuum pots and turned, feeling hunted. It was Friday afternoon, and he'd dashed from one task to another since breakfast—again. Every day had been like this. At night he showered and fell into bed without a minute for his books. Why should he feel guilty about grabbing two mouthfuls of coffee?

He waved a hand at the table. "I'm setting up for their break."

Catherine gave him her thin smile. "Looks like you're done. I need you at the gazebo. Come along."

She turned and walked away without looking back. He couldn't leave his cup here to clutter the table, so he took it with him. He snatched two more sips before they reached the reception desk, where he left it. Then he followed Catherine's quick, clacking steps out of the main doors and down the drive.

The gazebo was new since his interview—a wooden structure built over the stream where it looped between the bridge and the trees. The water ran under the middle of the floor, in a deep cleft visible through the gaps in the slatted wooden planks.

Catherine pointed to a thick roll of polythene lying on the grass. "I want that over the top. The chairs are coming, and we need them set out today. There'll be no time tomorrow. So in case it rains tonight, I want you to cover the whole roof and weigh it down with rocks or something. He'll help you"—she gestured towards a man sweeping the floorboards—"and the guy who brings the chairs."

"What time's the wedding?" Bennet asked.

Catherine ignored the question. "Set the chairs out in rows of six on each side with the aisle in the middle. Don't let the rows go right up against the walls, because you'll be covering the lattices with fresh flowers tomorrow. And make sure there's room for people to sit and pass between the rows."

He'd have worked that out for himself. Did she think she was speaking to a five-year-old?

"We need rush matting over the floor at the top there," she went on. "And find a lectern for the officiant—they never use them, but it makes the place look more like a chapel. Is that something coming?" She stopped still and listened. "It'll be the chairs."

Bennet followed her to the entrance. A van was approaching across the grass. Catherine shrieked and ran out, waving her arms to stop it.

The guy with the broom came to stand beside Bennet. "Oops. Vehicles aren't allowed on the lawn."

"There's no other way to get here," Bennet pointed out.

"But he should have gone all around the drive and then crossed carefully from the forest, not come straight across the middle." The van stopped. Catherine's canary figure reached it, arms still gesticulating. The driver got out. "Oh, he's new. She'll probably fire him."

The driver—or ex-driver—thrust his hands in his pockets and walked off across the grass towards the house. "See? There he goes," the guy added.

Bennet was shaken. Did she really fire people just like that? The man at his side sounded like he admired Catherine's ability to wield the job-axe. Bennet, not so much.

The clients' dreams might come true, as the advertising

promised, but what about the workers'? Several times over the last few days, he'd wondered what he was doing here. But it was a job—or it might become a job. Then he'd have to concentrate on keeping it.

They set up the chairs the way Catherine wanted them. Around 4 p.m., when he'd done that and a handful of other random tasks, he slipped away.

He'd stashed his climbing shoes and leggings in a locker in the basement, so he didn't have to go all the way to his room to change. He'd brought his gear to Pemberley thinking he might get some real climbing while he was here, but that wasn't going to happen outside of his dreams. No way could he make time for a day on the Peak or even a trip to a sports centre in Sheffield. But he was using the shoes all the same, at his rock.

That was how he thought of the place Giorgio had shown him: "his rock." He'd been back every day. It was nothing in terms of height, but that had its advantages. It meant he could climb there alone. He'd scrambled over it in five or six different ways, including circling the whole face and zigzagging back and forth.

Yesterday it had rained, and that had given him a whole new challenge. Today? He hadn't decided. Maybe a loop around and a rest at the top. The sky was overcast, but it was hot and humid, a good day for doing very little.

He changed his shoes and slipped out of his work clothes. Bare-chested, he grasped the first handhold and stepped up off the ground. This part was easy. He could have done it in his sleep. But halfway up there was a big patch of smooth rock that was harder to get around. He aimed for that.

He hadn't seen Giorgio again—which was good in a way, because there'd been a moment when he'd wondered if Giorgio might have a crush on him, and that would have added a whole new level of complication to his interactions with this family. But since that didn't seem to be the case, Bennet missed the young guy. Giorgio was bright and funny, and he seemed more real than most of the people here, with their Catherine-worship and their constant talk of dreams coming true.

Footsteps thudded along the path. Maybe that was him now. Bennet looked down with a smile already prepared, and froze.

Darius. Looking lean and hot and hungry, in his climbing gear.

Bennet needed to keep moving—he wouldn't be able to hold this position for long—but his arms and legs wouldn't do what they were told. Darius stared at him, and he stared right back. His fingers slipped from the crevice, and he felt himself falling.

He tried to make it look as though he'd meant to jump, but he landed heavily. He twisted and grabbed at the rock.

Darius was right there beside him, as if he'd moved with the speed of light. His strong hands held Bennet's bare shoulders, steadying him. A jolt of electricity surge through Bennet, and he jerked out of Darius's grasp.

"You startled me." *You bastard*, he wanted to add. Every time they met, Darius put him on the wrong foot somehow.

Made him see his defects—poverty, naivety. Made him see the chip on his shoulder, made him feel he didn't measure up, made him fall off this bloody boulder. And then sent these waves of desire through him.

"Are you okay?" Darius asked.

"Fine." The word came out like a gunshot. But he had to admit, Darius looked genuinely concerned. Maybe he hadn't intended to make Bennet fall.

Bennet brushed his hands off against his thighs and shook out his arms and legs. "What are you doing here?"

Darius raised one eyebrow in the way he had. "Do I need a reason to be here? I own this land."

The one place Bennet could fully relax at Pemberley, and Darius had to come along and remind him whose rock it was. Bennet didn't bother to keep the resentment from his voice.

"Your brother said I could climb here, but if Your Highness thinks I'm trespassing, I'll go back to being Pemberley Hall's lowest minion."

Darius took a step back, and something crossed his face. On anyone else, Bennet would have thought it was pain. "I didn't mean you weren't welcome."

*Playing mind games.* Bennet didn't have the energy to join in. He just wanted things out in the open. To know where he stood—and have Darius standing somewhere far, far away. "Okay. So I only have, like, one hour a day free, around this time, late afternoon, and that's when I come here."

Darius nodded. It looked like he'd got the message—if

he was here for the weekend, he could come out to this rock any other time of day and have the place to himself, but this hour was Bennet's. "You're working for Catherine?"

"Yes. No. Just until Sunday." Not that it was any of Darius's business.

"Right." Darius took his cool gaze from Bennet and walked up to the face of the rock. "It's a good place for bouldering. Have you tried going diagonally across the middle?"

He hadn't seen that route. "Not yet."

"Do you want to give it a go?"

Bennet thought of saying no and heading back to the big house. He'd told Darius he never wanted to see him again, and he'd meant it. But he'd only just started his break. Why should he let Darius drive him away?

He turned to face the rock. Maybe he could pretend Darius wasn't there. If he climbed, he wouldn't have to look at the man, and then he wouldn't feel so stirred up, so uncomfortable, so *sensitive*. Darius always turned him into a hedgehog, a ball of prickles around a soft, sore heart. How did he do it?

Bennet needed to stop thinking. He leaped at the rock, moving easily up to the middle. His Zen-like climbing mind kicked in, and when Darius followed him onto the gritstone edge, Bennet's tension was gone. Darius was just another climber, and Bennet had no thoughts beyond the next hand- or foothold.

They took a break on the grassy ledge at the top of the rock. Darius stretched out and settled back on his elbows. It wasn't a huge space, but Bennet kept his distance, sitting beside a stubborn hawthorn bush that had rooted next to the mossy path he'd scrambled up when Giorgio had first brought him here.

Darius said, "This is the first place I ever climbed—properly, I mean. Before that, I used to get on top of wardrobes and hang from banisters. Did you do that kind of stuff as a child?"

"All the time." Bennet gazed away towards the big house, barely visible through the trees. "Pemberley must have been awesome for that."

"It was. They found me on the edge of the roof one day. It's mostly flat, of course, and there's access from the back stairs, but I hadn't taken the easy way. I'd hooked an old rope over the balustrade and scrambled up from a bedroom window. I was lucky the masonry took my weight. My mother coaxed me back in, and one of my last memories of my father is of him looming over me, saying 'This is the last straw!'"

Darius barked out a laugh. "I expected some megapunishment, like being tied down with a ball and chain, but he brought in a climber who taught me it was uncool to take stupid risks. We started here, then I joined a kids' club that went out to the Dark Peak."

"I didn't have anything like that," Bennet said, envious. "School visits to the climbing wall was it."

"But you made the most of what you had."

Bennet shrugged. "You have to when you don't have much."

"Some people don't. They take from others, instead."

Bennet didn't want to be drawn into a discussion. He shouldn't be speaking to Darius at all. He turned towards the other man to say he was going down, but the words dried on his lips.

Darius lay on his back on the grass, long limbs glistening with beads of sweat. His eyes were closed, so Bennet's gaze was free to travel over the wide shoulders, the swell of his chest, the way his top fell into creases over the ridges of his abs. Below that, the soft bulge in his shorts . . . or was it soft? It reached almost to his waistband. Semi? Wouldn't take much to bring it all the way up. One or two slow strokes of Bennet's hand, maybe. So tempting.

An ant ran over Darius's leg. Bennet could reach over, brush that off, and then—

No. It was just physical. Way more trouble than he wanted to get into. *Think of the shitty way he's treated me. Think of Jamie.*

Instead, he found himself thinking of ropes and balustrades. "What were you saying about access to the roof?"

Darius's eyelids flickered and opened. "At the top of the back stairs. I'd show you, but I'm not supposed to wander around the building without giving Catherine notice."

But Bennet couldn't pass up the challenge of that roof. "You won't be wandering around it. You'll be going straight up the stairs and out. And then we'll climb down the side of the building."

Darius sat up. "What? No. We'd be spotted. It's a crazy idea."

Bennet rubbed his hands together. "We don't have to go all the way down. You've got ropes, right? And can you bring me a spare harness? Or mine's in my room. Which staircase is it?"

"Bennet . . ." But Darius was grinning.

"Come on, I don't have much time. Half an hour at the most." And Bennet wanted to be doing something in that time instead of sitting here just . . . gazing.

He clambered down the rock. He didn't change, just grabbed his bag of work clothes and set off. Darius followed, still arguing, but breaking into a run beside him when they reached the path.

Darius pointed out the staircase before he turned off towards Peak Lodge. It was the one nearest Bennet's room. There was a fire door at the bottom, but it only opened outwards, so Bennet and went in through the kitchens. A florist spotted him as he dodged along a corridor and raised her eyebrows at the way he was dressed, but he evaded her and made it to the stairs.

Down a few steps, and he was up against the inside of the fire door. He pushed it open. Darius was already in sight, jogging towards him half hidden by a hedge, carrying a bag. Bennet let him in, and they ran up the stairs as softly as they could.

From the ground the roof looked flat, but up here it was full of low structures. Long rows of sloping skylights ran along both sides, tiled ridges stuck up at random points, square shed-like constructions squatted between them, and a line of chimneys marched down the middle.

Darius's eyes glinted as he picked his way to a low brick wall near the back of the building.

"I haven't done this for years. Look, here are the bolts I put in one summer."

He checked their stability and reached into his back for the rope. Bennet put on a harness, then strolled over the lead-lined gaps between the structures to the front of the house.

Lambton and the fields and hills beyond were set before him like a buffet. He was higher than everything in this direction except the birds and the clouds. He stretched out his arms and threw back his head. He'd have whooped, but dumpy figures were moving over the lawn below, and he didn't want anyone rushing up to stop them.

He walked back around to Darius. "My room's under here somewhere." He peered over the rear balustrade. "I think it's this one. The window's open—maybe I can drop in."

Darius laughed. He looked like a different person in this mood. "You'd better make sure you have the right room. Okay, we're on. I'll go first, and—"

"Wait. Why?"

Darius opened his mouth to answer, then closed it. His gaze slid away.

Bennet folded his arms. "You can't think of a good reason, can you?"

"I want to make sure it's safe. If anyone's going to break their neck—"

"No necks will be broken. We have ropes, and we've

both done this kind of thing before."

Darius blew out a breath. "We don't have time to argue about it. In fact, I don't know if we have time to do this at all. Your half hour must almost be up."

"It's fine. Nobody important saw me leave, so I can take a few extra minutes. But since there may only be enough time for one of us to go over the edge, it should be me. You've had plenty of chances."

He glared at Darius across the space that separated them, and Darius glared back. Then Darius threw up his hands. "Okay. I'll anchor myself behind this wall. You'd better take the rope through the balustrade, not over the top, so you won't bring a great lump of stone down on your head."

They roped up and checked each other's knots, just like in Brighton. Then Bennet waited until Darius was in position, made sure there was nobody watching from below, and clambered over the balustrade.

That wasn't difficult, because there was a ledge on the other side. Then there was a drop of a couple of feet to the next projection, which was only just wide enough for his toes to grip. One more step down and he'd be outside the window that he thought was his. He let go of the first ledge and dropped his other hand to the second.

"This is as easy as going down stai—"

The stone crumbled under his fingers. At the same time, his foot slipped. He barely had time to yell, "Falling!" before he was sliding down the wall.

His stomach lurched, though his logical brain knew he was in no danger as long as the rope held. For a second he was in freefall. Then his harness jerked, caught, and held him. He crashed in against the building and hung there safely. Darius and the bolts had taken his weight.

"Are you hurt?" Darius called.

"No, I'm fine. Let me down a little more, and I'll be on a windowsill."

The rope lowered Bennet in short jerks until his feet were planted half in and half out of the gap at the bottom of a sash window.

"Is it your room?"

"I hope so. Give me more rope."

Bennet bent, pulled up the sash, and slid through. His computer was on the desk, his towel on the back of the chair. He stuck his head and shoulders back outside.

"Yes, it's mine, and I'm in," he shouted up.

The rope slackened, and Darius's head appeared over the parapet above.

"Oops," Bennet said, grinning. "I think I broke a bit off your mansion."

"I don't give a shit, as long as you didn't break any bits of yourself." Darius wiped his forehead with the back of his hand, his expression grim. "I'm coming down—by the stairs."

"That's probably a good idea."

"Can I take up the rope first?"

"Sure." Bennet fed it up to him. He told Darius where to find him, and a minute or two later, Darius knocked.

He came in and closed the door. He'd brought Bennet's bag of work clothes, which he dropped onto the end of the bed. The cramped space seemed too small for the two of them and too hot, despite the open window. Or maybe it was Bennet who was hot. He was in a bedroom with Darius only inches away, and they were both breathing heavily—from the shock, or the climb, or the running down stairs, obviously. Nothing else.

Because anything else would be impossible, and the thought of it made Bennet seriously uncomfortable.

"I should get back to work," he said.

Darius took a step closer, his eyes running over Bennet's limbs. "I need to know you're really okay. I must have been insane to let you do that."

"Bullshit. It was fun. I slipped, but I was never in any danger." Bennet spoke as breezily as he could, but he didn't feel great. He was shaking a little, and he wanted to sit down . . . or to have someone's arms around him.

What he'd said was true—he'd never been at risk—but only because Darius had done the right things at the other end of the rope. His life had been in Darius's hands, and he would put it there again in a heartbeat. Liking and disliking didn't come into it. He trusted the man.

Darius bent his head, frowning. "What's that on your elbow?"

Bennet looked down, twisting his arm. "Just a graze." It burned, though, and blood was streaked over the broken skin.

"You should wash it. Where's your bathroom?"

"These are the attics. No en suite facilities. There's a shared bathroom down the corridor."

Darius nodded, tipped a couple of apples out of a bowl that Bennet had borrowed from the kitchen, and went out. While he was gone, Bennet slipped out of the harness and changed into his work trousers. Then Darius came back with the bowl full of water, a bar of Pemberley Hall soap, and a toilet roll. Bennet sat down on the bed.

"Hold this here," Darius said, setting the bowl on Bennet's thighs. Then he knelt on the floor, took Bennet's arm in the gentlest of grips, and dipped the grazed elbow into the warm water.

*He's kneeling at my feet.* And it actually felt okay to have him there. A strange, heavy calm came over Bennet as Darius dabbed away the blood and cleaned the wound. Darius's head bent lower until his face was so close to the inside of Bennet's elbow that his breath fluttered over the skin like butterfly wings, sending sparks coursing through Bennet's veins and making his own breath catch raggedly in his throat.

It was too much. He jerked his arm away. His wrist jostled the bowl of bloodstained water, which splashed onto his trousers.

Darius went still for a second. Then he said in a clipped voice, "Sorry."

He staggered to his feet, strode to the door, snatched it open, and was gone.

# Chapter Twenty

Bennet couldn't sleep that night. His mind buzzed with thoughts of Darius, no matter how he tried to banish them and relax. He couldn't even stroke himself without being flooded with the memory of Darius kneeling at his feet or Darius's long body lying on the grass like a dish waiting to be tasted.

He got up and opened the curtains, looking out towards Peak Lodge. Under that roof Darius was sleeping—or was he? Did he feel the same tension? Was Bennet on his mind, haunting him, annoying him, keeping him awake?

Bennet went back to bed and gave in to his desire, imagining Darius's hand instead of his own, Darius's mouth on his lips, on his chest, on his cock. It didn't matter. No one would ever know. And then, finally, he slept.

The next afternoon, Saturday, Catherine caught him as he crossed the orangery.

"Bennet! Could you help us in here?"

He checked his watch. "It's my break." He'd been thinking about it all afternoon. He was going to the rock. Darius surely wouldn't be there, after the abrupt way he'd left Bennet's room yesterday, and Bennet wanted to scramble over it one last time.

"Nineteen years old, and he needs breaks!" Catherine's tinkling laugh echoed against the hundred panes of glass, setting his teeth on edge.

"I'm twenty."

"Right. Sorry. And that makes all the difference?" She looked round with glittering eyes at the other staff, who virtually stood to attention as they watched the scene.

What was it about her that had everyone at her beck and call? If she had magnetism, Bennet didn't feel it, but he tried to hide his wariness. He needed a job to come out of this.

"You can have a break in fifteen minutes," she said. "It's your last full day with us, isn't it? You're leaving tomorrow?"

"Yes." And he wasn't sorry. It would be a relief to get away.

"Then you must have dinner with us tonight. Come up to our suite at seven."

Wow. He hadn't expected that. "Okay, thanks."

Dinner with Catherine and Annabel had to mean a job offer, didn't it? He could delay his break for that. It didn't make any difference what time he went, anyway, since Darius wouldn't be at the rock.

*Stop thinking about Darius.* He followed Catherine's pointing finger and picked up one end of a table.

"Leaving you to it, team," Catherine announced to the room. She stalked out, heels clacking on the fake wood floor.

When the fifteen minutes were up, Bennet ran all the way to the rock, to make the most of whatever time he had. As he turned the last corner, he stopped short. Darius was here after all, stretched out against the face, climbing.

Bennet's heart thudded.

Darius turned his head, saw Bennet, and jumped down. At the foot of the rock, he brushed dust from his hands. His expression was cool, unruffled. "I thought you'd be here earlier."

"Sorry, I was delayed." Why was he apologising?

Darius nodded. "I have to go in a moment. I have a phone appointment with Giorgio's therapist."

So this was goodbye. Darius wasn't sticking around. Now maybe Bennet really would never see Darius again . . . which would be a relief, of course. Unless Bennet came to work here, when maybe they'd meet at the rock from time to time.

"I still have your harness," Bennet said.

"It doesn't matter. You can bring it . . ." Darius hesitated, then began speaking quickly, as if he needed to get the words out before he changed his mind. "I know tomorrow's your last day here. Would you like to come out with the local climbing club? We'll be going to Derwent Edge. I'll drive you there, of course. I'd just like to offer you some real climbing, after that mess yesterday. I won't bother you in any other way."

*Derwent Edge*! "What time do you go?"

"Fairly early, usually, but I could make it a bit later if you . . . Say nine o'clock?"

Bennet was already shaking his head. "I'd have liked to"—he wouldn't say no to Derwent Edge without a good reason—"but I've agreed to work here until midday."

"I could speak to Catherine," Darius offered.

"I'd rather you didn't. Does she know we've met?"

"Not unless Giorgio has told her."

"I'd prefer it to stay that way. I don't want any special treatment."

"I understand. I'll respect that." Darius hesitated. Bennet had never seen him as uncertain as this, as if Bennet had power over him in some weird way.

Without meeting Bennet's eyes, Darius added, "Do you have plans for this evening?"

Was that an idle question, or did he have a suggestion? A date, even, maybe?

A few days ago, Bennet might have led him on and then stood him up, to pay him back for that night in Brighton. But he couldn't play those games now. Something had shifted in these two days. It wasn't that Bennet liked the man, exactly, but he . . . respected him, maybe. He was wary of Darius still, but in a different way. And he had to be honest.

"I'm summoned to dinner with the Brackenbroughs."

"Ah." Darius looked—what? Relieved or disappointed? Both, maybe. It was hard to tell. He gave a short laugh. "Have fun."

"I don't think fun is on the menu."

"Maybe not, but you'll find a way to have some. You have a talent for brightening life."

Before Bennet could respond to that, Darius raised a hand and walked away. Bennet was left with what he'd wanted—a rock to climb, and no aloof, distracting presence.

But he found himself wishing that Darius had stayed.

BENNET SHOWERED, POLISHED his shoes, and dressed in his suit. If Catherine and Annabel remembered he'd worn the same suit for the interview, too bad—he only had one.

Their apartment covered a wing of the top floor. Bennet's nerves were on edge and his heart was beating a little faster than usual as he rang the bell.

Footsteps approached on the other side of the door. He squared his shoulders, straightened his back, and put a smile on his face. Who would it be, Catherine or Annabel?

Neither. When the door opened, he was greeted by a broadly smiling teenager: Giorgio.

Oh no. If Giorgio was here, Darius could be too. *Not now*, he thought. *Not tonight.* This was too important. He needed this job.

He followed the teenager down the hall, saying nothing, seeing nothing. They passed through an archway into the living room.

And there was Darius, standing stiffly by one of the big windows looking out over the park, dressed casually but not carelessly. The setting sun lit him up in gold. Bennet's stomach lurched and dropped, as if he were blasting off in a rocket.

He took a deep breath. *You can do this. Just don't be fazed. If he criticises, pretend he's an awkward customer. Stay cool, stay polite, stay on top of the situation.*

But what was Darius doing here? He'd said nothing about it this afternoon. In fact, he'd implied he was free.

Had Giorgio arranged it? It was possible. In fact, Giorgio might have set up this whole weekend. He could have asked Darius to come up without saying why, then sent Darius out to the rock yesterday.

But if Giorgio's plan was to bring them together, it was doomed. It seemed a shame to disappoint him, but there was no way Bennet and Darius would ever be a couple. And Bennet would make that clear by switching into professional mode—just as soon as he could stop staring at Darius. Which would be any second now, right?

"Glad you could come, Bennet." Catherine's voice jolted him out of his rabbit-in-the-headlights act. He hadn't even noticed she was in the room. He fixed his smile back on and turned to her.

She moved smoothly into formal introductions. "Darius, Giorgio, this is Bennet Rourke, a student who's on work experience placement with us this week. Bennet, this is Darius Lanniker, Pemberley Hall's landlord, and Giorgio Moorhouse, my nephew and Darius's half brother."

Giorgio winked from behind Catherine's back. Darius stepped forward and held out a hand to shake. "How d'you do."

Bennet took the outstretched hand. The firm clasp sent warmth rushing through his body. He disengaged from it as soon as he could.

Catherine cut in, saving him from making awkward conversation. "I discovered Darius was visiting and invited him to dinner, since he seems to be busy every other moment this weekend. So it's lucky you're here. You can be our waiter."

*Okaaay. She invites me for a meal, and then tells me I'm to serve it.*

"Isn't he a guest?" Darius said.

"He'll eat with us, of course," Catherine said airily. "It's just to give Annabel a hand taking things to the table."

"I can do that," Darius said.

"Sweet of you! But no. Bennet will want to show us his skills. You don't mind, do you, Bennet?"

"No." What else could he say? And maybe Catherine was doing him a favour. He'd rather have something to do than stand here with Darius acting like a stranger.

Catherine dismissed him with a flutter of her hand. "You'll find Annabel in the kitchen." As he left the room, she added, "The meal's a surprise, Darius. She hasn't even told me what she's making. But I think you'll be impressed—she's an excellent cook."

Bennet closed the door on them and located Annabel by the clatter of dishes. The room was a big, bright space, half kitchen and half dining area, separated by a serving island. Annabel had her back to him, doing something at the counter.

All the surfaces were clean and clear. Impressive. She must be the kind of cook who washed up as she went along. But his mum did that, and she still made more mess than this.

"Hi," he said from the doorway.

She jumped and spun round. The salad tongs in her hand dripped oil onto the floor. Behind her were two big bowls—one plain white, like they had downstairs, and one blue with polka dots. She'd been transferring salad from the white bowl to the blue. She didn't look happy to see him.

"I'm here to serve," he said.

He half expected her to send him away, but after a moment she waved the tongs at the fridge. "I suppose you can put the smoked salmon on the table. It's in there."

He crossed the tiled floor and opened the fridge door. There was nothing in it but a flat platter covered with plastic film, a cheesecake on a blue plate, a trifle in a glass bowl, a few jars of sauces, and two bottles of wine. No raw food at all. Maybe she'd taken everything out to stop the desserts smelling of onions? Either that or they had another fridge somewhere.

Thinking of odours, he couldn't smell anything cooking, either. He glanced at the stove. Yes, the oven light was on. The door seals must be extra effective.

He lifted out the platter and set it on the round wooden table that was laid for five with candles and flowers in the dining area.

"You can open the white wine," Annabel said.

He took a bottle from the fridge, loosened the cork, and set it beside the Burgundy, already open on a steel tray on the windowsill.

"Okay, that's it," Annabel said. "Close the door as you go."

"If you're almost ready, I'll wait," Bennet said. He was in no hurry to go back to the awkwardness of being in a room with both Darius and Catherine.

Something pinged, and a light came on above the counter where Annabel stood. What was that—a built-in microwave?

"Not yet. Come back in five minutes," Annabel said.

He went out, but he didn't close the door all the way. He peeked.

She opened a hatch and lifted something out. It looked like a stainless steel pot, but it couldn't be metal, if that was a microwave. Another, smaller one came out from behind it. In their place she put the white salad bowl, which must be empty now. Weird. Why would anybody put an empty bowl in a microwave?

She took a ladle and transferred the contents of the larger pot (definitely metal, he heard it clang) to a ceramic casserole and tipped the smaller one into an open dish. Now the first aromas wafted to Bennet's nose—lamb. He felt the movement in his stomach that meant it was about to growl, and tightened his abs to keep it quiet.

When Annabel was done, she put the empty pots back into the hatch beside the white bowl, closed the door, and pressed a button. The light came on again, and something made a whirring noise. She turned away to open the oven doors. The full ceramic casserole went in the bottom oven and the open dish in the top, beside a stack of plates.

*Ha.* He'd got it now. Lamb ragù with gnocchi was on the menu downstairs tonight. The hatch was a dumbwaiter. She hadn't cooked a thing—it was all sent up from the hotel kitchens.

He took Catherine at her word and acted as waiter, walking round the table with the dishes, then slipping back into his seat between Catherine and Giorgio. It meant he didn't take much part in the conversation, because he was always either serving or eating. He was fine with that, because his seat was opposite Darius, and if he had nothing to do, he felt awkward whether he was looking at Darius or not looking at Darius.

"The next course?" he asked Annabel when he'd finished his salad.

"Oh, yes." She hadn't said much, either. Those were almost her first words since they sat down. "It's in the oven. If you could lift it out—"

Darius pushed his chair back. "I'll do that."

"Bennet can manage, unless he has no biceps at all," Catherine said sharply.

"I didn't intend any slur on Bennet's biceps," Darius said over his shoulder. "I'm sure he's well-endowed with them."

Giorgio spluttered at *well-endowed*. Darius frowned a warning at him and added, "I'd like to be of some help myself, that's all."

Bennet carried the plates to the kitchen area, scraped the remains into the food bin, and opened the dishwasher. By the stove, Darius put on oven gloves and lifted out the casserole. He hesitated with the pot in his hands, looking around for the best place to put it. Bennet took an iron trivet from a shelf and set it on the counter for him.

Did Darius cook? Was he like this at home? Was this how it would be if they lived together and were serving this meal to their guests?

Where the fuck had that thought come from?

He stood still. His breath came fast and his stomach felt jittery. Right now he wanted to be there, in a kitchen that was his and Darius's, more than he'd ever wanted anything.

*Click out of it.* Back to reality. Him and Darius living together? No way was that going to happen.

"Do you really want to work for her?" Darius whispered.

Bennet let out a breathy laugh. "I'm short of options right now."

"All right. I'll see what I can do. I'm sorry about tonight, by the way. I didn't plan to muscle in on your evening."

Bennet shrugged. "I guessed that. It's okay."

"What do you want done with this?" Darius asked aloud, nodding towards the counter.

The casserole. Right. Bennet should be serving dinner. Why wouldn't his brain work? He looked over at the table. Giorgio met his eyes—he'd been watching them. Catherine and Annabel had their heads together, talking.

"I'll serve it from here, if you could take the vegetables to the table." Bennet opened the top oven and handed the dish of broccoli and carrots to Darius, who headed back to join the others. Bennet lifted out the warm plates and spooned ragù and gnocchi onto the top one. His hand shook a little. Without even looking, he was aware of every move Darius made.

"Tell us about the Parsons case, Darius," Annabel said, as

Bennet slid a steaming plate around her elbow and onto her place mat.

Darius frowned. "You heard about that?"

"Of course, it's been reported everywhere," Catherine said. "Darius is a barrister, Bennet."

He almost said *I know*. He closed his mouth just in time.

"Such a difficult case. It must have been a challenge," Annabel added.

"It was, but it's not the best subject for the dinner table." Darius slid his fork into his portion of ragù. "This smells delicious."

Catherine pulled the dish of vegetables towards her and took some broccoli. "Come on, Darius. We're dying to hear the juicy details."

Darius's eyes met Bennet's for a second, then flicked to Giorgio, who was sitting perfectly still with his hands in his lap, looking down at his plate where broccoli, carrots, and stew were grouped in three separate islands. He'd slipped his spoon under one side of his plate to tip it, so no sauce would run onto the vegetables.

Bennet's intake of national news was patchy, but hadn't some guy called Parsons been accused of a sex-related murder? The victim had been a male teenager. Darius was right. This wasn't the moment.

He settled into his own place and tried to shift the conversation to safer ground. "Do you appear in the news a lot?" he asked Darius. "Do you open websites or newspapers and see your own face?"

"Not often." Darius gave him a grateful glance. "Training

takes several years, so I'm still quite new to the profession. But it does happen. We have a tracking service that picks up any mention of our names, and of course sometimes I see cameras outside court."

Giorgio picked up his fork and began to eat, starting with the carrots.

Darius turned to Catherine. "Is Bennet coming to work here permanently?"

Catherine was chewing. She waved a hand at Annabel, who said, "We can't really discuss personnel matters at the table."

"I see. He seems the kind of guy who'd fit in easily anywhere, though, doesn't he? I'm sure he has plenty of offers." One of his eyelids flickered, like a secret hint of a wink that nobody else could see. "Am I allowed to ask what you're hoping for, Bennet?"

*You*, was the answer that sprung up from the depths of Bennet's mind. Wait, what? No. What had happened to his brain?

He cleared his throat. "A challenge. Something I can learn from and grow into." *What a cliché*. But he was way too stressed to think of anything better.

Catherine swallowed. "We'll be in touch with you when we've finished the reorganization. Talking of which, Darius, we need to put a mezzanine in the old library and create another office up there, with a door through to the projection room behind the main conference hall."

"I'll have to see the plans," Darius said. "I don't like the idea of doors cut into the walls at that level."

"It's only a partition wall." Catherine turned on her charm, and Bennet relaxed. He wasn't needed in this conversation. Giorgio finished his vegetables and started on the meat. Annabel's plate was almost clean. Bennet got up to offer them more.

---

HE AND DARIUS didn't speak again until they left. Even then, out in the corridor with the Brackenbroughs' door closed behind them, Bennet couldn't think of anything to say. So they walked side by side in silence, with Giorgio close behind. Bennet was in a strange state of mind—both hyped up and exhausted, as if the smallest thing might make him laugh or yell or even cry.

There'd been no job offer. Catherine had said nothing more about his possible employment. So why had she invited him? Maybe they would have discussed it if Darius hadn't been there. Or had she just wanted to put him in a potentially stressful situation to see how he reacted?

Darius started down the stairs. Bennet stopped and gestured at the corridor ahead. "I go this way."

"Oh, yes, of course." Darius came back up one step, his gaze lowered.

Giorgio nudged his brother. "Climbing."

"Right." Darius seemed to break out of a daydream. "I wanted to ask you, Bennet—how about tomorrow afternoon? I have a few things to do here, so it works out better for me. The main climb will be over, but we can still go up. And I can introduce you to people before they leave, so you'll have contacts in the local club if you come to work here."

Giorgio hung at Darius's elbow, eyes darting from his brother to Bennet, as if he was holding his breath waiting for Bennet's answer.

If only Bennet could say yes . . . but there was no way. "I can't, even in the afternoon. There's work on the rail tracks. I have to get two buses and three trains, and it'll take hours. If I stay up here all afternoon, I'll miss the last connection to Meriton."

Darius's hand moved as if he wanted to brush away all objections. "That's not a problem. I can drive you home afterwards. I'll be going back to London, and it's not far out of the way."

Bennet stared. Darius would drive him all the way to Longbourn? Did he mean that? Two or three hours alone together in a car—wouldn't that be beyond awkward? Or would it be fine now? Were they moving into something like a friendship?

Darius had been looking over Bennet's shoulder, his brow furrowed as if he was puzzled or fascinated by the striped wallpaper. Now, just for a second, his eyes flicked across and met Bennet's.

Bennet answered the question in those eyes, not even thinking about the climb. "Yes, okay."

A tremor passed across Darius's face. What was that? Relief? It was gone before Bennet could decide. Darius nodded in his usual expressionless way. "What time can you leave?"

"One o'clock? Or let's say one thirty. They find extra work for me all the time."

"All right. It's probably best if you come to Peak Lodge."

"Yes." Then no one at Pemberley Hall would see him with Darius. Later, if he got the job, he wouldn't care, but right now he preferred people not to think there was something between them—since there wasn't.

Darius turned away. "Tomorrow, then, at the Lodge. We'll have a sandwich and go. Come as early as you can. The more time we have, the better."

Bennet could have sworn he'd almost said *the more time we have together, the better*. But no, he couldn't have meant that. Climbing time, he meant.

"Okay. Thanks, I'll be looking forward to it."

"Me too." Darius gave one of his rare smiles. Then he was gone, heading down the staircase.

Giorgio flashed Bennet a grin as he followed. "Good night."

"Yeah, good night." He watched them to the turn in the stairs, then went on to his room.

It felt strange to be alone now—felt like Darius should still be with him. Like something was missing from his life, though it had seemed full before, and he hadn't lost anything. It wasn't lust, or not only lust, but something deeper.

It was impossible, of course. Even if Darius hadn't cared about the differences between them, there were other barriers—like Jamie.

Jamie! Guilt stabbed at Bennet. He hadn't thought about

his friend all evening. Jamie hadn't recovered from Tim—hadn't even started to recover. How would he feel, seeing Bennet jump out of Darius's car tomorrow? It would be the worst betrayal.

Should he go after Darius and say he'd changed his mind—no climbing, he was going back by train? Probably he should.

But the temptation was too much. He'd have Darius drop him at the end of Longbourn Lane and walk from there. That way, Jamie would never know.

Tomorrow. One more morning of work, then climbing in the Dark Peak. Derwent Edge, no less. He'd dreamed of that since he'd first discovered how much he loved to climb. And yet right now, he was looking forward to the journey south more than anything else—to Darius driving him home.

# Chapter Twenty-one

BENNET WAS HELPING to set up a wedding breakfast towards noon the next day when his phone rang in his pocket. He ignored it and went on tying flowers to columns under the direction of a fussy wedding planner. He took a bathroom break a few minutes later and checked his call log. He didn't recognise the number, but there was a voice mail.

"Bennet, it's Philippe Hennice. I want to see you. Call me back. Do it right now, I don't care what else you're doing."

He sounded furious. Bennet's pulse quickened. What could it be? Had Catherine made some complaint about him?

He found a quiet corner and selected Callback.

"Bennet. Where are you?" Philippe barked down the phone. "Nigel says you've gone away. What the fuck are you playing at?"

The f-word? He had to be seriously pissed off.

"I'm at Pemberley Hall. Where else would I be? You fixed it up yourself."

Philippe swore under his breath and added, "I want you back here."

"What's this about?"

"You know what it's about. This thing you've done with Wyndham Moorhouse."

"Wyndham Moorhouse? I haven't done anything with him." Not recently—and then it wasn't much. None of Philippe's business, anyway.

"Just get your arse back to Meriton."

"All right. I'm coming back tonight. I'll see you at college tomorrow."

"No. I mean *now*, Bennet. You call a taxi, you grab your bag, and you get on the very next train."

"But Catherine—"

"I'll square it with Catherine. I'll speak to her now. Come straight to college from the station. I'll be in my office."

It made no sense, but Bennet didn't argue. His hands were shaking as he went back to the orangery to make his excuses to the wedding planner. What had he done—or what had Wyndham said he'd done? No way to know.

Luggage first, while Philippe talked to Catherine. Bennet headed for the lift. He was less likely to meet other staff there than on the stairs.

He so didn't want to leave now. Making a bad impression here was the tiniest part of it. No climbing Derwent Edge—and no journey home with Darius. His legs felt dull and heavy as he tramped along the corridor to his room.

He put the open bag on his bed and started filling it. It didn't take long. One last look around the room (the room where Darius had got down on his knees), then he slung his bag over his shoulder and went to look for Catherine.

He asked a couple of people, who pointed him outside, and he found her in discussion with a delivery driver around the side of the building, by the kitchen door.

"Bennet," she said. "Not a great time. Philippe's explained."

What had Monsieur Philippe said? "I know, I just—"

She gave him a wide, dismissive smile that didn't reach her eyes. "We'll be in touch."

She said no more. Not even a thank-you for all the exhausting days he'd worked here for free, but maybe last night's dinner was meant for that—the privilege of spending an evening serving Annabel's fake food.

Whatever. He put Catherine out of his mind and went on towards Peak Lodge.

He heard someone coming towards him around a bend in the path. It didn't sound like Darius's stride, and he didn't want to see anyone else right now, so he slipped off the path into the trees. It was Annabel, walking with her head down. She didn't look in his direction.

He let her pass and walked on, then remembered he hadn't called the taxi. He felt for his phone but didn't pull it out. Another couple of minutes wouldn't make much difference.

Darius was loading ropes, shoes, and crampons into his car. He straightened at the sound of footsteps. "You're early. Excellent. Sling your bag in."

But Bennet dropped his bag on the ground and thrust his hands into his pockets. "I can't go with you. I have to go straight back to Meriton."

A cloud passed over Darius's face. "Why?"

"I don't know. They want me at college."

"On a Sunday?"

"Yes, on a Sunday."

Darius said nothing for a moment, looking at him. Then he bent to pick up one last crampon from the side of the road. With his face turned away, he said, "If it's because you don't want to spend time with me, I'd rather hear it straight."

Bennet took out his phone, hit up voice mail, and passed it to Darius.

"What's this?" Darius said.

"Listen."

Darius put the crampon on top of the ropes in the car and held the phone to his ear. He glanced at Bennet when Monsieur Philippe's voice began, sounding tinny to Bennet at this distance, but still spitting with anger as he demanded that Bennet call him back.

Darius passed back the phone, frowning. "Are you in some kind of trouble?"

"Sounds like it, but I don't know what or why. I spoke to him, and he insists on seeing me this afternoon. I need to get the next train."

"Okay." Darius was brisk. "Come in the house. We'll have some lunch, and I'll take you. Or have you eaten?"

Bennet gazed in through the window of the Audi. The passenger seat seemed to beckon. But . . .

"I should really go right now. He told me to call a cab." The words dragged on his lips.

Darius was brisk. "It'll be quicker if I drive you. Lunch won't take long—it's only salad. I don't eat a heavy meal before I climb. You can surely spare fifteen minutes?"

Bennet relaxed. A taxi would take more than fifteen minutes to get here. If they ate in that time and Darius dropped him at Sheffield station on his way to the Peak, he'd be there at the same time. He set his bag in the car, next to the ropes, and followed Darius through the sunny garden and into Peak Lodge.

The door was so low, he felt the beam brush the tips of his hair as he stepped into a hall as big as his parents' living room. The floor was dark oak, partly covered by a thin, faded carpet. A vase of dried flowers sat in the big open fireplace, and the bricks were sooty, as if they had real fires there in winter. But the room was dominated by oil paintings of people in old-fashioned clothes, some of them almost life-size, in massive gilt frames.

Darius crossed to the wooden stairs that twisted up in one corner and called, "G? Bennet's here. If you still want to be in charge of lunch, we need it now." A distant voice answered, and Darius went on up.

Bennet closed the front door and turned at the sound of someone coming down the stairs—Giorgio, whose face broke into a wide smile.

"Bennet! Come through, and don't let the forefathers overwhelm you." The boy waved a hand at the paintings. "This is nothing, really. We had tons more when we lived in the other place. These are just the ones that weren't worth selling because they aren't by anyone famous. They're his people, of course, not mine—his Lanniker and Darcy ancestors."

Bennet looked more closely at a young couple posed with a dog outside a vague, pale mass that must be Pemberley. The guy had a look of Darius—not so much in his features, but in the tall, spare figure and the tight control that gave the impression of arrogance at first glance.

"Except this one," Giorgio went on. "She's mine too."

Bennet followed him into the next room, where Giorgio pointed to a bright, modern picture of a laughing dark-haired girl in a white dress dotted with poppies.

"Our mother."

She looked no older than Bennet. Maybe she hadn't been, at the time. And gone now, leaving part of her dancing spirit in this picture and in her two sons.

What would she have thought of Bennet? Would she have cared what his parents did and where he went to school, or would she have looked beyond all that and seen the person inside?

They'd put her in a good place. Roses bloomed outside the window, and sunbeams danced through the leaded panes. An upright piano stood in another corner, with its lid up and music on the stand.

"Who plays that?"

"Darius. Hasn't he told you? He's good. He could have gone to music college, but there's more money in lawyering."

"Thank you for making me sound so mercenary," Darius said, coming in behind them with a bag that Bennet recognised from the day they'd climbed the cliffs in Brighton.

"Music was never more than a hobby. I thought you were getting lunch? Bennet's in a hurry."

"You said you weren't going until half past one," Giorgio protested.

"Change of plan."

They followed Darius through another door and down a step into a big kitchen with blackened beams and a stone-flagged floor. A wooden table that must have been twelve feet long stood in the centre of the room, with an old oak dresser against the wall beside it. Opposite was a fireplace that held a cast-iron stove.

Darius walked straight past the table and out of the back door. Giorgio opened the fridge, lifted out a quiche, and shook salad leaves into a bowl.

"How old is this house?" Bennet asked.

"We're not sure," Giorgio said. "It's a cool kitchen, isn't it? We think these walls are sixteenth-century, but the front rooms may be seventeenth. It's older than the big house, anyway. This was the main lodge for the old Pemberley manor house, which they knocked down in the eighteenth century to build the new place." He turned the salad and added, "I lived there when I was little, you know."

"In the big house?"

"Yes. But it was always so cold and scary. This one's much nicer."

So much for Wyndham's story of a bullied teenager imprisoned in a hovel.

When Darius returned, they sat around one end of the table and ate. Bennet's mind drifted back to Monsieur

Philippe's call. What could he want? Should Bennet phone him again from the train?

He was still distracted when they set off in the Audi. He'd wanted this journey to the station with Darius, and yet now he had nothing to say. His mind was blank, and his limbs felt stiff and awkward. He stared out of the window.

At first Darius took the same route as the bus, but after a while he stopped following the Sheffield signs. Bennet thought he must know a quicker way, a short cut, until they reached the M1 and Darius turned onto it.

Bennet stared at the blue sign: *The SOUTH*. "You're going the wrong way."

"I don't think so. Hertfordshire was south of here, last time I checked." Darius eased the Audi into the stream of traffic between two vans.

Bennet's heart thumped. "Aren't you taking me to Sheffield?"

"No, I'm taking you to Meriton. I told you I'd drive you home on my way to London, and that's what I'm doing."

"What about your climb?"

"I cancelled. No point going without you."

Of course, he'd missed the main climb with the club, and he couldn't go up alone. That would be what he meant. But the way he'd put it made Bennet's face feel unexpectedly warm.

Darius turned his head for a second. "Thank you for being so good with Giorgio. Most people aren't that relaxed around him."

Bennet shrugged. "I don't need thanks for that. I like

him. He's never going to be an average guy, but the world has plenty of those already."

"A *happy* guy is what I'd like him to be."

"He seems pretty happy."

Darius glanced up at the rearview mirror. "Yes, until something scares him, or worries him, or doesn't go his way."

"What did the therapist say yesterday?"

Bennet half expected Darius to tell him it was confidential, but he answered as if Bennet had a right to know. "She's not allowed to tell me much, but she said he's making progress . . . slowly."

"Maybe slow progress is the best kind. It gives him time to build on each step. He's less likely to be thrown back if something goes wrong."

"That's a good way to look at it."

Darius pulled into the fast lane. The motorway was busy, and this wouldn't be much quicker than taking the train. Or maybe it would, with the works on the rail line. No going back now, anyway.

Bennet was jittery. Nothing to do with Darius—he'd grown weirdly comfortable with Darius over this weekend. No, his nervousness was all to do with Monsieur Philippe and whatever was going on at college.

He'd have liked to tell Darius about it, if he could have done it without mentioning Wyndham. But what else was there to say? He knew so little. Wyndham's involvement was the big deal.

He watched the traffic go by until what started as an easy

silence had stretched out too long. Then, just for something to say, he asked, "What was that about the Parsons case last night?"

"I defended him. It was a brutal crime, but I don't believe he did it. He'd done some stupid things that put him in the frame, but he hadn't killed anybody, in my opinion."

"And you got him off?"

"I did. It hasn't made me popular in some circles. The community wanted someone convicted—never mind if it was the wrong person."

"So who was the real killer?"

"It's an open case. We may never know."

Another detail struggled up from Bennet's hazy memory. "Where did it happen?"

"The murder? In Brighton."

That was what he'd thought. His arms came up in goose bumps. Brighton, and the killer was still walking around. If Bennet had gone clubbing alone, if he'd gone home with some random guy . . .

Which hadn't happened because Darius had fucked up his weekend—or so Bennet had thought at the time. Who knew what he might have been saved from?

Silence fell again until Darius said, "Shall I entertain you with stories of my victories in court, like Othello?"

Othello? Shakespeare, right? How was that relevant? Should Bennet bluff it out, pretend he knew what the hell Darius was talking about?

No, he didn't have the energy. He didn't care if Darius saw how ignorant he was. He hadn't gone to some posh boarding school where the teachers had time for everyone, and the kids sat quietly and let a boy learn. He'd had to focus on the subjects that mattered to him and let the rest go.

"Was Othello a lawyer, then?"

"No, he was an army general." Darius didn't take his eyes off the road. "He wooed a beautiful girl by telling her about his battle victories. She must have been much younger than him, but she admired him so much, she fell in love and married him."

Like Annabel last night, hanging on Darius's words, except she wasn't that young.

Or wait, did he mean Bennet? He wanted to woo *Bennet* with his stories?

Bennet's breath caught. Darius checked the mirrors, indicated, changed lanes, all with no sign of emotion. No, couldn't be.

Anyway, wasn't *Othello* one of the tragedies? "It didn't end well, did it?"

"Unfortunately not. He never felt he was worthy of her. He thought he'd talked her into marrying him, and sooner or later she would regret it. So when somebody told him she was having an affair, he believed it on the flimsiest evidence and killed her." Darius glanced across and gave his wry smile. "Maybe it's better if I keep quiet."

Bennet laughed. It did sound like he meant something personal with all this. "Don't worry, Philippe's first in line for killing me."

But Darius shook his head and said no more.

They came to the Meriton exit sooner than Bennet expected. Too soon. He wished he could have the journey over again and tell Darius more of what he felt—about Pemberley, about Wyndham, about Jamie, about Darius himself, even. So much to say, but all so scrambled in his head, he couldn't find the place to start. If it came out wrong, Darius might misunderstand feelings that Bennet barely understood himself. And there was still Jamie to think about.

Darius slowed the car as they approached Longbourn Lane. "You live down here, don't you?"

"Yes, but could you take me to the college?" It would get him there quicker, and Jamie wouldn't see the car.

The silence between them grew heavy as they drove into the town. Bennet's limbs stiffened as they passed Tim's gallery. Back here, everything seemed awkward. Real life took over, separating him from the romance of Pemberley—and putting a wedge between him and Darius.

Philippe's car was in the college car park, along with a couple of others. Darius stopped the Audi outside the main doors.

Bennet cleared his throat. "Well, thank you for the ride, I appreciate it."

"You're welcome. Shall I wait? If it's something serious and you want advice when you've seen him—"

*Not if Wyndham's involved.* "No, I can call you if I need to."

"You still have my number?"

"Yes."

Darius's lips twitched. He hadn't missed the subtext. *Yes,*

*I told you I never wanted to see you again, but I didn't erase your number, and I know that for sure. I don't have to pull out my phone and check.*

"Don't hesitate to use it." Darius opened a small compartment in the dashboard. "Take this too. It has the office number on it."

He handed Bennet a card. Their fingers brushed and somehow got mixed up and hooked together, sending a warm glow up Bennet's arm. Not holding hands but linking fingers.

Darius's grip lasted long enough for Bennet to know it couldn't be accidental, and then he let go.

# Chapter Twenty-two

THE MAIN DOORS were locked, so Bennet walked around the building. Monsieur Philippe's office was on the ground floor. He could tap on the window.

A flowerbed was in his way, but he squeezed through rose bushes to reach the glass. They were both in there, Philippe and Nigel, standing on opposite sides of the room like antagonists. Arguing. The words weren't clear through the double glazing, but Bennet couldn't mistake the tone.

He knocked. Two pale, startled faces turned to the window. Philippe glared and tipped his head to the left, towards the side entrance to the kitchens. Bennet made his way there, wiping mud off his feet on the grass. Philippe stood back to let him in.

"What's all this about?" Bennet asked.

"You really don't know? You'll see soon enough." Monsieur Philippe's jaw was set, his lips tight. He turned his back and led the way to his office without another word. Bennet closed the side door and followed.

"Hi," Bennet said to Nigel. Nigel nodded to him without speaking. He stood apart from Philippe as if a chasm had opened up in the floor between them.

Philippe picked up a tablet, tapped the screen, and handed

it to Bennet. A video began to play.

Two guys in a dark corner, kissing. Actors? He didn't recognise them. Wait, he did. They were students. One of them was in Jamie's class. A smooth voice started up—Wyndham's voice.

"For centuries, gay men led disadvantaged lives—but have the tables now turned?"

The video changed to show the back of the college and the lawn, the shot they used for the TV series, with a title superimposed: *Bridgemaston Gays*.

Bennet spluttered.

"You think it's funny?" Philippe's voice was dangerously high.

"It's a joke, isn't it?"

"Is that what you thought? Is that why you got involved?" Nigel pounced on Bennet's words as if they excused him.

Bennet's hands clenched on the tablet. "Involved? I'm not involved. I've never seen this before."

"It's no joke," Philippe said. "Keep watching."

The camera moved inside the college, showing Philippe at his most pompous, frowning down his nose at a female student, then bending to admire the work—and possibly the lower body—of a male student. Unfair, but Bennet couldn't hold back a quick grin.

The voice went on: "Are the powerful connections of the gay subculture, formed for protection when it was needed, now being used to dominate and exclude women and straight men?"

Now it showed Leon—Leon and Kofi, eating, drinking, and cuddling at Nigel's dining table, and Nigel looking on. Just for a second, but spliced to make his kind face look like a voyeur's. Bennet's mouth dropped open. What the fuck was this?

"We go behind the scenes of one of the most respected institutions in the hotel and catering industry to expose the prejudice, bias, and corruption at the heart of our vocational education system."

Bias and corruption? At Meriton College? Was that what it meant?

The video ended. Bennet looked up. "Where's the rest?"

Monsieur Philippe took the tablet from him. "So you know there's more?"

"I don't *know*. I'm guessing, because there's nothing to this. A few students kissing. So what?"

"That's just a trailer," Nigel said. "Philippe's seen the whole thing. It is what it says: an exposé, so-called, designed to destroy the reputation of the college—and destroy Philippe."

Philippe looked as haggard as if his destruction was halfway complete already. Bennet felt bad for him, but he didn't get why he'd been summoned back from Pemberley. "What does this have to do with me?"

"This man Moorhouse can't have done it alone," Philippe said. "He hasn't been following me around the college with a camera. I'd have noticed. Someone inside must have helped him."

"He could have set up a surveillance system," Bennet

said. Like he'd done with Giorgio.

"No. Some shots literally follow me. The camera is moving. Anyway, how would he know what to film? What gave him the idea—or rather, *who* gave him the idea?" Philippe stared at Bennet, his scowl an accusation.

Bennet took a step back and put his hands up. "Not me. I barely know him."

"Ha! *Barely* is the word." Philippe gave a bitter laugh.

"You're in it," Nigel said. "Having sex with him—at least, it might be him. It's definitely you."

Bennet was in the video? Having sex with Wyndham? None of this made sense.

"That's not possible. It must be faked. I haven't had sex with him. I haven't had sex with anybody for—I don't know. Months." Which was none of their business, but this felt surreal.

Philippe said, "It doesn't show actual sex, but you're stripped down to your underpants, discussing condoms."

Oh, no. Bennet went cold. Wyndham messing with his phone, wanting the bright overhead light. They'd gone no further, but anybody seeing that would think they had.

And Bennet had wanted to. He'd *liked* Wyndham. He'd trusted him. He'd taken his word over Darius's.

"The bastard. I can't believe he'd do this." But deep down, he did believe it. His heart was thumping. Wyndham had tricked him, used him. "What's the point of it? Is he trying to blackmail you?"

"No, he's trying to sell it to a television company," Philippe said.

"This is going to be on national television?"

"Apparently. We only heard about it because it crossed the desk of someone at the BBC who knows the principal from a film that was shot here a few years ago. They gave the principal the access code so he could watch it, and he called me in this morning."

"You mean the *college* principal? He's seen me—He's seen it all?"

"Oh yes," Philippe said.

"Philippe's job's on the line," Nigel put in. "They've hinted at early retirement."

"Hinted strongly," Philippe said. "And for me it would be preferable to a long and stressful inquiry, with or without dismissal at the end of it."

Bennet shook his head. "That's crazy. You *are* this college."

"Kind of you to say so, but some people wish I wasn't." Philippe sat down in his swivel chair and made a steeple of his fingers. "So you're denying involvement in this? You didn't help him?"

"No. No way." Bennet turned to Nigel—Nigel, whose house he'd lived in for two academic years. "How could you believe I'd do that?"

Nigel threw out his hands. "Philippe thinks it must have been one of my tenants. There's so much footage of you all. You in your room, Kofi and Leon in one of theirs—that's even more explicit."

The bank robber session. It hadn't been for porn—it had been for this.

"And there's a whole scene filmed in the dining room the day the Moorhouse man came to lunch," Nigel went on.

Monsieur Philippe's lips tightened. This was evidently why they'd been arguing. Philippe accusing, Nigel defending "his" boys.

"I didn't have anything to do with this," Bennet insisted.

Nigel ignored him. His hands were shaking. "Moorhouse has edited his conversation with me to give the impression that Philippe and I are using Philippe's position to fill my house with handsome young men to satisfy our middle-aged urges. I'm apparently conspiring with Philippe and the college administration to make extortionate profits by renting rooms in my house—as if the college wasn't leafleting the whole town begging householders to find beds for you all. I only do it to help out. I don't even charge as much as the college suggests!"

Nigel's voice rose high. Philippe held up a hand to calm him. Nigel turned back to Bennet.

"Charlotte wasn't there that day. Did he make a point of coming when she was away, so it would look like I only have male students, or was his lucky star shining on him?"

"I don't know. I didn't invite him."

"Then who did? I wasn't expecting him. Nobody told me he was coming."

Bennet struggled to remember. "I think he invited himself."

"He must have arranged it with somebody," Nigel said.

"Leon?" Philippe asked.

"It could have been," Bennet said. Yes, Leon had told

Wyndham he could come. But that didn't mean Leon would have followed Monsieur Philippe round the college with a camera.

Nigel turned to Philippe. "Leon would have done anything to be an extra in *Bridgemaston Days.*"

"Yes, but he never *was* in it, was he?" Bennet said. "If he'd helped with this, he'd have had his reward. And he's not great at keeping secrets. If he knew someone was filming an undercover documentary, he'd have dropped so many hints it would have been all over college in no time. Anyway, you're misjudging him. Leon's sound."

"Then how did this Wyndham Moorhouse hear about us?" Nigel said. "And how did he know there was anything between Philippe and me?"

Bennet's heart sank. "That might have been my fault. It was totally unintentional. I brought him back once. We didn't have sex."

"I really don't care if you did," said Philippe.

"Whatever," Bennet said, his temper rising. Philippe wouldn't take his word for anything! "He asked me a lot of questions about you and the house. He must have been pumping me for information. I'm sorry, okay? I had no idea he'd use it this way."

Maybe Wyndham had never wanted to have sex. Wasn't attracted to him. Used his nice-guy looks to have himself invited back to the house, where he got the information he wanted, took the shots of Bennet half-naked, then staged the whole condom thing to give him an excuse to leave.

Bennet clenched his fists. "There must be some way you

can stop it. Doesn't he need consent to broadcast this?"

Nigel clasped his hands together. "He has it. That's the whole problem. When he came to the house, he told me he was taking pictures for a freelance spread he planned to pitch to magazines. I've looked at my copy of the document I signed, and it doesn't limit him to still photos. And at lunch, don't you remember how he said he had a camera in his bag and we could all be in *Bridgemaston Days?* Or did he say *Bridgemaston Gays*, I wonder? Leon was all over him, and the rest of us thought he was joking. Certainly none of us objected. That could be taken as permission, and he'll have it all recorded on camera."

Bennet's legs wobbled as if the ground was shaking beneath them. None of this seemed real. He turned to Monsieur Philippe. "*You* surely didn't give him permission."

"It seems I did, and you were there," Philippe said. "You've been everywhere these things have happened."

Bennet opened his mouth to deny it, but the scene sprang into his head before he could speak. That day in the training restaurant, over the spilled lentils. Wyndham with papers in his hand, pressing Philippe to sign.

"Plenty of other people were there too," he said. Who were they? He thought back. "Richard Jones, for example. I was just following along—I'd come from your office with you. But he was in the restaurant creating havoc, making the mess worse, putting you under pressure so you'd sign without reading every page."

"Richard Jones?"

"Yes." The more Bennet thought about it, the more

certain he was. "Remember his 'gay mafia' comment? I can imagine him and Wyndham cooking up this plan over a pint in a pub."

But Philippe put his head in his hands. "Then there's nothing we can do. If it had been you, we could have shown you it wasn't in your interest to let this go out, and maybe we'd have found a solution. But Richard's not gay. He won't be touched by it, and we can't touch him."

"But that's crazy. That's totally unfair. Can't you threaten to expel him for... for bringing the college into disrepute?"

Philippe shook his head. "*I* can't expel anybody. You overestimate my power—as your Wyndham has done."

"He's not *my* Wyndham."

Philippe dismissed that with a wave of his hand. "The college won't discipline Richard, even if we were sure it was him. There'd be no point. He'd have the right to come back to take his exams, so what would he lose? It would only add fuel to the conspiracy theories. Can't you see the headlines? 'College expels whistle-blower.' No. And I'm not going begging to him."

"I wasn't asking you to."

"And *you* won't tackle him either." Monsieur Philippe turned steely eyes on Bennet as if he could see the resentment bubbling in his chest. Bennet didn't know where Richard Jones lived, but he could find out. He'd like to go round there and punch him in the face. It wouldn't solve anything, but it would make Bennet feel better.

Philippe added, "I don't want you making this worse.

You're not to say anything to Richard or to anyone else in the college."

"Give him your word, Bennet, please," Nigel said.

Bennet's fist thumped the side of Philippe's desk. He'd like to do that to Richard's head. And he hated having to keep secrets, but who would he tell? "Okay."

"You'd better go." Philippe looked exhausted. He turned to Nigel. "You too."

Nigel moved closer to him and asked in a low voice, "What will you do?"

"I don't know. Retire, I suppose."

Bennet hesitated in the doorway. Philippe said, "Are you still here?"

"I just want to check . . . You believe me, that I wasn't involved?"

"I wouldn't say you weren't *involved*, from what you've said. You had a part in it, didn't you?" Philippe gestured at the door. "Just go."

---

BENNET'S FEET CRUNCHED over gravel, his mind whirling with things he'd like to do or say, to Richard, to Monsieur Philippe, to Wyndham. He leaned on the side of the bike shelter, looking at the abandoned bikes in the otherwise empty racks. Where was his? At home, of course, because Darius had brought him.

He couldn't have cycled with this heavy bag, anyway. He shifted it to his other shoulder and started walking, heading for the path to Longbourn.

If this broadcast went out, everyone in the industry would watch it. How could he hold up his head in interviews after that? If he got a job, how would he feel at work? How could he face the snickering, the loaded questions?

Only one person had to recognise him half naked with Wyndham for his name to be all over social media, to haunt him for the rest of his career. And even if that didn't happen, he'd always have the college's name on his record.

Meriton College meant something in the hotel and catering industry. Mentioning it in a job application had always been a plus point. Donna Clare at Distinctivent had offered him an interview on the strength of it.

Not any more. That reputation would be shot to shit as soon as Wyndham's show aired. And if Bennet got the distinction he hoped for, people wouldn't know if he'd deserved it. They'd wonder if Philippe had favoured him because he was gay.

Richard Jones wouldn't suffer. He had a job lined up in Dubai, and a British television documentary couldn't touch him there. Maybe he was even proud of his part in it. But the rest of them—what would it do to their career prospects?

As for Monsieur Philippe... Nigel was right, it would destroy him. They'd make him retire, and all his experience, all his energy, would be lost to the industry. Okay, he could be pompous at times, but he was a great teacher. It hurt to think of everybody laughing behind Philippe's back, of his department's reputation crumbling to dust.

And some of it *was* Bennet's fault. He'd been so eager to hear Wyndham's tales about Darius, he hadn't considered what he was revealing in return.

Flames of humiliation and fury flared in his chest. How had he ever fallen for Wyndham's bullshit? The man had a nice smile, so he had to be a nice guy? Please. A ten-year-old could have seen past that.

Wyndham, with his cute puppy-dog look. Wyndham, who'd tricked his own young brother into losing his virginity on camera—no question about who to believe on that story now.

Bennet gritted his teeth. He'd been such a fool. He'd prided himself on his cleverness, thinking he knew what was what. He'd disliked Darius because Darius hadn't fallen at his feet the first time they met, and he'd trusted Wyndham because he had charm. And all the time Darius was the honest man.

Darius could be infuriating, and he'd messed with people's lives in a way he had no right to do, but he'd always told the truth as he saw it. While Wyndham . . .

That night when Bennet had brought Wyndham home from Rush, who'd picked up whom? Bennet might have made the first move, but Wyndham had obviously recognised him from that day in the college restaurant. In the club he'd made eye contact, and when Bennet had approached him, Wyndham had started straight in with questions about Monsieur Philippe.

And Bennet had listened to Wyndham not because he'd liked him so much, but because he'd disliked Darius. The more vicious Wyndham's stories were, the happier Bennet had been to believe them.

Now look where his prejudices had got him. He'd landed a starring role in the movie that could destroy his career before it had even begun.

# Chapter Twenty-three

THE LIGHT OF dawn showed through his curtains before Bennet fell asleep that night. When he woke, he was lying on something that stuck to his skin. He reached under his ribs and fished it out—Darius's card.

Memories flooded back. Sometime in the night he'd switched on the light, fetched the card from the pocket of his jacket, and lain in bed stroking it with his fingertips like a kid with a crush. His face grew warm at the thought of it.

He stared at the digits of Darius's office number. Darius had offered advice. He wished he could take it, but how could Darius help? This wasn't illegal, like the video of Giorgio.

Or was it? Bennet had never consented to being filmed in his bedroom. Maybe Darius could use that to stop the thing being shown on TV? No, Wyndham would just edit Bennet out of it, or not even that. *Sue me*, he'd say. Wyndham would love a court case—awesome publicity. Then Bennet's name would be all over everywhere, which would be worse... if he could even afford to sue, which he couldn't.

He passed the phone from one hand to the other. What was he thinking? Darius mustn't know anything about this.

And there was a chance he wouldn't, as long as Bennet kept quiet and didn't ask for his help. Darius hadn't heard of *Bridgemaston Days* until he came to Meriton. He'd told Leon he didn't spend his evenings watching TV.

But if Bennet involved him, he'd have to see it. Then he'd think Bennet had had sex with Wyndham and lied about it in that text he'd sent after Darius's voice mail. Or even if he didn't think that, he'd still have seen Bennet doing something he now regretted deeply.

And that bothered Bennet. He was surprised to find how much. It mattered to him way more than it would have before this second trip to Pemberley. Darius had got under his skin in the last few days. Bennet cared what Darius thought of him now, cared so much that he felt a pain in his gut.

And Darius wasn't the only person he cared about. What about his family? He got out of bed and paced around the room. Darius might not watch TV, but they did. Marlon would never let him live this down.

And his mum—his poor mum, so proud of her first and fatherless son, boasting to her friends about Bennet being at the college that was used for *Bridgemaston Days*. He imagined her seeing a trailer, a shot of the building she knew so well from her favourite show, and settling down to watch the documentary.

"It's about Bennet's college," she'd say to his dad and Marlon. "He might even be in it!"

They'd grumble, but they'd flop down on the couch with her, if they were home. And then what would they see, and how would she feel? She'd shrink to nothing as she watched. If Monsieur Philippe would never get over it, nor would Bennet's mum.

God, it made his blood boil. He slammed his fist into the wall. Pain blasted his hand, adding fuel to the smouldering rage in his chest. He couldn't sit here and let this happen.

He stood before the open window, blind to the world outside. Darius knew the law and he knew Wyndham. He was their best hope. Bennet had two options: he could put this in Darius's hands, or he could do nothing.

Going to Darius would cost him his pride but not much else. If Darius never wanted to see Bennet again, what difference did it make? Nothing could happen between them anyway, because of Jamie.

But what would he say if he called Darius? What did he really know? He'd only seen that trailer. He couldn't give Darius access to the documentary or even tell him much about what was in it.

Someone else would be able to, though, someone who knew more—Philippe or the college principal.

If Bennet put Darius in touch with them, it would be out of his control, which he didn't like. He wouldn't know what was happening—he might never know. And it wouldn't necessarily help. There might be nothing Darius could do.

But Bennet couldn't fix this by himself. If he wanted any part in putting things right, he'd have to suck it up and let Darius find out. His limbs felt like lead at the thought of it, but he had to try, for the college, for Monsieur Philippe, for his mum.

At least he could put in a word for himself first. He picked up his phone and found Darius in his contacts. His fingers trembled as they typed the text: *You may see something with me and Wyndham. It isn't how it looks.*

Bennet dressed, showered, and checked his phone, but there was no answer. Not surprising. Darius would be working at this time on a Monday. He'd be in a meeting, in court, whatever. No point waiting for a reply—he could be hours. Bennet needed to do this before he changed his mind.

He jogged down the stairs and out to his bicycle, then pedalled fast through the lanes to the college.

---

THE DEPARTMENT SECRETARY told him Monsieur Philippe was in a meeting in the principal's office. "Come back later," she said.

He could have used that as an excuse to delay, but he'd burned his bridges when he texted Darius. Even as he told her he'd be back at lunchtime, he knew he had to act now.

He went on towards the principal's suite. The corridors were empty—everyone was in class. His shoes rang so loudly on the tiled floor that he had to resist the urge to walk on tiptoes.

His phone buzzed as he approached the office. Darius. Bennet's hands felt stiff and his mouth was dry. He opened the text: *Message received.*

He had to laugh. Anyone else would have asked what the hell Bennet meant, but not Darius. He didn't question it, but he didn't say anything reassuring either. Totally noncommittal.

*Okay.* Bennet took a deep breath and pushed open the door to the large outer office. "Excuse me, I need to see Philippe Hennice. I think he's with the principal? It's urgent."

The principal's PA typed a few more words and clicked her mouse before she swivelled her chair around to face him. "What's the emergency?"

"It's not an emergency, exactly. I have some information related to what they're talking about."

"And what's that? What are they discussing?"

"It's connected with filming in the college."

She stared at him for a moment, then looked at her watch. "All right. Coffee should be coming in five minutes. When I take it in, I'll let Mr. Hennice know you're here. What's your name?"

"Bennet Rourke."

He sat down to wait on one of three low chairs. Magazines lay on a low table, and butterflies fluttered in his stomach. It felt like being at the dentist's, only worse.

Wheels squeaked and crockery rattled in the corridor outside. Bennet jumped up and held the door for the catering student pushing a trolley laden with tea, coffee, and biscuits.

The principal's PA got up and said, "That's fine, thanks. I'll take it from here," and the student left. Bennet stood to help with the inner door, but the principal's PA waved him away as if she suspected him of trying to follow her inside.

He sat down again on the edge of his chair.

A few seconds later, Philippe came out alone, closing the door behind him. He looked smaller, hunched and haggard. His face was lined and weary, his brows drawn together in a frown.

"Bennet. What is it?"

Bennet stood up. "I think I know someone who can help."

Philippe sighed and crossed the office to another door, marked *Vice Principal*.

"Come in here. The VP's with the principal."

Bennet followed him in. The office was gloomy, its blind closed against the sun.

Philippe shut the door firmly behind him and said in a low, angry voice, "I was told you were here about the filming. You're not supposed to know, remember?"

"You can say I heard about it from Wyndham."

"I'll have to." Philippe stood beside the VP's desk, tapping his fingers on a filing cabinet. "So who's this person who can help? Who's the good fairy who's going to wave a magic wand and make everything all right? Be quick. I don't want them making decisions without me, although they will anyway. They're taking no notice of anything I say."

Bennet had prepared a whole speech while he waited, but it fled from his mind under the stress of Philippe's scowl. "It's Darius Lanniker. He's a barrister."

"Lanniker? I know the name."

"You met him at the opening of the art gallery. He knows Wyndham—"

"The owner of Pemberley. Of course." Monsieur Philippe rubbed his forehead. "But they're related, aren't they? We can't use him. He's more likely to be acting for Moorhouse."

Bennet's words rushed out. "No, he'd never help Wyndham. He's come up against him before in a similar situation. I can't give you the details, but Wyndham filmed somebody without their knowledge and was planning to sell the video, and Darius stopped him. He'd do it again if he could. I think he'd be glad to. The college could negotiate through him, offer Wyndham money—buy the rights or something. There'd be a cost, but it would be worth it to keep the college's reputation."

But Philippe shook his head. "This is a publicly funded institution. We can't instruct random barristers to bribe Moorhouse, which is what you're suggesting, isn't it? Everything has to go through the proper channels, and every penny must be accounted for. The county solicitor's in there with the principal and the VP now."

Bennet's heart sank. "So what are they planning to do?"

"Approach Moorhouse, threatening to ask the courts for an injunction to delay the broadcast until he makes some edits. They're hoping he'll do the edits without going to court."

"He won't," Bennet said.

"Of course he won't." Philippe paced back and forth around the desk. "The question, as I see it, is whether an injunction is worthwhile for us. We could probably achieve some cuts, and the college would win the right to make its own statement at the end. But that won't help me, and I don't believe it will help the college."

He walked to the window and pulled the cord of the blind to let in some light. "I think it would be better to let it go out as it is. It's so obviously biased that the major TV channels will turn it down, and it won't be taken seriously in the catering industry. We don't want to end up with something that's still crushing but appears fair. But I can't make the principal or the county solicitor see that. They're talking about damage limitation. They think if I resign, the reputation of the college as a whole will survive." Philippe shrugged. "They may be right."

"No," Bennet said. "They're wrong."

"*Whatever*, as you students are so fond of saying. They won't listen to you. They won't even listen to me. I'm too *emotionally involved*, apparently." Monsieur Philippe turned away from the window. His cheeks sagged and his eyes were bloodshot. "I must get back in there."

Bennet took a step forward. "Darius would help you. He'd advise you, at least—you personally, if the principal isn't interested."

He held out Darius's crumpled card. Philippe took it, frowning.

"It's worth a phone call, isn't it?" Bennet said.

"Perhaps." Philippe sounded dismissive, but he put the card in his top pocket before he went back to the meeting.

# Chapter Twenty-four

TENSION HUNG IN the college corridors like fog. The pressure of it weighed Bennet down. Most of the staff and students had no idea of the threat that hung over the place—for them, all the stress was about the coming exams—but Bennet felt something extra, as if the ceilings were heavy with shame.

Monsieur Philippe did call Darius, then went to London to see him. Nigel went with him, which was how Bennet heard. The next day, all Nigel would say was that Darius had made no promises.

The next weekend passed with no news. Charlotte was away again, Jamie was monosyllabic, and Kofi and Leon had taken to cavorting naked in the garden under the lawn sprinkler. Bennet's mind wouldn't focus on his books between shifts at the Black Lion, so he cycled in loops around the town.

The following Tuesday, he ate lunch in the training restaurant with Charlotte. She went up to the hot food counter while he found a table. He'd brought sandwiches from Longbourn.

"Don't tell me," she said, looking at his plastic box. "Peanut butter and cucumber?"

Bennet took his first mouthful, crunching the cucumber. "Call it comfort eating if you want. I think I'm entitled."

She assumed he meant the exams. "At least it's HR first. They're easing us in gently . . . which of course you'd know about."

She waggled her eyebrows at him. He didn't react. She stirred sauce into her pasta. It smelled good, but it looked overcooked. Bennet was happy with his sandwich.

"You'll never guess who I saw at Longbourn last week," Charlotte said.

Bennet stopped chewing. Wyndham? No, Charlotte didn't know him. Darius? His heart thumped. "Who?"

"The residential partner from Credlands."

His shoulders relaxed and he swallowed. "So what?"

"So Nigel's having the house valued, that's what! He must be thinking of selling. Can you imagine, after the way he talks about all the generations of his family who've lived and died there? I thought Monsieur Philippe would move in when he retired, and they'd spend the twilight of their years in blissful togetherness, pruning the roses and adopting a houseful of cats, with no more noisy students to cause havoc in their lives. Didn't you?"

This didn't sound good. He watched her twirl spaghetti onto her fork. "Perhaps he's having it valued for insurance."

She shook her head. "You need a building surveyor for an insurance valuation. Residential agents only deal with sales and lettings."

Then they must be thinking of making an offer to Wyndham. Bennet put down his sandwich. His stomach was in knots at the thought of Nigel selling his beautiful old house and Wyndham getting all the money.

"How much do you think it's worth?"

Charlotte pursed her lips. "One and a half million? More, maybe. Properties of that age don't often come on the market."

"Jesus." They couldn't give Wyndham all that . . . could they?

"Maybe he's only planning to let it," Charlotte went on. "But either way it means Nigel's moving out. I bet he and Philippe have had a massive fight and he can't bear to live in Meriton any more. Haven't you noticed how devastated they're both looking?"

Bennet didn't correct her.

He tried to speak to Nigel that night, but his landlord waved him away.

"Stay out of this now," Nigel said. "Philippe's seen your friend Lanniker, and Lanniker's doing what he can."

"But I didn't mean *you* should pay for it!"

"Perhaps I want to. Now run along. It's out of your hands."

Out of his hands? Yes, and that was the problem. What had he unleashed? He didn't want Wyndham walking off with over a million pounds. Damn Darius and his negotiating skills, if that was what they achieved. Bennet wished he'd never mentioned the man's name.

The nights were warm and he was restless, kicking off his quilt and pulling it back, searching for a cool spot to lie on. Whenever he felt close to dropping into slumber or fantasy,

Wyndham would come back into his mind, making his fists thump the mattress and his sweat-coated legs thrash against the sheets. The sky lightened early so close to summer solstice, and daylight often came before he slept.

His last shift in the training restaurant was dinner on Friday of that week. Term would continue into July, but his class would finish earlier. How long would the restaurant survive if Monsieur Philippe left? Without his dedication, its reputation in the town would fall, and soon it might be nothing more than a lunchtime cafeteria. The end of an era was coming, and nobody seemed to know it but Bennet... and Richard Jones.

Richard was maître d' this evening. Bennet, as sommelier, had planned to stay out of Richard's way. He took an order for a bottle of Burgundy and went to the cellar to fetch it. But when he turned back to take the wine to the diners, Richard was lounging against the door, blocking his exit.

"Got a job yet?" Richard's smile was wide, but his eyes flashed with malice.

Bennet had heard nothing from Pemberley Hall. He'd made a couple of other applications but still had no offers. "Why should you care?"

Richard put his hands up in front of his chest, as if to ward Bennet off. "Whoa, just being friendly."

*Yeah, right.* Bennet took out the cellar keys. "Excuse me, I need to lock up and serve this wine."

Richard shrank against the doorframe with one arm across it. He was tall, so there was space for Bennet to pass, but not without coming too close for comfort. Their HR courses taught that a move like that could lead to claims of sexual harassment, but Richard's motives with him weren't sexual.

Bennet squeezed through the gap without meeting Richard's gaze. His elbow "accidentally" jabbed Richard's ribs.

Richard whispered, "Wearing your Calvin Kleins tonight?"

He'd been wearing CK underpants that night with Wyndham. So Richard had seen the video. He couldn't know it would mean anything to Bennet now, but clearly he wanted Bennet to remember this moment when it was broadcast.

Bennet took a deep breath, waited for Richard to move aside so he could lock the door, then walked away as if he hadn't heard.

He delivered the Burgundy to a well-groomed man and woman who were holding hands across the table. The woman's face and neck glowed cherry-pink with sunburn. Bennet let them taste the wine, then poured for them.

He glanced up and saw two older men coming in. He blinked. Nigel and Philippe? They never ate here together—another of Philippe's rules for not mixing his private and his professional life. But here they were, standing with stiff determination at the maître d's station, while Richard's flustered hands turned over the reservation sheet.

Richard seated them and took their wine order himself. He approached Bennet and said with a sneer, "Champagne for table twenty-six."

Bennet's heart pounded. Champagne? Darius must have

reached a settlement with Wyndham. He glanced over at the table. Nigel winked.

"They may regret that," Richard added. "You've all got a little surprise coming."

*Or you may have a long wait for something that's never going to happen,* thought Bennet. But what had it cost Nigel and Philippe?

He fetched the champagne—the college's most expensive vintage—but they said nothing as he opened and poured it, and in his role, he couldn't ask.

---

NIGEL SPENT FRIDAY and Saturday nights at Philippe's. Bennet had to wait until Sunday morning to speak to him, and then they only had a moment alone in the dining room while Bennet laid the table for lunch.

Nigel was gleeful. "Moorhouse has been arrested. He'd been supplying underage porn. The police have impounded all his equipment. Of course he might not be convicted, and we don't know what will happen to the film about the college, but no reputable television company will be interested after this. Such a lucky coincidence!"

That wasn't luck. Darius must have tipped off the police. Had Giorgio agreed to give evidence? No, the footage of him hadn't survived. But Bennet was certain Darius had made this happen.

"I'd told Philippe all I had was his, including the house, and I meant it, but I must admit I'm relieved we won't have to sell," Nigel went on. "We haven't had to pay a penny.

Darius Lanniker didn't charge for his time. I suppose Moorhouse was arrested before he could begin negotiations. And Philippe won't have to retire. Isn't that wonderful?"

Before Bennet could answer, Charlotte came in and announced she was getting married.

To Callum.

Bennet's jaw dropped.

Nigel clapped his hands with glee. "Wonderful! We'll celebrate at lunchtime. Now, how are those boys getting on?"

He went out to the kitchen, and Bennet told Charlotte, "You have to be out of your mind."

She shrugged. "He'll be a good father."

"*Father*? You're not—"

She nodded. "Must have happened the first time, or almost."

"Oh my God."

"Shh, I don't want everyone to know. It's not due until next year."

Engaged *and* pregnant? It didn't seem real.

Nigel came back, looking for his keys. Bennet shook his head at Charlotte and went into the kitchen, where Leon was preparing lunch with help from Kofi and Jamie.

Leon slid a side of salmon out of the oven and turned back the foil to give it a final baste.

"Wow," Bennet said. "Is that genetically modified?"

"I know, massive, right?" Kofi said. "I did tell him there are only six of us, but he's, like, 'No, got to have the biggest.'"

Leon snickered. "In all things. Bennet, since you're here, you can make yourself useful. Wash this green stuff for the salad."

Bennet took the pack of leaves to the sink. At the counter beside him, Jamie was arranging chocolate shavings around halved blueberries on the smooth surface of a cheesecake.

"That looks amazing," Bennet said.

"Charlotte's request." Jamie stood back to assess his work. "It's done. Can I wash my hands?"

"Sure." Bennet pulled handfuls of leaves out of the water, shook them, and dropped them into a salad bowl.

Leon slapped his hand. "Don't put it in yet. It's too wet." Kofi snorted with laughter.

Bennet sighed. Everything was a dirty joke to these guys. "So where's the whizzer thing?"

Leon danced around the table, singing, "My whizzer thing, my whizzer thing, I want you to play with my whizzer thing!"

The doorbell rang.

"You know what I mean," Bennet said. "The salad spinner."

"I'll get it." Jamie finished drying his hands. He dropped the towel on the counter and went out into the hall. He'd meant the door, not the salad spinner.

Bennet found what he needed in a cupboard full of baking tins. The spinner was the old-fashioned kind with no outer bowl, so he dumped the wet leaves in it and headed out into the garden.

He stood near Nigel's roses and spun the wire cage above his head, sending a fine spray over the peach-coloured blossoms and their glossy dark leaves. The sun burned in a cloudless June sky, bees buzzed around the flowers, and butterflies zigzagged out of the way of this unexpected man-made rain. He switched arms—not that the weight of the lettuce would have any effect on his muscles, but out of habit—and turned his face up to bask in the heat.

"That's enough!" Leon yelled through the kitchen window. "We don't want sun-dried lettuce, thank you!"

Bennet whistled as he walked back inside and shook the leaves into the bowl. He still had no job, and if Charlotte and Callum were adding to the world's population he'd have no chance of getting any money out of Callum, ever. But he'd mostly given up on that already, and he wished them well. Other things were more important.

Wyndham had been arrested. The college would keep its reputation, Nigel would keep his house, Monsieur Philippe would continue to teach, and Bennet's mum would stay happy and proud of her firstborn son. If the path ahead of Bennet himself wasn't clear, he should see that as an opportunity. The last few months had been weird, but he could put them behind him and move on.

Kofi added avocado, tomatoes, and peppers to the bowl. No cucumber. Good. The place for cucumber was between two slices of bread, with a salty, crunchy peanut butter coating.

Bennet smiled to himself and wandered into the dining room, where Nigel was pouring wine and Charlotte hovered over the table. She waved away a glass of wine, poured herself some water, and grabbed a piece of bread. "I'm starving."

Bennet winked at her. "Guess why."

"Shh."

Kofi came in holding the bowl of salad up high, like an offering. Leon followed, pink from the heat of the oven. They took their places.

"Where's Jamie?" asked Charlotte.

Bennet hadn't seen him since he went to answer the doorbell. "I'll fetch him." He slipped up the stairs to knock on Jamie's bedroom door. No answer. He knocked again, then peeped in. Nobody there.

Back downstairs, Bennet checked the living room. Empty. He began to worry. Jamie must have gone out—not a good sign. He might not be eating much these days, but he was always at the table for Sunday lunch.

Bennet opened the front door. Jamie couldn't have gone far. His bicycle was still there, propped against the garden fence.

One door was left—Nigel's parlour. Bennet opened it, and there they were, Jamie and Tim, standing in the middle of the gloomy room with its antique furniture and unopened curtains, locked together in the world's deepest kiss.

Bennet's first thought was Darius. Where Tim went, there Darius would be, right? But not this time. No strong, slim figure lurked in a corner.

Bennet cleared his throat. Loudly.

Jamie turned and gazed at him as if from another world. His lips were swollen and the light was back in his eyes. Tim went on kissing his ear, his temple, his neck.

"What's this?" Bennet said.

"Tim's back," Jamie said.

"Right, but . . ." Bennet cleared his throat again. When that didn't get Tim's attention, he said, "Tim?"

Tim turned to face him without letting go of Jamie. His face was as blissed out as Jamie's.

Something told Bennet he was wasting his time, but he said, "You can't just walk back in here as if nothing's happened. Where the fuck have you been for the past two months?"

"I misunderstood," Tim said. "I've said I'm sorry. I'll make it up to him."

"Yeah, but—"

"I love him," Tim added. "I've never stopped thinking about him, not for a minute."

"He's told me all this, Bennet," Jamie said.

"And Jamie's agreed to marry me," Tim added.

What could Bennet say? They stood there, the two of them, united. It was what he'd wanted for Jamie, but he'd never thought it would make him feel so . . . alone.

Kofi appeared in the doorway. His jaw dropped, but he recovered faster than Bennet had. "Luncheon is served, gentlemen."

---

KOFI LAID A place for Tim next to Jamie's and found an extra chair. They sat with barely room to pass a sheet of paper between their shoulders, and their hands brushed every few seconds. Nigel's eyes were damp with emotion.

Tim fed Jamie morsels of avocado and salmon from his own fork. He must have felt how thin Jamie was. But whose fault was that? Tim's. And now Tim was back, Jamie accepted every mouthful as if it were a gift from the gods. Unfair.

When Jamie got up to find another dessert because there was wheat in the cheesecake base and Tim couldn't eat it, Bennet followed him.

"I hope you had him crawling on the floor before you forgave him," he said.

Jamie laughed. "You don't need to give him such a hard time. It wasn't all his fault. I never showed him how I felt—I waited for him to say everything first."

"Except when you texted him a hundred times and he never replied."

"It wasn't a hundred times. Five, max, and he didn't even see all of them, because Quentin had his phone. Anyway, those messages were just, like, 'Are you okay?' Not 'I love you, I miss you, please come home.' I see how he misunderstood." Jamie crushed blueberries with a fork and stirred in some yogurt. "I'll talk to him properly this afternoon and make sure we're on the same page. We both have to learn to discuss these things instead of hoping and assuming."

"But you've already said you'll marry him?"

"Yes, because I know we can work it out. Everything's good now. I can feel it." Jamie touched Bennet's shoulder. "Do you think you could stop scowling at him and be happy for me?"

"I *am* happy for you." And he was, by the end of the meal. He couldn't hold a grudge against Tim when the two of them looked like the poster couple for St. Valentine.

After lunch, Nigel excused the lovers from any part in the cleaning up. They vanished down the front path to Tim's Lotus, hand in hand. Nobody had mentioned Darius.

Bennet cleared the dining room. Kofi stacked the dishwasher. Leon, the cook, had done his work and lay outside in the sun.

"Coffee?" Bennet asked. Usually they had it at the table, but that hadn't happened today.

Nigel passed Bennet the supplies, and Bennet set up the machine. He fetched mugs while the machine gurgled. Black for Nigel and Leon, white for Kofi and himself. Leon took sugar, but—

"Is there any more sugar?" Bennet said.

Nigel took the empty canister out of his hands. "All gone. You boys! My cupboard would be bare if I didn't lock it."

"Oops, I meant to buy some," Kofi said.

"Leon, there's no sugar!" Bennet called through the window.

"Jamie'll have some," Leon shouted back.

True, and Jamie wouldn't mind Leon having a few spoonfuls. At the back of the shelf where Jamie stored his cake-making supplies, Bennet found a bag of something white. He checked the label. No, that was coconut flour. Jamie had used it in his birthday cake and in all the other things he'd made for Tim. Now he'd be needing it again.

Here was the sugar, in this plastic tub. Bennet tasted it on his fingertip to be sure, then stirred some into Leon's coffee and put the tub back. As the cupboard clicked shut, he heard a voice in his memory: *"You mean he's a pastry cook?"*

Darius had said it, at the party at Tim's gallery, and Bennet had thought he was sneering. But could it have been something else? Maybe Darius had only thought it ironic that Tim, with his wheat allergy, should fall for someone whose best creations all contained flour?

Darius had found fault with Rush, the college, Leon . . . the whole town. And Bennet himself, of course. But maybe there'd been times when he'd meant no criticism, and Bennet had misjudged him.

Tim was back, and that was good. It might have taken Bennet an hour to get used to the idea, but it was Jamie's dream come true. And Bennet wasn't losing anything. He and Jamie would still be friends. Not as close as they'd been in this house, perhaps, but their college days were ending anyway.

Had Darius told Tim how Jamie felt? He'd split them up—had he also brought them back together? Bennet had wanted to ask Tim, but not in front of Jamie.

He took his coffee upstairs and replayed the three voice mail messages that he still hadn't deleted. Yes, they were all about Darius and his family, but it sounded more like confession than self-obsession now.

Maybe he and Darius had more similarities than differences, after all. Darius's home might have been fifty times the size of Bennet's, but wouldn't Darius have been as miserable with Wyndham at Pemberley as Bennet was with Marlon in the cramped terrace in Beldon?

It was an unhappy story. Darius's father dies, his mother remarries, the boy is sent to boarding school. When he comes home for the holidays, another boy his age is there—an interloper, as unhappy as he is, and vicious. Later he loses his mother too, and he fails to protect his vulnerable little brother from that other boy.

Was it surprising if he grew up defensive, meeting challenges head-on? Wasn't it natural that he'd be fiercely protective if he thought a close friend was in danger of being hurt?

Wouldn't he be, in fact, a lot like Bennet?

Bennet's eyes smarted. He rubbed at them, digging his knuckles in.

Darius had done what he'd done for Tim's sake, and if Tim was here now, it must mean Darius was prepared to admit he'd been wrong. He might be back in Meriton soon.

Bennet dropped his phone on the bed. He was tempted to call, but what would he say? He'd have to leave a message. Darius wouldn't sit around doing nothing on Sunday afternoons. He'd be climbing, or preparing a case, or on a date with some guy.

Darius had only ever wanted one night to get Bennet out of his system, and one night wouldn't be enough for Bennet now. Better if it never happened.

# Chapter Twenty-five

THE STUDENTS JOSTLED each other coming out of their law exam, letting off tension. Bennet's phone was almost knocked out of his hand.

He grabbed it and opened a text from an unknown number.

*Coming your way tomorrow, can we meet? Your college or home? C Brackenbrough*

Catherine Brackenbrough wanted to see him—and was prepared to come to Meriton? It wasn't a major diversion if she was on her way to or from London, but all the same, it must mean a job, or a good chance of one.

He texted her straight back: *Happy to meet. I have an exam in the morning, home from 12.30.*

She arrived soon after three, wearing peacock blue. He'd asked Nigel for permission to take her into the parlour. Nigel fussed about, welcoming her and opening the curtains, which he kept closed to stop the furnishings fading.

Bennet made coffee. When he came back with it—two cups, not three—Nigel was in full flow on the subject of the portrait of his great-great-grandfather above the fireplace. Catherine stopped him in midsentence with a brilliant smile, and he scuttled for the door.

Bennet put her coffee on a low table by one of the couches, but she didn't sit down. She took an envelope from her shoulder bag.

"I have a contract for you here."

Bennet's cup shook in its saucer. A contract! He put his coffee beside hers and pulled the papers out of the unsealed envelope. Four pages, plus a job description headed *Internship—Assistant Coordinator.*

An internship, not a real job? His pulse slowed back to normal.

She must have seen his face fall. She added, "It's a paid position—a little bit of everything. You'll learn the whole business."

He nodded and turned the first page. He'd get minimum wage in theory, but they'd deduct a big slice for the room and meals that they'd provide. Still, it would cost him less than living in Sheffield, and the job would be a stepping stone. He had to start somewhere.

He flipped back and read the offer properly. Responsible to the facilities manager and marketing manager. Assisting with publicity—he'd enjoy that. Liaison with the wedding planner, kitchens, hotel reception, statutory bodies—what would those be? Health inspectors, the marriage registrar?

He'd be doing a lot of running around. But as she said, it would be good experience. Better than struggling to survive in a rented room on the hours they gave him at the Black Lion.

She hadn't signed the contract. Both of the spaces for signatures were blank.

"It's conditional on passing your HND, of course," Catherine said. "But Philippe expects you to get a distinction, so I imagine you'll have no problem achieving a mere pass."

He nodded again. The exams were going okay, and it wasn't the moment for modesty.

Catherine took a mouthful of coffee and bent to replace the lipstick-stained cup on its saucer. "There's one small thing I wanted to talk to you about, since I'm here. It's a little delicate."

He stopped reading and raised his eyes. This "small thing" would be the reason she'd come in person, instead of emailing this to him.

She went to the mantelpiece, picked up one of Nigel's miniature ebony elephants, and examined its tusks. "You met Darius Lanniker when you came to dinner. I didn't realise you already knew each other . . .?"

Bennet swallowed. He made himself relax, to keep his voice under control. "We'd met before, yes."

Her head lifted. She still held the elephant, but she was examining Bennet now. "So my nephew tells me."

Her nephew? Giorgio or Wyndham. Giorgio, most likely. What had he said?

She pursed her lips. "You know Darius is our landlord, and our families are connected?"

"Yes."

"There's no actual blood tie, but an alliance with my daughter is planned. Has he mentioned that?"

"Sorry?"

"Marriage. To Annabel."

Bennet's world shook, as if a rift had opened in the floor between them.

"But he's—" He broke off and closed his mouth. Who was he to say Darius was gay? He might be bi, like Callum, or pansexual, or anything. Bennet had never asked.

Catherine said, "Oh, I know he has certain *tastes*, but I think this fashion for categorising everyone by orientation is a huge mistake, don't you? We're all much more flexible than we give ourselves credit for. He's in London all week, so he can do what he likes there and come home to Pemberley at weekends."

"So he—You're telling me he and Annabel are engaged?" He needed it spelled out.

"He'll want children, Bennet. You can't know him well if you don't know how important family is to him. Family, and Pemberley. He'll need an *heir*, don't you see?"

Bennet thought of the messages he'd played again last night, for no other reason than to hear Darius's voice. She was right, it was all there—the pride in centuries of ownership, the insistence on Pemberley staying in the Lanniker line.

And hadn't Bennet seen Annabel coming away from Peak Lodge on the day he left Pemberley? He'd assumed she'd been to see Darius on business, but how likely was that, on a Sunday morning? Had she gone after she'd sent all their empty dishes back to the kitchens the evening before, and spent the night in his bed?

Darius had asked Bennet to go climbing on Sunday, but

he hadn't invited him back for coffee on Saturday night. He'd asked what Bennet was doing for the evening, but that was earlier in the day, before Catherine and Annabel knew he was there.

Bennet crossed his arms and dug his fingernails into his flesh. The physical pain distracted him from the turmoil inside. If only he could have five minutes to himself, so he could think!

Catherine was still talking. "Annabel will inherit the business, and he owns the land and buildings. It's perfect. Everything will come together for the next generation."

"An alliance." Bennet couldn't do more than repeat her term for it. She wasn't saying Darius was bisexual—she was saying he'd do anything for his property. He felt sick.

"Exactly." Catherine's smile didn't reach her eyes. "But I was speaking to my nephew, and he implied there was something between you and Darius, which would be a nuisance if you were working at Pemberley. So I'd just like to be clear about the situation."

He could imagine the conversation—Giorgio teasing Catherine, letting her think the relationship was much more than it was. Not difficult, since it wasn't a relationship at all.

"Right. Yes, you've made it clear." He tried to keep the bitterness out of his voice.

"No, I mean I want to understand *your* situation. How *close* you are. Is it sexual, or a friendship, or what?"

"It's nothing. Not even a friendship." Now he did sound bitter. "We'd met a few times because his friend Tim Wilson was—is—dating a friend of mine. That's all."

"So you haven't had sex?"

"No." Not that she had any right to know—but maybe Annabel did.

Catherine's shoulders relaxed and she gave a tinkling laugh. "Oh, that's a relief! I thought you *must* have... because you belong in such different *circles*, don't you? I couldn't imagine it being anything but a physical attraction. And you won't? Because I do hope we can get this signed and sealed today." She pointed a pink nail at the papers in his hand.

Her words stung. She was right, of course—it had never been anything but a physical attraction on Darius's side. Bennet knew that. So why did his gut twist so painfully when he heard it said aloud by this woman, his potential boss?

"Bennet?"

"Sorry, what did you say?"

"I just need you to assure me that you won't."

"Won't what?"

"Goodness, you don't seem as bright as I thought." Her smile was brittle now, and her eyebrows shot up. "That you won't start something sexual with Darius at Pemberley."

Bennet swallowed, trying to get the sour taste out of his mouth. "You mean when he's married?"

"Before or after the wedding."

Darius wanting him or him wanting Darius in those circumstances seemed so unlikely that he almost gave her the assurance she wanted. But the first shock was over. His defences hardened against her.

"Are you implying I have to make this promise to get the job? To be honest, without wishing to offend you, I don't think it's any of your business."

Catherine came a step closer, as if she wanted to snatch the contract back. "But it is. It's exactly that, my business. The smooth running of Pemberley Hall depends on it. What he does in London needn't affect my daughter at all, but if he had someone at Pemberley... Don't you see? We're so insular. Everyone would know. How shame-making for Annabel. And it might mean no babies, divorce—the whole plan could fall apart."

He shook his head. "I don't think it's a reasonable request."

"But you've already said there's nothing between you."

His logical brain kicked in. Words tumbled out. "There's a difference between telling you what's happened—or not happened—in the past, and making promises for the future. It's not about him. I just don't believe an employer has the right to veto my personal relationships."

She folded her arms, and the fingernails of one hand drummed against the opposite sleeve. "Bennet, please don't be obstinate about this. I have no wish to exercise any influence over your private life in any other respect, but I do think I should be able to expect that my employees will not try to seduce my future son-in-law."

"Yes, you should be able to expect that. So you don't need guarantees."

"But there's no reason for you to refuse, unless you are planning something."

"There's also nothing to stop me making the promise and then going ahead and seducing him, as you put it. So why ask me?"

"Because I think you're a young man of your word."

She was right, and that was the problem. If he made this promise, he'd feel bound by it. And if Darius came to him someday, as he did every night in Bennet's half-waking dreams—if Darius came to him, even if it was years from now, and Bennet had moved on from Pemberley, and Darius and Annabel were long divorced—even then, some part of him would hold back because he'd given his word. Loving Darius would always seem wrong.

He shook his head. "Sorry."

"You mean—"

"I won't make that promise."

"So there *is* something between you."

"I didn't say that." He gave her back the contract.

She stared at it, then at him. "But that's ridiculous!"

"I don't think so."

She gave an exaggerated sigh of impatience, but she must have heard the finality in his voice. "Well, Bennet, I'm disappointed. I was looking forward to having you on our team."

"Me too."

He could think of nothing more to say and nor, it seemed, could she.

She waited for a moment as if expecting him to change his mind. When he didn't, she turned on her high heels and left the room. The front door banged behind her. After a moment, her car started up outside, and tyres crunched over gravel.

Nigel appeared in the doorway, his face full of expectation. Bennet picked up the coffee cups and pushed past him to the kitchen.

He'd thrown away his only job offer—and for what? He'd never want to be some married guy's bit on the side. So why hadn't he made her that promise? He had to be crazy.

No, wait. If he were working at Pemberley, he'd have to help organise Darius's wedding—and that would only be the start. He'd be around Darius's wife every day, watching as her belly swelled. He'd see Darius coming to visit her in the quirky old lodge with its sunlit garden. He couldn't have handled that.

He'd done the right thing.

He washed the cups and told Nigel everything was fine. It wasn't far from the truth. He didn't want Catherine's stupid internship, and he was glad she hadn't offered it with no strings.

He'd had a narrow escape. Pemberley Hall was not the place for him.

---

HIS MEETING WITH Catherine focused his mind. With exams almost over, it was time to put some serious effort into job hunting.

Charlotte put her head round his door when she came back from college. "Coming to the pub?"

"No, I've got my last exam tomorrow."

"Okay." She came in. "I hope you'll keep in touch."

"Yeah, sure." He flicked through another list of jobs on the internet. So many, and yet none of them was right. Was he too picky? He'd found a couple more trainee hotel positions—he'd settle for one of those now, if they'd have him.

She sat on the bed beside him. "I think we'll be living in Beldon. It would be good to know someone."

He looked up from the screen. "I won't be there, Charlotte. Whatever happens, I'm not going back home. I'd rather stay in Meriton."

"You can't live here. Monsieur Philippe's moving in, now they've gone public, and they want to be alone."

"I know, but there's Philippe's house. Nigel said he'd speak to him about letting Kofi and Leon rent it. I could share it with them."

"You want to go on living with them?" Charlotte asked.

"Why not? Better the devil you know, right?"

He searched a job vacancy site for Distinctivent. Nothing. Why was it so hard to let go of the things he wanted?

Charlotte leaned forward, clasping her hands. "But anyway, you'll visit, won't you? I mean, you'll visit your mum and dad. And we could meet up then?"

"Of course."

"You won't blank me out because of Callum?"

"No." He turned to her and rubbed her shoulder. "What's wrong? You shouldn't get married if you don't want to. You don't even have to live together. You could have the kid on your own."

She sighed. "No, we'll give it a go. We owe it to the baby to try, at least. We do seem to click. We know where we are with each other, you know? I'll be as happy with him as anyone."

"Sounds practical," Bennet said. Not exciting, though. He typed the address for Distinctivent's website. One last check, and then he'd forget it.

"I've heard of them," Charlotte said, looking at the screen.

"Yeah, I had an interview with them last term."

"No, it was something else . . . Aren't they involved in that massive sponsored danceathon in Trafalgar Square?"

"Are they?" He typed *sponsored dance* in their search box. "There's nothing on their site." He widened the search across the internet and found a news report about it.

"You're right. It's on Friday, and they don't have it on their website. Their business must be ballooning beyond control. They need me." He grabbed his phone.

---

DONNA CLARE WAS too busy to speak to him, so Bennet caught an early train to London on Friday morning. He found her on the steps of the National Gallery. Music was already pounding.

"I'm Bennet Rourke. You offered me an interview before Easter, but you weren't able to be there for it. I wanted to—"

"I'm sorry. This is a bad time."

"I know, that's why I'm here."

She laughed and ran a hand through her hair. "You

picked the worst possible time on purpose?"

"I want to show you what I can do. Couldn't you use an extra body today?"

She put her hands on her hips. "We certainly could, if you're willing to work. Who did you say you were?"

"Bennet Rourke. I'm at Meriton College, leaving in a week or two. We talked on the phone a few months ago."

A uniformed roller dancer came skating over and clumped up the steps. "Donna, the caterers want to see you. Urgent."

"In a minute. Did you say Meriton, Bennet? What are you studying?"

"Hospitality management."

"All right. If you want to wear yourself out today like the rest of us, you're welcome. Yes, I'm on my way, Emma. Can you take Bennet and give him to Jake? Tell him to sign him up as a volunteer and put him on water."

So Bennet spent the morning wriggling through a growing crowd of dancers of all ages, sizes, and costumes, helping them to refill their water bottles. At lunchtime he was promoted to water fountain logistics. It was hectic, it was fun, the buzz energised him, and he saw new faces all the time. He had a permanent grin on his face.

Donna Clare came by in the late afternoon. "How's it going, Bennet?"

"Awesome." She'd remembered his name.

"Glad to see you're still smiling. Will you shoot me your application again sometime? We've been offered another big contract today. No promises, but I like your style."

"I'll send it tonight."

"And have they told you there's a new shift coming on at six? You can go when they're here."

He watched her walk away, then he punched a triumphant fist into the air. She liked his style! Exactly what he'd hoped for. The day couldn't have turned out any better.

Unless . . . since he was in London, why not give Darius a call?

Now that Tim was back, Bennet was uncomfortable about some of the things he'd said the night Darius had come to the Black Lion. It sounded like Quentin had been the real driving force behind Tim leaving. Darius must have played some part or he wouldn't have accepted the blame, but Bennet might have gone too far with his accusations. He had an uneasy feeling that he owed Darius an apology.

He ought to hear Darius's version of the Annabel story too. Why had he taken Catherine's word for that? He'd trusted Wyndham against Darius, and he'd been wrong. He didn't want to make the same mistake with Catherine.

And if Darius wanted to meet up to talk about it, Bennet wouldn't say no.

---

HE WALKED NORTH until the music had faded to a vague *thrum* below the traffic noise. He found a small space planted with trees, sat on a stone wall, and looked at his watch. Six twenty. Mobile or office?

Londoners worked late. He found the website on his phone and called. His thumb shook as he pressed the screen, and his heart raced as he waited to be put through from the switchboard.

He reached a languid male voice. He didn't catch the name, but it wasn't Darius.

"He's left for the weekend," the guy said. "Can I help? What's it about?"

"It's personal. I'll try his mobile."

"You have the number? Okay, yeah. It'll be switched off for another couple of hours—he doesn't take calls when he's driving. But try later, or text him, or whatever."

"So he's not in London?" The energy that had kept Bennet running all day flooded out of him. If Darius was driving for several hours . . . "Has he gone to Derbyshire?"

"That's right, yeah. He's been up there a lot lately. Must be the third or fourth weekend on the trot."

"Thanks. No, no message."

Bennet's limbs felt so heavy, they might have been chained to the ground. What had Darius said—he went to Pemberley once a month at most? And now he was there every weekend? Maybe he *was* engaged.

Bennet dropped the phone into his pocket, then headed for the nearest Tube station. He wouldn't text. If he wanted to know for sure about Annabel, he could ask Tim. As for apologies, they could wait until Jamie's wedding, if they were needed at all. Darius was at Pemberley, where his past and his future lay. Nothing Bennet said or did could touch him.

# Chapter Twenty-six

H E WOKE LATE on Sunday morning, some distant noise pulling him out of sleep. Summer rain dripped on his open window. He kicked his quilt into a crumpled heap, rolled off the mattress, and staggered down the corridor into the bathroom.

He needed a shower and a shave—bedhead, stubble, not a pretty sight—but his stomach wanted food first. He'd take care of his appearance after breakfast. Or lunch, since it was almost noon. He pulled on a pair of jeans and a cleanish T-shirt, and headed down the stairs barefoot.

The house felt airy and empty. Charlotte was gone. She'd cleared her room yesterday. Nigel spent more time with Philippe now, and Jamie would be with Tim. The silence meant Kofi and Leon must be out too. Bennet had the place to himself. Perfect. He could raid whatever bread was in the kitchen and replace it later.

His phone buzzed as he sprang off the last step onto the dark polished boards of the hall. Email, from Donna Clare.

He straightened, his heart thumping. He opened it and skimmed the words. Good to meet him. Something to offer him—call tomorrow. Start as soon as possible.

*Yes!* He let out a whoop that echoed around the house.

And the parlour door opened, and Darius was there.

Bennet couldn't believe what he was seeing. Was this a dream? His breath came fast, and his need for coffee and food was forgotten.

Darius was in his climbing gear—knee-length shorts and a deep crimson shirt of the brand he always wore. Why come here dressed like that? Hadn't Bennet told him there was nothing to climb in Meriton?

"What are you doing here? How did you get in?" The words tumbled out of Bennet's mouth.

Darius passed a brown envelope from one hand to the other, almost like he was nervous. "Your landlord let me in. He was on his way out, but he said I could wait."

"For Tim? I haven't seen him this weekend. If he and Jamie aren't at the gallery, I don't know where they are."

Darius cleared his throat. "They're getting on all right, then? Tim told me they were engaged, but since then I've hardly heard from him."

Bennet ran a hand through his hair, trying to smooth it down. Why had he skipped his personal grooming? "Yes, they're doing great, I think. I haven't seen Tim, but Jamie was here last night. They're busy planning to bring light and love to the world with their art and their pastries."

A flicker of a smile crossed Darius's face, and he advanced one step into the hall. "That's good."

"Was it you who told Tim to come back?"

"I didn't do as much as that. It took me a while to reach him—he'd changed his phone number and stopped using social media—but when I did track him down, I only had to hint that Jamie missed him, and Tim was on the first plane home."

"Thank you."

Darius shrugged. "I don't think it made much difference. Tim was pining. He'd have been here sooner or later, whether I said anything or not."

"Later might have been too late. We'll all be leaving college soon."

"Tim would have found him, wherever he was."

Bennet grinned, imagining Tim chasing Jamie from restaurant to restaurant around the country. Then he thought of Annabel. The smile left his face, and he squared his shoulders. "I believe I should congratulate you."

Darius's muscled arms relaxed. "What, on the thing with Wyndham?"

Heat rose in Bennet's chest. How could he have forgotten Wyndham and the college? The brown envelope must hold papers for Monsieur Philippe. That was what Darius meant about waiting. He was waiting for Philippe.

"I was lucky with that," Darius said. "I had to trawl through some disgusting shit, but I saw something that looked like the room where he'd filmed Giorgio. So I went to see him, to check my memory of it. I let him think I was there to negotiate for the rights to the film about the college and offered him ten thousand pounds. He asked for two million."

"Two million? Jesus. Would Philippe and Nigel have paid it?"

"Not through me. When they suggested selling their

homes, I said if they planned to do that, they should keep the money and move away. Leave the country, if they really couldn't face it."

"But you found evidence and had him arrested?"

"Not evidence, exactly, but I saw enough. Young teens, they looked like, filmed in his living room." Darius winced, pacing back and forth across the hall. His brow was furrowed and his mouth a thin line. "I'd told a friend in the police what I planned to do in case I fell into one of their nets and got into trouble for browsing the sites myself, so I went back to her with what I'd seen, and they got a search warrant."

It must have raked everything up again for him—all the anger and worry and pain he'd felt over Giorgio.

"You did a good thing. Your clients are over the moon."

Darius turned to him in surprise. "Hennice and his partner? They aren't my clients. I told Hennice I'd do what I could, but I couldn't act for him in any formal sense. I had personal interests in the case that might have conflicted with his."

Bennet was confused. "What about the ten thousand you offered Wyndham? Wasn't that on their behalf?"

"No. I let Wyndham think so, but only because I knew he wouldn't accept as little as that."

"But what if he had?"

Darius stopped near the stairs and drummed his fingers on the oak banister. "Then I'd have paid it myself. A bargain."

"Ten grand, just to stop him making a name for himself?"

"Not only for that, no." Darius caught his lower lip between his front teeth. "For you."

Bennet couldn't speak. He could hardly breathe. *He doesn't mean that the way it sounds. Or if he does, it's nothing serious. Remember Annabel.*

"Hennice said you gave him my name," Darius went on. "You wanted my help to keep your body off the nation's screens."

"Yeah." The word came out like a cough. "But it wasn't what it looked like. I didn't go any further with Wyndham than what you saw."

"I didn't see anything," Darius said. "I didn't need to. You'd told me you hadn't had sex with him, and I didn't think you'd lie to me. You've never had trouble speaking your mind."

Bennet's heart thudded. Darius had believed him, trusted him, in spite of the evidence. He'd never expected that. All his defences fell away . . . and that was dangerous.

He drew himself together. "But when I said congratulations, I meant to congratulate you on your engagement."

Darius took a step back. "My *engagement*? Who's the lucky guy?"

Bennet drew in a sharp breath. Did that mean . . . "You're not going to marry Annabel Brackenbrough?"

"Good God, no. I'm gay, Bennet." Darius's eyes twinkled. "I thought you knew what I liked."

A weight rolled off Bennet's chest. Of course he knew. The memory of Darius's body moving against his in the Brighton club filled his mind and raced through his bloodstream. His stomach fluttered, and lower down, his jeans began to feel tight.

"I didn't want to make assumptions," he said. "I called your office on Friday, and your assistant said you'd been to Pemberley every weekend."

"Yes, because of Giorgio. I wanted to tell him about Wyndham's arrest before he heard about it from his father or saw it in the news. He didn't take it well. It's brought up some disturbing memories, and he's needed extra support. But I think it will make him stronger in the end. Closure, as his therapist says."

Darius put his hands in his pockets. His mouth flickered with amusement. "So you thought I was going up there to see Annabel?"

Bennet's cheeks flushed with heat. How could he have believed that for a minute? "Catherine said you wanted children—heirs for Pemberley. It made sense."

"Oh, heirs . . . It's true I want the estate to stay in the family, but gay men can have children. And if I don't, there are plenty of Lanniker cousins. Catherine's a fantasist. She'd love to get her hands on the freehold to Pemberley, but some dreams won't come true for her, no matter how hard she pushes." Darius laughed. "Is this what you were discussing when—she alleges—you refused to promise to keep your hands off me?"

Bennet's face was flaming now. "She told you that?"

"Yes, this morning. That's why I'm here. I'd arranged to go climbing today, but she caught me at the car, all indignant. What did I think I was doing, messing with one of her potential employees? In her view, you've turned down the opportunity of a lifetime for my sake. So instead of driving to Stanage, I found myself heading for the motorway, to see how much truth there was in it. One never knows, with Catherine."

Darius clearly found this highly entertaining. Bennet scowled. "It was a matter of principle. I didn't think it was any of her business."

The corner of Darius's mouth twitched. "Oh, so you'd have said the same whoever it was? What if she'd asked you not to play around with Tim?"

"With *Tim*? My best friend's fiancé? What kind of person do you think—" Bennet stopped, seeing the trap he'd fallen into. The heat rose to his face again. Bloody lawyers.

Darius gave him a wicked grin. "So, not a matter of principle at all, but a question of what you might want to do with the man concerned—i.e. me."

Bennet folded his arms. He wasn't admitting anything. "She had no right to try to control my private life."

"Absolutely, and I said so. In my view it was discriminatory. She wouldn't have asked it of a straight man. I told her that I intended to find out if you wanted to take the matter to a tribunal, and that if you did, I'd be happy to represent you. As a result, I have a job offer for you." He handed the brown envelope to Bennet. "I have to say, though, I think you could do better. She can't be the easiest person to work for."

The envelope wasn't sealed. Bennet pulled out the papers. It was the same internship she'd offered him before, but this time the contract was signed.

She'd have to wait. He didn't plan to do anything about this until he'd spoken to Donna Clare.

His stomach growled again, and Darius raised his eyebrows. "Should we get you some food?"

"Yeah, maybe." Bennet needed to get his head round some of this. "Do you want something? Toast, coffee?"

"Coffee would be perfect."

Bennet dropped the papers on the hall table where Nigel left the mail and led the way to the kitchen. His limbs felt out of his control, as if Darius were pulling their strings. Hard to believe Darius was here, instead of halfway up a rock in the Peak District, just because Bennet had said no to Catherine.

And he wasn't engaged to Annabel. Bennet's heart skipped. Catherine must have invented that story because she wanted it to happen.

Darius had spent long hours searching for evidence against Wyndham for Bennet's sake. He'd been prepared to pay thousands of pounds. And now he was here, not to see Monsieur Philippe, but to see Bennet.

Nigel's canister of ground coffee was out on the counter, and a new filter sat in the machine. "Looks like he was interrupted," Bennet said.

"No, I did that. He told me to help myself, so I started setting it up, but I couldn't find the measuring spoon."

Bennet opened the right drawer and flicked the plastic scoop up onto the counter. He searched around until he found the end of a loaf of bread. It was dry but not mouldy, so he put the last slice and the crust into the toaster.

Darius spooned coffee into the filter. "Then I went looking for you, but I didn't like to go upstairs. I didn't know which was your room, and you might not have been alone."

Darius's back was turned and slightly bent, as he focused on the coffee machine. The fabric of his shorts was pulled tight over his glutes and thighs, revealing hard, knotted muscle. Bennet couldn't tear his eyes away.

"I'm alone." Bennet's voice came out gruff.

"I'm pleased to hear it." Darius straightened up.

Bennet turned away to hide the quickening of his breath. "I do have a chance of another job. A good chance, I think."

"Really? Where?"

"An events company, based in Richmond."

"West London or Yorkshire? I hope it's not Virginia. I'm not qualified to practise law in the USA."

Bennet laughed. "Richmond in London."

"Excellent. I can get at you there," Darius said calmly. "That's if Catherine's right, and you've changed your mind about never wanting to see me again."

So Darius wanted to get at him? The idea sent blood rushing through Bennet's veins.

He needed something to do—something that didn't involve meeting Darius's eyes. The toast had popped up unnoticed and was sitting in the toaster, going cold. Bennet picked up a knife and reached for the peanut butter.

Before he could get the lid off the jar, Darius strode over to the toaster and pushed the lever. He waited a few seconds, flicked it back, and dropped the slices onto Bennet's plate.

They were hot.

"I'd never have thought of doing that," Bennet said.

Darius was right up beside him now. "What?"

"Reheating the toast." He slathered peanut butter over it, trying to pretend Darius wasn't standing so close that Bennet could feel the heat coming off him.

"I have my uses," Darius said. "No cucumber?"

How did he know about the cucumber? That day on the cliffs at Brighton. It was months ago, but Darius had remembered.

"This isn't a sandwich," Bennet said. But cucumber had crossed his mind. He'd have added some if he'd been alone, but he didn't want to seem obsessed.

He took a bite. It wasn't the same without the cucumber—too sticky. And now his mouth would taste of peanut butter if anything happened, like a kiss, which was starting to seem possible. A quiver ran down his spine.

The coffee machine gave its long, protesting, final gurgle and stopped. Darius took a couple of mugs from the drainer and filled them from the glass jug. He put milk in Bennet's without asking. He must have remembered that from Brighton too.

Bennet had trouble swallowing his toast with Darius right there watching him, both of them hyperaware of every move. But somehow he managed to eat most of both slices, washing them down with coffee.

Then he caught sight of his reflection in the microwave's glass door. Shit, what did he look like? He tried to pull his hair into shape.

Darius took two steps to come up close beside him. "Leave it, you look gorgeous. Like you just got out of bed. Makes me want to take you back there."

Heat lit Bennet's core, but he didn't want to show it. He twisted away. "Still trying to get me out of your system?"

Darius shook his head. "Not possible. You're in there to stay. I realised that when I saw you at Pemberley. I want you in my life, not out of it. So tell me, do I have a chance with you?"

Bennet couldn't look at him. His eyes would give him away if he did. "What do you think?"

"Truthfully? I think if I didn't, you'd have thrown me out by now."

Bennet laughed. "That's kind of hard to do when you're standing there in your climbing gear all lean and muscled and . . ."

"And irresistible?" Darius finished for him, with a smile in his voice.

Bennet didn't deny it. But he said, "We shouldn't do this. We'll kill each other."

Darius gave a gasping laugh. "I don't think we'll go that far. We're two proud and passionate men, it's true, and I'm sure there'll be fireworks from time to time, but I wouldn't have it any other way. Would you?"

"Well, no. If you put it like that." Nobody else had ever come close to rousing him the way Darius did. It wasn't always comfortable, but anything else would seem like second best.

Darius's eyes were fixed on his face. "We've always been

honest with each other. We'll make it work . . . Won't we?"

All the arrogance was gone, and Bennet saw only the man. A man who wanted him . . . a man pleading. The only man who mattered.

"Come here," Darius said.

Bennet didn't have far to go. He twisted around, and with one step he was within kissing distance of Darius. Still they didn't touch until Bennet ran the back of one fingernail down the front of Darius's shirt. Darius sucked in his breath.

Bennet couldn't hold back any longer. He hooked an arm over Darius's shoulder and felt Darius's breath on his cheek. Their lips met, bumped, connected. Contact. What he needed.

Darius's mouth was hot, firm, and dry. Bennet took Darius's top lip between both of his and began licking and sucking, caressing each half inch and moving on to the next. Darius's fingers dug into his back, as if he planned never to let Bennet go.

Bennet ran the tip of his tongue around the oval of Darius's parted lips, and a tremor ran through Darius's back. So he could do that to Darius—could get through his armour, under his skin. Good to know. He'd thought it only worked the other way around.

Darius slid a hand up Bennet's spine.

"I haven't showered yet," Bennet said.

He only meant to explain any possible smell, but Darius said, "Lead the way."

# Chapter Twenty-seven

BENNET DARTED FOR the kitchen door, swung through it, and slammed it behind him, but Darius was out in a second. They ran up the stairs, Darius's shoes drowning out the dull thuds of Bennet's bare feet.

Bennet fell into the bathroom, bumping up against the wall. He grabbed Darius's designer shirt and pulled him close. He got why Darius liked this gear. It felt good to the touch, shiny-silky soft.

Darius reached out with one foot and kicked the bathroom door closed, shutting out the rest of the house, the rest of the world. His hands settled on Bennet's hips. Bennet's flesh grew warm in response.

"Are you glad I'm here?" Darius asked in a teasing voice.

"What do you think?"

Darius bent his head and ran his tongue over Bennet's earlobe, sending feverish shivers radiating through him. "I want to hear you say it."

"Yes," Bennet said. "Yes, I'm glad." Weird how vulnerable it made him feel to say the words aloud. And yet it was okay, like it was safe to open himself up to this man.

He ran his fingers over Darius's abs through the thin, clinging fabric of his climbing shirt. The muscles trembled, flinching—he was sensitive there. *Good. I'll use my tongue there sometime.* Later today or some other time, because there would be other times. No question about that. This was only the beginning.

Darius nuzzled Bennet's neck as he slid one hand up under the front of Bennet's T-shirt—strong, sure, and supple, a climber's hand. His fingers found Bennet's nipple and pinched it. Bennet gasped, and every hair on his body stood up, electrified.

"You like that?" Darius said.

"As if you have to ask."

Darius's grin mirrored Bennet's own. *We're a good match*, Bennet thought. They'd push each other's boundaries, but they'd keep each other in line, and they'd always connect.

He yanked his T-shirt over his head and kicked off his jeans. He tugged at Darius's clothes, but Darius held him off and stared down at Bennet's naked body. "You're gorgeous," he said, his voice thickening. "I knew you'd be gorgeous."

He made a grab for Bennet, but Bennet could tease too. He turned the water on, dodged Darius's hands for a few seconds while it ran warm, then jumped into the shower so Darius couldn't come near him until he'd stripped off his clothes . . . except Darius didn't play by those rules. He threw off his top in one fluid motion, then stepped out of his shoes and into the cascading water with his bottom half still clothed.

"That's cheating," Bennet protested.

"Durable and quick drying." Darius did a convincing imitation of an advertising voice-over. "Shower-resistant, the label says. I assume they meant rain showers, but let's see how they hold up in here."

Darius ignored the water that ran in rivulets down his face, coming so close that Bennet could sense the warmth of his body above the heat of the shower. He smelled of the outdoors, of earth in springtime. A sprinkling of dark hairs accented his chest. The water made them glisten and straightened them out so they gathered into a line pointing irresistibly downward.

Bennet traced the wet hairs with one finger as far as the waistband of Darius's shorts, which had failed this test of their waterproofing. They clung to Darius now, soaked, revealing every jutting bone, every curve, every ridge of muscle, and the long, hard, swollen rod that drew Bennet's gaze like a magnet. Seeing it framed in the wet fabric, straining against its prison, unleashed a pulsing need in his own groin whose intensity took his breath away.

Darius took one more step and pressed the whole length of his body against Bennet's, pulling him into a kiss, hard and hungry. Their hips scraped, and Bennet's cock throbbed as it grazed the front of Darius's saturated shorts. He'd thought of getting them off, but instead he found himself gripping under the cheeks of Darius's arse. He began to rock against Darius, sliding his cock against fabric as smooth and soft as wet skin.

Darius grunted and thrust the tip of his tongue into Bennet's mouth. *Yes.* Bennet leaned back against the tiled wall, revelling in the sensation of his own desire and Darius's matching need for him. Their bodies were crushed so close that they moved as one. The hairs on Darius's chest were like silk threads twisting over Bennet's nipples, sending shock waves from his chest to his groin.

For a long moment this was enough; then it wasn't. He wanted to suck more than the tip of Darius's tongue. He pushed one hand between their hips, reached down, and cupped the base of Darius's cock through his shorts. Not rock-hard like a statue—it had some give in it, some warm responsiveness, a living thing. He ran his palm over it, squeezing, loving the feel of it filling his hand.

Darius gasped and jerked his head out of the kiss. Fingers like iron gripped Bennet's wrist and dragged his hand away. "Jesus. Not so fast. You're killing me."

"Ha. Didn't you just tell me you wouldn't have it any other way?"

Darius closed his eyes. "I don't remember anything I said. I plead diminished responsibility. You've turned my brain to mush."

He buried one hand in Bennet's wet hair and sent the other hand lower, following the stream of water running down Bennet's crack. He squeezed out some shower gel and began stroking around the hole, then slipped in a probing finger.

Bennet gasped. The sudden invasion made every nerve in his body light up, energy rushing through him, a natural high. He tried to move harder and faster against Darius's groin, but Darius gripped his hip and pushed him away. His finger slipped out. Bennet groaned in frustrated protest.

"Condom?" Darius said.

"In the bedroom. You mean you didn't come prepared?"

Darius gave him a wry grin. "No, I don't carry condoms when I'm climbing. Though I might have to start, if I'll be climbing with you." He turned off the water and grabbed Bennet's hand. "Where's this bedroom?"

They slipped across the landing, leaving wet footprints on the carpet. Bennet's room was a mess, but Darius didn't seem to notice or care. He tugged off his soaked climbing shorts and dropped them on the floor. God, he was gorgeous naked. The sight of his long, strong limbs took Bennet's breath away.

Darius slipped an arm around Bennet's waist, and they fell onto the rumpled bed side by side. Bennet's arm was trapped under Darius's shoulder. He pulled it out with more force than it needed, tipping Darius onto his back.

"Oh, you want to fight?" Darius growled.

Bennet twisted away, laughing. Sex had never been so much fun. There was something about Darius, about all their messy history together, that meant Bennet didn't have to put on an act. Darius had seen his bratty side and still kept coming back for more.

"I want to fuck you," Darius growled. "I wanted to fuck you the first time I saw you."

Bennet narrowed his eyes. "Oh yeah? Was that what *just about fuckable* meant?"

"You deserved that, eavesdropping on us. And I loved the way you stalked furiously across that roof. You are the hottest thing on earth when you're angry, you know that?"

"No. I'm the hottest thing on earth *all* the time."

Darius laughed, relaxing his grip on Bennet. *I'll get you now*, Bennet thought, and he flipped over to pin Darius on his back. He held him down by one shoulder and ground his cock into the hollow at the top of Darius's thigh.

That felt so good, Bennet forgot to defend his position. Darius grabbed his wrist and jerked it away, freeing himself. In seconds, Bennet was on his stomach in an armlock. Darius's thighs pinned his legs down, while Darius's cock was hot and hard, branding Bennet's arse.

Darius breath was heavy in his ear. "Surrender? I could push it in and fuck you right now."

It would be hot as hell if he did. But the darn condom . . . They'd have to save that game for another time.

Bennet let his limbs go limp. Darius rolled off onto his side and ran his hand over Bennet's back.

"I was right," he murmured. "You're lickable, suckable, and . . . yes . . . definitely fuckable."

He got up onto his knees and parted Bennet's legs, then pressed his cheeks apart. His tongue glided over Bennet's hole, warm and wet, making him quiver. Bennet closed his eyes, giving himself over to the sensation.

He shifted on the bed, rubbing against it as he moved. Heat shot through him. He grabbed Darius's hand and tried to guide it. One touch and he'd be gone.

But Darius pulled back, as if he could read Bennet's mind. "Not yet," he murmured. He swivelled around to lie on his side, bringing his legs up. His cock lay stiff on the sheet, begging for Bennet to take it in his mouth.

Bennet couldn't resist that. He manoeuvred his head

between Darius's legs and fluttered his tongue over the slit, where beads of pre-come mingled with droplets of water from the shower. It tasted like Darius—sharp and salty. Darius groaned.

Bennet gripped Darius's hips and took the thick, slippery tool deeper into his mouth. He was dizzy with arousal and elated by the knowledge of his own power. Darius was all his, and it felt amazing, like nothing else ever had.

"Come here," Darius said, reaching for Bennet's hips.

Without letting up on his attention to Darius's cock, Bennet shifted his body around to give Darius access.

Darius slid over the sheets until his head was up by Bennet's hips. "Hmm, what shall I do with this?" he murmured, running one finger along Bennet's cock from base to head and back. Then he followed it with his tongue, circling the head.

Bennet's stomach contracted and his balls drew tight. He was about to come, and he didn't want to. Not until Darius fucked him.

But he didn't tell Darius to stop. He clenched his thighs and stilled, waiting for the moment to pass. Darius's firm, sweet mouth on him there was heaven on earth. He wanted this to go on forever, but he wanted everything else too.

Darius's body gave a tremor, and he withdrew from Bennet's mouth. He let Bennet's cock slip from between his lips and rose to his knees. "Where are the condoms?" he asked, his voice rasping like sandpaper. He pulled at the drawer. "In here?"

"Yeah." Bennet let Darius open the packet, then stole the

condom from between his fingers. He pinched the tip, settled it over Darius's cockhead, then took the head back into his mouth and unrolled the condom all the way down with his lips.

"Party trick?" Darius asked.

Bennet drew his mouth back and off. "One of many." He started to turn over onto his stomach, but Darius stopped him.

"On your back. I want to watch you."

Bennet hesitated. He'd never been fucked that way. He'd always been able to bury his face and hide his reactions. With his heart beating fast, he lay back and let Darius part his knees. He felt more vulnerable like this, but it was okay. Exciting, even, because if Darius could watch him, he could watch Darius.

Right now Darius's face was tense with concentration. His hand, slick with lube from the drawer, found Bennet's hole and eased in—two fingers, quick and rough, opening him up. Stretching the raw bundle of nerves, finding that special place, sending Bennet's mind reeling, and setting his breath free from his body.

Darius moved in closer, and his fingers were replaced by something much thicker pressing at the place. Bennet tipped back his chin, letting himself relax and open up down there. He moaned when he felt the head enter him.

Darius was gazing down at their coupling. *That's my man, the one who'll stay*, Bennet thought. How was he so sure? But he was. As if he'd been waiting all his life for this, and now he could let go. He didn't need to bottle up this moment and keep it in his heart forever, because this was just the beginning.

Darius met his eyes with an intense, fiery gaze. "You don't know what you do to me," he muttered.

His hand went back to Bennet's cock, rubbing him, and at the same time he began to push further in. He moved in short thrusts at first, pulling out a little way and easing into Bennet inch by glorious inch, deeper every time. Fucking him. Filling him.

Bennet drove his shoulders down into the bed. Oh, it felt good. Something in him loosened and let go, as if a door had opened.

Darius's thrusts began to accelerate, and his hand on Bennet's cock speeded up at the same rate. Warmth built around the base of Bennet's spine. His gut pulsed. His head spun. Darius groaned and fucked him harder, faster, until both of their bodies trembled with it.

"God, it's too much," Darius groaned. "I want to make it last but I . . . *Jesus*."

He broke and cried out as he came, deep inside Bennet. His hand faltered. Bennet grabbed it and forced it to keep the rhythm. One stroke, two, a jerk of Bennet's hips, and Bennet, too, was over the edge, spurting onto his belly. Spasms so strong he was lost in their potency, gasping, all his muscles clenching.

Bennet's heart pounded in his chest like a drum. He felt a little panicky, like he always did right after. But it was different this time. He didn't want to get away. He'd just wait for it to pass. He closed his eyes and let his breathing slow.

After a few minutes, when Bennet's mind had settled, Darius asked, "What are you thinking?"

From anyone else he'd have hated that question, but from Darius it was okay. "Weird that it turned out to be you."

That didn't sound like it made much sense, but Darius said, "Mmm," like he understood.

"Same for you?" Bennet asked.

"Kind of, but I've known for a while. Thought I'd fucked it up, though."

"Yeah, I thought you had, too."

Darius gave a short laugh, and silence fell between them. Bennet cuddled up against Darius's back. Darius didn't move. Was he asleep?

A design was etched on his shoulder in black—no, dark green—almost hidden against the mattress... the tattoo Bennet had glimpsed in the club in Brighton, half a lifetime ago.

It wasn't a Celtic knot. A pattern, but not symmetrical. Bennet laid a palm flat on Darius's back and pressed gently, trying to see it better without waking him.

Darius said in a deep voice, "Are you touching my tattoo?"

*Not asleep, then.* "Looking at it. What is it?"

Darius turned onto his stomach, exposing the shoulder. "The maze at Pemberley."

"I can see the way to the middle." Bennet traced the path with the tip of his tongue, ending at a checkerboard pattern in the centre. He tasted salt on Darius's skin. A memory surfaced. "Your brother told me if I went in there, I'd be lost forever."

Darius rolled over to face him. "And are you?"

Huh? Oh, right—was he lost forever? Maybe. But he wasn't going to say it. He bit his lip and turned his face away.

Darius laughed. He leaned in and nipped Bennet's shoulder with his teeth. Bennet took his hand and settled down to sleep.

---

HE WOKE TO a knock on his door. Sunlight streamed into the room, warming his bare legs. No disconnect—he knew at once that there was someone in his bed and who it was, though he lay facing out, towards the door, with Darius behind him.

The door handle turned. They'd kicked the quilt onto the floor, and nothing but the corner of a sheet covered his hips. He tugged at it to make himself decent as Jamie's head appeared in the opening.

Jamie's face went blank with shock that morphed into horror. Kind of an overreaction, since they were only lying there.

The door closed swiftly but silently, and Jamie's steps retreated over the creaky landing floor.

Bizarre. Bennet moved to slip off the bed, but an arm snaked around his waist and held him back.

"I'll be two minutes," he said.

Darius grunted, and the arm released him. Bennet sat up and looked around. Darius was watching him through one eye. The other was squashed against the pillow. Darius smiled, and a shiver went through Bennet as he thought of the things they'd done and the things they hadn't yet done. He'd have lain straight down again if he hadn't also needed to pee.

"Any longer and I'm coming to get you," Darius threatened, as Bennet pulled on underpants and jeans.

"Okay."

He padded down the hall to the bathroom first, then knocked on Jamie's door. Footsteps crossed the room towards him, and Jamie yanked the door open.

He looked upset. Weirdly so.

"What's wrong?" Bennet asked.

Jamie took a couple of sheets of paper from his desk and pushed them into Bennet's hand. "I found this downstairs."

The contract from Catherine. "Yes, so?"

Jamie stepped away and tugged at his own hair. "I know you need a job, but you didn't have to prostitute yourself."

"Prostitute? What are you talking about?"

"I saw him in your room—Darius. You slept with him to get this internship, right?"

A bubble of laughter rose in Bennet's chest. He'd have let it out if Jamie hadn't looked so dismayed. "Oh no, Jamie, that's not how it is. He doesn't have anything to do with this. He did bring it, but he has no control over who they hire at Pemberley Hall. And I don't plan to accept it. Distinctivent have made me an offer—or they're going to, I hope. I'd rather work for them."

Jamie's expression didn't change. "So what's he doing in your bed?"

"What do you think?"

Jamie turned back into his room. "I'm sorry, Bennet. I'm trying to understand, but I don't get how sex can mean so little to you. Casual sex with a stranger, okay, but when it's someone you hate . . ."

Bennet followed him in, leaving the door open. "I don't hate him. Not any more."

"Since when?"

Bennet crossed his arms over his bare chest, hugging his ribs. "I don't know. I always secretly thought he was hot. I just hated him at the same time, until recently."

"Because you thought he wasn't interested?"

"No—Well, maybe." Bennet didn't want to get into the other reasons and open up old wounds for Jamie.

"Why didn't you tell me?"

"It was complicated. I didn't think anything could ever come of it."

"You still could have said." Jamie had relaxed now. He was even smiling. "Or didn't you want to admit you'd been wrong?"

"Yes, that too."

Jamie started to say more, but then he saw something over Bennet's shoulder. His jaw dropped. He covered his eyes and laughed.

Bennet turned. Darius was coming along the landing, and he hadn't put any clothes on. His body was all grace, strength, and muscle. His half-erect cock bobbed against his leg. Something in Bennet cracked open and flooded him with warmth. What a gorgeous guy, and all his.

Darius was grinning back at him, shameless. "Six minutes. Too long."

Bennet walked towards him. "Can't cope without me?"

"No. You'll definitely have to work in London."

"I was thinking the same."

Bennet met him on the landing, pulling Jamie's door shut behind him. Darius hooked his arms around Bennet's neck. As their lips met, so did their thighs, and Darius's cock pressed against Bennet's jeans.

Bennet broke away when he heard the stairs creak. Nigel had stopped four steps from the top, his head level with their hips.

"My dear boy," Nigel said faintly. He appeared to be speaking to Darius's cock.

Bennet grabbed Darius's arm. "Sorry, Nigel, this one's mine."

# Epilogue

GIORGIO WAS MAKING himself invisible. He could do that, sometimes, if he stood against a background like this trellis at the back of the gazebo, stayed very still, and looked down. He'd be right there before people's eyes, but they wouldn't see him because the brain only notices things that move—one of the few useful things he'd learned at school.

He hadn't expected to come to the wedding, although he'd had an invitation . . . so pretty, with the gold lacy paper and the pressed flowers, and his name beautifully inscribed in real black ink. Jamie had written them, Bennet said.

Giorgio had thought Darius must have asked Tim to invite him, but Darius said no. Tim had thought of it by himself.

"So what did you say?" Darius had asked, as Giorgio stroked his invitation with his little finger.

This was yesterday, in the garden. Bennet had come up with Darius, but Jamie and his parents hadn't arrived yet. Giorgio had brought out the card to show them.

"Say?" Giorgio repeated.

"Didn't you reply?"

Giorgio let his finger rest below the letters *RSVP*,

embossed in gold. "I wanted to, but I didn't know whether to say yes or no. Of course I won't go, so it wouldn't be right to say yes, but on the other hand it seemed rude to say no, when they sent me such a lovely card."

Bennet said, "You could come and be, like, on the edge of things."

Could he?

"Right at the back," Bennet added, "or even further, if you want. Outside, behind the gazebo. You could take pictures, then you'd have a reason to move around."

He'd been torn. He did want to see Darius and Bennet being best men, and he was beginning to feel better around strangers now. But the wedding wouldn't have just a few new faces. It would be full of people he didn't know, people who might stare.

He didn't decide until the last moment. He waited until everyone was there, even the grooms, then crept up to watch.

He counted one, two, three empty chairs. He didn't want to sit down—standing at the back felt safer—but it was good to know they'd kept a place for him, even if he hadn't replied. He wasn't an interloper. He was an invited guest.

Tim's pink face beamed over his white suit. Jamie, dressed in red with a halo of golden curls, was so dazzling that it was hard to look at anything else. Giorgio almost wished he could be so beautiful, but someone like that could never be invisible.

Darius was in grey, and Bennet in black—not matching each other, but contrasting with their grooms, and it worked. The difference made them fit together better, somehow.

Giorgio had been right. They were good together.

He'd hinted, yesterday, that Darius and Bennet might have their own wedding at Pemberley sometime. Sometime soon, even.

Darius had said, "No way."

*Oh. That sounded final.* Giorgio had sneaked a look at Bennet, to see if he was disappointed too, but Bennet's eyes had crinkled in a smile.

Then Darius had added, "Catherine's having nothing to do with our wedding," and Giorgio'd had to laugh, even though it meant he'd have to go to London to be a witness, if he wanted to . . . which he wasn't sure of, yet.

Up at the front, Darius passed Tim the first ring.

# Acknowledgements

I'd like to send out a huge thank-you to everyone who helped me and other authors to self-publish our books after we withdrew from publishing contracts with a commercial publisher.

For practical help with services at that difficult time, I especially want to thank Megan Derr, Nospheratt, Heidi Cullinan, Rachel of Signal Boost Promotions, Jay of JoyfullyJay.com, and Katie of WantonReads.com. There were many other offers, but those were the ones I needed the most.

I'd also like to thank everyone who was involved at different stages of a long writing and editing process: Sarah, Alex, and Mala; Michelle Spiva; Mark who helped with the first chapter, and Lucee Lovett who has helped all the way.

Many thanks also to Natasha Snow for the gorgeous cover design.

And I'll always be grateful to the organisers of the UK GLBTQ Fiction Meet (Charlie Cochrane, Clare London, J.L. Merrow, Liam Livings, Josephine Myles, Elin Gregory, and Cathy Laird), who have made me feel I'm not alone or crazy since the first meet I attended, and Anna Butler, who has been a wonderful writing friend to me at the meets and elsewhere.

# About the Author

Megan Reddaway lives in England and has been entertained by fictional characters acting out their stories in her head for as long as she can remember. She began writing them down as soon as she could.

Since she grew up, she has worked as a secretary, driver, barperson, and article writer, among other things. Whatever she is doing, she always has a story bubbling away at the same time.

Website (with two free stories if you sign up to the newsletter):
meganreddaway.com

Facebook Page:
facebook.com/meganreddawayauthor

Goodreads:
goodreads.com/author/show/5753619.Megan_Reddaway

Twitter:
twitter.com/meganreddaway1

# More from Megan Reddaway

*The Luck of the Irish*
*A free male/male romance ebook*

Kyle is English and he's lucky. He's going to Dublin for St Patrick's Day, and his boss is paying.

Declan is Irish and he's unlucky. His friends are off to Tenerife for a weekend of gay clubbing, and Declan will be stuck in Dublin alone on St Patrick's Day. But bad luck is nothing new for Declan. He's been plagued with it ever since he was cursed by a leprechaun on the night he was born.

When the two of them meet, there's magic as well as mayhem. But can Declan escape his bad luck long enough to make a real connection with Kyle before Kyle has to fly home to England?

Free to download when you sign up for Megan's newsletter: meganreddaway.com/luck-of-the-irish

## *Shelter Me*

*Gay romance in a not-so-distant future*

**Love and survival—is it too much to ask?**

Leo Park is an empath on the run. He's escaped the secret research facility where he's been held since he was six years old, but how can he survive without being captured? He has no money, all his ideas come from old movies, and he's carrying his baby brother, smuggled out in a carton.

Cole Millard lives by his own rules in the Oregon woods, refusing to fear the world war that's coming closer every day. Now his freedom is threatened by a naive 19-year-old with a baby in tow and a spooky way of knowing what Cole is feeling. But Leo is vulnerable and desperate. What's a guy to do?

**Shelter Me** *is a dystopian gay romance novel with a hot backwoodsman, a desperate fugitive, a six-month-old baby, and the world on the brink of an apocalyptic war.*
meganreddaway.com/shelter-me

## *Big Guy*
*A sweet and funny gay romance novella*

Overweight Truman Rautigan and his mom are about to be made homeless, but she's a top slimming salesperson who could win her dream house if Truman comes through with some sales of his own. Instead, he's stashing food in his bottom drawer and indulging in late-night binges.

When his mom sends him to infiltrate a rival weight loss group, he meets the gorgeous Brad, biker, mechanic and successful slimmer. But Brad couldn't be interested in Truman, could he? What if he knew Truman's real reason for being there? Truman could lose everything if his shameful secrets are exposed…

meganreddaway.com/big-guy

Printed in Great Britain
by Amazon